JUST WATCH ME

JUST WATCH ME

DAVID JACOBS

Just Watch Me

Published by Wheatmark®
1760 East River Road, Suite 145, Tucson, Arizona 85718 USA
www.wheatmark.com

ISBN: 978-1-62787-162-4 (paperback)
ISBN: 978-1-62787-204-1 (ebook)
LCCN: 2014951842

CHAPTER 1

JOSH RYAN, a hot-looking yet obnoxious hunk of a jock—I mean jerk—was picking on the tuba player from marching band at our high school. Josh is tall, weighs about 160, and is totally ripped. His bronze skin offsets thick blond hair and blue eyes quite well. And his hair is not a washed-out blond, but rather a striking bright blond with naturally dark highlights and dark eyebrows.

But bullies, even good-looking ones, make me really angry, and when I get angry, I sometimes react in ways that I live to regret. This can be especially problematic since I'm trying to cope with mysteriously odd yet powerful new abilities that I have yet to control, let alone master.

Josh and the tuba player were standing near a neat row of palm trees. At first there was silence, not a leaf moved. Then the wind started; gusts of twenty-five miles per hour made the palm trees whoosh and sway. I grabbed on to the wind with my mind. I felt the wind and melded it to my breath: I embodied the element, collected it, compressed it, vibrated with it, and then flung it out of my being. It was almost like the infamous Tacoma Narrows Bridge that collapsed in 1940. In that case, the bridge started to vibrate slowly and benignly but accelerated so that its movement grew and magnified until the bridge snapped.

In my rage as judge, jury, and executioner who presumed Josh's guilt, I amplified the wind into a 120-mile-per-hour gust that blew

Josh Ryan into a wall. The band kid tried to hide his face and clung to his instrument as the wind blew his hair back, leaving papers and dust swirling.

I'm Katie Jackson. I'm seventeen and can't wait until I'm eighteen, so that my parents can't tell me what to do; plus, I am going to vote.

I've led a fairly ordinary, white-bread, sheltered, suburban, teenage life in a sleepy, high-desert Arizona neighborhood. Some of the kids around here are high on drugs. Not me.

I'm not from the planet Krypton, nor have I been bitten by a mutant spider. People do have to be careful around here, though, as there is no shortage of venomous insects and snakes. One time a rattlesnake bit our dog right on her nose. We got her to the vet in time, and she pulled through. Her face swelled to three times its normal size after two vials of antivenom. She was never quite the same after that. When she got liver cancer three years later in my junior year of high school, my parents refused to take her in to be put down. Instead, we took care of her at home until she died and then buried her in the backyard. It was so sad, like losing a family member. Plus, digging a grave in the desert was no easy task; the ground was so hard and rocky that we had to use a caliche bar.

Our dog's death was the impetus for my first extraordinary experience. A few months ago, my mom won a trip to play tournament poker in Las Vegas. On a silvery Vegas afternoon, while my mom was downstairs gambling at the casino, I had a vision. Before that, I had lucid dreams in my sleep, but this one happened while I was awake.

Mother, like so many others in the windowless casino, lost track of time at the craps table, yelling out numbers in between poker games. She was an excellent Texas Hold 'em player who read books about tells, pot odds, table position, and nut cards. She would talk about the importance of having good hole cards. Back home she played in a local tournament every Tuesday night. My dad was somewhat uncomfortable that she was the only female player, but I think he was jealous. The tournament met in the private dining area of a local eatery. The top four winners were sent to Las Vegas. Mom was in fourth place and determined to move up.

She made sure to drink coffee; she liked it when the guys got drunk, since drinking made them play sloppy. Unfortunately, Mom's coffee drinking made her need to go pee. A few times she lost her money because she had to go during betting time. I guess that's better than losing your water.

Sometimes she complained to us about how annoying, drunk, or arrogant some of the other players could get, but it made her that much happier to take their money. When she talked like that, Dad felt better about her poker playing.

Occasionally my parents would argue about Mom's poker night because my dad didn't like it when she came home after midnight. There were nights when Dad would storm out of the bedroom with his pillows. My mom thought his behavior was ridiculous. She would tell him not to get his underwear in a twist.

I was grateful for my driver's license when the atmosphere got too tense at home.

Casinos are not alluring to me. They smell permanently of cigarette smoke with a perfume-like undertone. Plus, I saw too many downtrodden folks who arrived with their walkers or in wheelchairs, oxygen tanks trailing behind them, mindlessly spending their Social Security checks at the slot machines that chimed and tinkled coins just frequently enough to keep these Pavlovian addicts coming back for more. Bleary-eyed patrons holding cigarettes that were burned down to ash went there to forget how they got this way. Someone told me that there is a slot tournament that people train for. Please.

Admittedly, Vegas had developed a family theme-park motif as well. Kids and teens like me could see great shows, shop, look at tigers and dolphins, and pretend that we didn't see the porno leaflets strewn all over the streets. No doubt the energy and impulsiveness formed a potent aphrodisiac that seduced folks all over the world big time.

My dad, on the other hand, was attending an aerospace engineering convention. He cheered Mom on at the craps table in between attending lectures or working out at the gym.

I don't know how he sat in a dark ballroom that doubled as a lecture hall hour after hour, listening to PowerPoint presentations about the tensile strength and stress points of space-age polymers, and so on. I think the only reason people didn't doze off while looking at graphs and equations was that the rooms were kept freezing cold.

Dad and I were planning to go shopping at the Fashion Show Mall and then do dinner and a show. This was my idea of a good time. My dad liked the South American all-you-can-eat carnivorous steak place with scantily clad waitresses. I wanted new jeans.

My parents' activities left me in the room alone at the hotel for a while. There was plenty to do. I wasn't lonely. I like solitude, especially from the parental units. It's not that I don't love them a lot. We are a tight little family since I'm an only child.

Even so, I was quite content with my computer, books, music, and—yes, I'll admit it—the minibar. It was one of those minibars where if I even thought about moving the snack, we were charged. I was eyeing the trail mix. I tried to figure out how to read what was in it without lifting it from the pressure-sensitive electronic shelf. I wondered if we'd be charged if I quickly grabbed it with one hand and put a shoe in its place with the other. I was going to eat it regardless, so I tried the shoe trick. Guess we would find out at checkout time if it worked. If all else failed, there was room service.

Brushing the knots out of my hair and inspecting for split ends, I noticed our room from a new angle in the mirror and realized it was done in respectable taste. I then rummaged through my suitcase looking for my T-shirt. I hadn't bothered to unpack. Looking up, I especially liked the blue accent wall and thought that when we got home I might try to paint one in my room with Dad. Parts of being in a hotel room are sketchy—like the sheets, for example: Where were they yesterday? Who was on them? What were those people doing that led to the expression "Whatever happens in Vegas, stays in Vegas"?

Coffeemakers concern me, too. They look like science experiments, but I'm a bit of a germophobe anyway. The drinking glasses on the counter in the bathroom really got to me when I wanted to brush my teeth. How well does housekeeping wash them, and who drank out of them? And what had been in those glasses? Dentures? One time we were in a hotel, and the glass in the bathroom had lipstick on it. I heard somewhere that it's more sanitary but much less stylish to have paper cups in a hotel room. I decided to ask the front desk to send up some paper cups so I could brush my teeth.

Our room didn't face the strip. Being in back afforded an expansive view of sky out the hotel window, past a sea of shimmering cars and what seemed like endless acres of tar rooftops. Vegas was enjoying a cold snap. The distant mountains took on a red hue, their tops snow dusted. I heard an aircraft and looked up. Maybe I would catch a glimpse of something from nearby Nellis Air Force Base streaking by.

Staring out the window at the big sky while lying on the king-sized bed and listening to music, I munched trail mix minus the raisins. I don't like them—they're sad, scrawny, and wrinkled. Just eat the grape and get over it. I flicked them across the room to see if I could shoot them into the garbage pail. Out of ten raisins, two hit the pail and made a metallic ping, one went in, and one bounced, landing on the windowsill; the other six went flying randomly. I needed to work on that.

I walked over to pick the raisins off the floor and sill. Outside my hotel window, the sky was titanium gray mixed with quickly moving white cotton clouds over the mountains. I love to stare at the clouds. It's peaceful and reminds me that the earth is moving. Occasional patches of blue peeked out between the clouds. One of the cloud formations looked like my golden retriever who had died. She had been seventy pounds and almost made it to thirteen; had a thick, shiny coat; was a great escape artist; and was quite mischievous, except when there were thunderstorms. Then she would hide. I loved her and still missed her terribly.

For a moment, the cloud looked like her big head and floppy ears. Then it was gone. The cloud formation dissolved. I didn't like that one bit. I wanted the cool blue-and-white patch that looked like my dog back. I wanted to recall my dog some more.

I closed my eyes, letting my mind become clear and my body calm. It was like I was observing my own thoughts and the outside world from some deeper place. I breathed, pulling and pushing air deeply and slowly, picturing the pattern in the clouds as it had been moments ago. I felt it. I was it. I inhaled the sky. When I opened my eyes, the clouds had reversed direction, and the image of my dog was back again. I was able to keep the clouds from moving as I looked on in amazement at the dog-shaped image in the sky. I was able to play with it, too. I moved the clouds forward and backward, so the ears moved, and I was sure I had lost my mind. The cloud image of the dog hung over the mountain for a while. I cannot tell you if it was a second or infinity. At first I laughed, but then I cried and at last got scared, and the cloud was gone, shriveled like the raisin. I was afraid to tell anyone about this. Certainly not my parents. I searched on the web for my symptoms of madness, hallucinations, and seeing things. Was I ill, delusional, or plain nuts? What was next, alien abduction?

This is what I'm talking about. These kinds of occurrences were becoming more frequent and concerning to me. For example, I recently acquired the unnatural ability to influence certain elements, such as wind and water, which freaks me out. I'm not sure if what I have is a talent or a curse. It's up there with moving the clouds around. I'm trying to get a grip on what's been happening.

One day, just after the Vegas hotel room experience, as I was coming home from school, I stopped to pick up an iced tea at Starbucks. I was about a block from home on a quiet suburban road. There were no pedestrians and few cars. I noticed a lonely mesquite tree that looked depressed. I must have passed it a thousand times and never even saw it, let alone paid it any mind. It was young, and the county had recently planted it off to the right of the shoulder after widening the street. The main trunk was no bigger around than my arm. It had barely established roots in its new home. Standing only six feet high, it scarcely merited the name *tree*. It wasn't doing a very good job of creating shade, maybe a little spit of shadow. Cars occasionally whizzed by it. Poor thing. If it could talk, it would ask to be sent back to the nursery from where it came. It hadn't had the time to realize that it was fully part of and integrated with the sun, wind, water, and earth. A dull plastic bottle lay on the ground next to it. Its nearest neighbor was a creosote plant.

If a tree could worry, this one would. The leaves were parched, which is atypical for this hardy species. Around here in Arizona there are precious few big-leafed trees. Everything has adapted to survive the desert. So instead of big green leafy things, most everything is sharp and pointy to reduce surface area and survive the harsh unforgiving climate. Still, these skinny leaves were kind of frowning. It really made me feel sorry for it even though I'm not exactly a tree hugger. I hate to recycle at home even though I should. I take showers that are way too long for someone who lives in the desert; I'd much rather drive a Corvette than a Prius, and I'm a meat-and-potato girl. I guess this may make me unpopular with some, but I don't care. My parents are the recycling tree huggers, especially Mom.

Still, this poor tree got to me. I felt a connectedness, a longing to help a fellow earthly life form. I wanted to nourish it. As I stood next to it, my eyes grew moist with tears, and suddenly it began to rain, soaking the tree. As if a cloud had burst forth from my own tear drops, it rained big, slow, splashing drops on only one side of the street where the thirsty tree and I were standing. Focal spotty rain can and does happen in Arizona where we live. Sunny here, rainy there. No big deal, right?

I felt so happy—and wet. My face glistened with fresh water and salty tears of joy. I laughed and looked up into the colorful sky pulling my wet hair back off my face. I rubbed the nearby creosote leaf between my fingers and touched it to my face. After rainfall the fragrance of the desert is intoxicating. I think there is something in the creosote bush that does this. One day I'm going to bottle the fragrance of desert rain, make a body wash out of it, and become a zillionaire. I felt light and expansive, like I had done something good and useful. I was proud and less scared. I was standing in the sun, soaking wet. I wasn't imagining this. It was real, whatever that means. Feeling less apprehensive and more confident, I imagined that I could harness this, control it. Being different wasn't so bad.

About a month or so after Vegas, still in the first part of my senior year in high school, I had two more episodes, after which time I couldn't stand to keep it a secret anymore. I was getting so stressed out by my abilities that I had to tell someone. The excitement was bursting through my chest. I felt alive, happier, with more to look forward to, yet I was developing a secret second life and looking over my shoulder, nervous that someone would see. It was like being a caterpillar in a chrysalis waiting to burst out and fly.

Our house is up in the foothills, backed up against the Santa Catalina mountain range. Most of our property is vertical, unusable, arid, and rugged, but still quite beautiful. The desert landscape is lush with plump green saguaro cacti that stretch skyward. A bosk of mesquite trees provides some shady respite and houses cardinals, hummingbirds, doves, and the occasional hawk. We have a two-story home where from upstairs we have great mountain views over the treetops. My favorite is the view of Thimble Peak, which looks like an inverted thimble on a mountain top. From the second-floor patio, it feels like we live in a tree house.

While sitting on that patio listening to music on my phone, texting, and doing homework, I noticed a rosebud in the garden down below. I stood and leaned over the ledge, going from looking at it to really seeing it someplace far within me. I realized that it has thorns to protect its delicate beauty. I was in awe and wonder that a clump of dirt and roots could create this miracle. My breathing slowed. A heavy knowing, like the rose and I were sharing the same energy frequency, informed my being. My mind began to empty, except for a sense of love and light. The rose opened. I wasn't exactly keeping track of time. I didn't set a stopwatch on my phone. This wasn't a race; it wasn't even intentional, but more than two minutes could not have gone by because the song I was listening to was not yet over. I nearly passed out and fell over the ledge but caught myself. My head swam; my knees were weak.

There's really nothing that unusual about me; I'm just an ordinary kid. I'm not a vampire and don't have a thing for bats. We have tons of bats that zip around in a frenetic blind flight every sunset. One time a bat flew down our chimney and into the house, which was a big deal. Animal control advised us that this is abnormal bat behavior and that the bat could have rabies. We had to make sure we didn't come in contact with the droppings. My dad chased it into the spare bedroom with a towel. My mother and I screamed while the dog barked. After Dad had it cornered, he ran out and closed the door behind him before animal control came to catch it with a net. For months I was sure that I would become rabid and start frothing at the mouth. I requested rabies shots, but my family doctor said that it wouldn't be necessary.

I had asthma as a kid, but have grown out of it, which is ironic for someone who's learning to play with the wind like a new instrument.

I'm not athletic. I love indie, electronic music and candles, especially the scented kind. My mother doesn't like me to light incense when she's having a migraine because the smells make her feel worse.

I do not have a boyfriend. It's not that I would mind having a boyfriend, but most of the boys at school are immature idiots. One of my friends has had the same boyfriend for two years, which seems like a lifetime for someone in high school. Some parents would say that it's getting way too serious and ask if he's planning to go to college. I think parents want to know if a potential suitor has future earning potential and good enough DNA stock for their daughter, as if it's never too soon to think about the future. Gross.

Conversely, one of my friends just messaged me on Facebook that someone asked her out. Not asked out on a date, but asked to be her boyfriend. So she's been "in a relationship" for an hour now, but it won't last until the weekend.

My dad says soul mates are meant to be together after you finish your education. He thinks that the whole high-school sweetheart romance can be wonderful for other kids, but not his daughter. In general he believes, however, that when people meet earlier in life their roots grow together, as opposed to meeting late in life where the most one can hope for is that the canopy of leaves may touch. "Okay, sure, Dad, whatever," I told him. I rolled my eyes and put my head down, covering my face with my hair and a hand.

Dad said if a boy asks me out, he has to come to the house, where there will be a very conspicuous shotgun on the table until he passes muster. My dad likes my male friends just fine, as long as they are not dating me.

This year I am not going to the fall formal unless a boy asks me, and the relationship has to last more than a few hours or days.

My best friend Sara thinks that's just plain wrong. She says a lot of the girls will be going stag, and even if they have boyfriends, they promise to dance with me. I don't know. Maybe I'll wear combat boots in defiance if I go single.

I met Sara in first grade. We were lined up outside Miss Penny's classroom. I was the new kid. I had transferred over from a different preschool and kindergarten.

All the other kids had backpacks except me. I didn't know I needed one. My mom should have known. Sara came over to me and asked where my backpack was. We have been buds ever since. It's been a friendship that has grown deep roots just as Father said. We have been through everything together from skinned knees to our first periods.

She has great grades and loves theater.

Sara's parents divorced when she was in elementary school. I remember how difficult that was for her. Her dad decided to grow his hair out, play guitar, and move in with the athletic trainer. Personalized training.

Sara is drop-dead gorgeous with model good looks. Mom used to tell her she should try to get modeling jobs right after her braces came off. Sara would say that she had higher aspirations than modeling. My dad cheered her on when she gave that answer.

I get good grades, too, and play the piano. I'm not one of the sketchy problem kids. I stay out of trouble and have no qualms about being from a white-bread, middle-class, suburban, two-parent household. I think hanging out at the mall is way dumb. I'm planning to start college next year. I want to leave Arizona and go out of state, much to my parents' chagrin.

I wear a retainer every night. I don't wear makeup. My hair is down to my waist and wavy, except when my friends and I straighten it.

I'm a little worried about putting on the freshman fifteen next year; I can easily put away two desserts at a time.

As a kid, I remember having odd experiences that no one would believe or allow me to forget. These occurrences happened often when I was a child, so much so that I don't even remember how or when they started. Having them wasn't always fun.

Sometimes while lying in bed at night with my eyes closed, I felt as though I could leave my body in bed to go play elsewhere for a while. I had dreams that were no less real than being awake but with more control over the dream than I have in my mundane daily life.

When I was seven, I started having recurrent lucid dreams where I knew that I was dreaming. I created the scenes like the director of a movie. My favorite was where I was a ball of light without my body surrounded by a 360-degree screen on which images played out. If I didn't like what I saw, I might walk through a wall or fly away and leave it behind. From rooftops I would watch scenes below. While being chased, I could run on all fours, escaping like a large and cunning beast, leaping and soaring high into the air with my back arched. It all seemed so natural.

Flying was my favorite. At times I dreamed of joyfully pedaling my legs and floating away.

Sometimes the nightmares would come, though. I dreamed that I was really awake in my own home hovering about in the dark like an apparition and could watch my own sleeping body paralyzed in bed. Terrified, I was unable to move or call out, sure that I had died. Suddenly, with a loud buzzing zap, I snapped back into my sleeping body. After really awakening, I would run into my parents' room and ask Mom for help. Mother would make nothing of it. She was familiar with what I was experiencing, which was a great relief and very validating. I also think that she just was trying to calm me down. My mom, Rena, would say, "*Pobrecita*"—which sounded like *pobre cheetah*—"it's okay. You're having an out-of-body experience. It's a special gift." She also grew up thinking that such occurrences were as normal as a tortilla because these qualities ran in our family but were kept hush-hush for fear of being considered crazy by their tight community. She would sit me down with a glass of warm milk and recount stories that her grandparents told her about how some of our relatives had these experiences, too, and I shouldn't fear them. Mother encouraged me to relax and embrace such gifts. She told me that her grandmother could see the dearly departed. Today, she would have been a famous medium.

Although I dreaded it and found it thoroughly mortifying, I finally told my parents what I was experiencing.

My insane abilities were giving me anxiety. Blowing Josh through the wall was the tipping point. Roses and a burst rain cloud I could deal with. But now I was getting panic attacks, and it felt like my asthma might come back. When I thought about what I could do, my chest tightened, and my heart sped up. I was positive that I was losing my mind but wasn't quite sure how to break it to my parents. I'm closer to Mother, which makes Father sad. I tell her practically everything. We even get our period at the same time.

I decided to talk about it over dinner.

It had been a stressful day for my father at work—designing bombs or whatever it is he does. He frequently tells me about the time when he was a student and designed a prototype rocket but accidentally placed a negative sign where a positive should have been, which resulted in a wing being placed upside down.

Like most engineers he's left brain dominant, which means he's concrete and scientific. He's also a real skeptic and hardwired to believe that if there isn't a schematic or a mathematical explanation, then it isn't so. I don't know if the schooling does that to engineers, or if the field attracts them. He's talked to me about studying engineering. Not going to happen.

No one wanted to eat at home, so we went out to the diner. My mom loves breakfast for dinner—an egg-white veggie omelet and maybe one pancake.

In the car I was trying to figure out what to say. They were bickering in the front seat about something.

"Hello up there, I'm going crazy back here."

"Do you hear that, John? We're making her crazy. We can continue this discussion later."

"No, Mom, you don't understand. I am literally going crazy."

My dad liked to make jokes. "Well, Katie, if you go crazy, be back soon. We're going to eat in a few minutes."

I shook my head as we walked through the parking lot.

The waitress wore a name tag on her chest. Darlene. Her shirt was tight and low cut. There was a lot of spandex going on, which I guess made for good tips. She didn't write anything down. I find that to be a marvel. With her memorization skills maybe Darlene could ace my biology exam. My dad was amazed. I don't think he was really smitten by Darlene's memory. It seemed more like her mammaries to me. Mom bristled; she didn't care for Darlene not writing things down because that usually means mistakes, and she's a picky eater who won't hesitate to send the food back. In Darlene's case, if Dad didn't stop smiling, I thought Mom might throw the food back. Food that gets sent back makes dinner awkward. Do we now wait for food to be remade while ours gets cold? I gave that up a long time ago. As I stuffed my face, Mom would say, "Don't wait for me. Eat, eat." Father would slowly pick at a potato, being polite. He could make one french fry look like an entire meal that way.

The food arrived. Salsa on the side, no bacon, dry whole-wheat toast. Darlene got it right, thank goodness. Dad was a bit too complimentary, if you ask me.

"Mom, Dad, I have to tell you both something."

My dad said, "Sweetie, can you pass the sugar-free syrup?"

"John, listen to her. I think something is wrong." Mom turned to me. "Honey, do you feel sick? Are you having trouble at school?"

My dad winked. "Boy trouble, kiddo?"

"Eww, Dad, please."

"Oh my God, John, maybe she's on drugs."

"I'm not on drugs, Mom. I'm not in trouble."

"Tell us, dear. Are you pregnant?"

"Mother, really."

"John, put the pancake down this instant," Mom ordered Dad. Then she turned to me and said, "You can tell us everything." My father frowned and crossed his arms. Mom's eyebrows were up the whole time exaggerating the wrinkles in her forehead. She'd be upset if I recommended Botox.

The food got colder, but I felt hotter. Dad went back to picking a potato. Mom became a little misty. Darlene came back. She looked at Dad and asked if we were still "enjoying" our food. That's the new catchphrase. Can't they ask if we're done yet? So I told her we stopped enjoying the food ten minutes ago when the flies started setting up shop in the French toast. Mom shushed me. Dad ordered coffee. I mumbled barely a whisper and looked down. Moved my food around. Regressed like a child.

"Speak up," said Dad. I tried to be matter-of-fact, glib. No eye contact. My plan was to summarize in a concise manner what had transpired, and while I simply wanted to share the news with my family, it was nothing to worry about. Play it down, feel them out. Win support. All the while, I was trembling inside.

As I recounted the new things that were happening to me and my surroundings, the skin on my neck and throat became red and blotchy. This got Mom's attention because she knows this only happens when I'm very upset. She placed her hand on my forehead, as if she were checking for a fever. It was cool, soothing, and reassuring. I didn't pull away. I tried to appeal to my father by saying that these instances probably have a logical explanation and that there is nothing to really worry about. Right? By the time that I explained my perception of what happened with Josh Ryan, I was biting my nails, crying, and my lips were quivered. I was very upset with myself for crying. I was determined for this not to happen. Be strong, I told myself. Mom moved around to my side of the table and hugged me.

"Mom, Daddy, help me," I cried.

After I got done explaining everything, my mother proclaimed that they would find me the best psychiatrists and neurologists. Dad thinks shrinks are quacks who experiment with people by prescribing the latest psychoactive drugs.

Mom said that her friend Sandy's daughter began seeing things, but now she's finally on the right medication. Maybe I shouldn't have told them.

CHAPTER 2

GETTING TO the doctor's office on time was a logistical feat. We almost missed our first appointment trying to find the office in the maze of buildings that were not numbered well. We drove around and around looking for it then walked everywhere. Anxious and dehydrated, we thought about walking into the urgent care center to seek immediate relief. Finally, we had to ask someone. A man in scrubs scurried by, wearing a lanyard that said patient care tech—whatever that means.

Mom shouted out, "Yoo-hoo, excuse me." Now I was totally embarrassed. "Do you know where suite three oh seven is? Where the neurologists' offices are?"

By then I wanted to crawl in a hole. The man stopped, turned, looked at us, and pointed the way.

"We should have left earlier," Mom said.

I wanted to, but no—they never listen.

We were now getting on each other's nerves.

～～～～

The neurologist with a red bow tie and a long white coat told my mother that he was ordering tests, including a brain scan. He was a bit robotic, but I liked his fountain pen since I had never seen one before. It was bright red like his tie. His hands were cold, and he had long skinny fingers, a white-gold wedding band, and sparkly eyes. They were comforting, and his expression was empathetic. The doctor seemed like a caring man, but he took himself too seriously and needed to relax.

I giggled when he tapped my knee with his hammer and made my legs jump. He called it a reflex. I didn't know if he meant the knee or the giggle. He said he wanted to tell me a secret. He found that about 15 to 20 percent of people of all ages, but mostly females, laughed when he checked their reflexes. It was only the legs, not the arms. He didn't know why, but he thought that the laughers were the nicest group of people. He asked me not to share this with the grouchy nonlaughers.

I passed the part where I had to walk one foot in front of the other like the test cops use to see if a person is drunk. Then he checked to see if I could remember five things after five minutes, which was kind of interesting. I had perfect recall.

I tolerated the MRI, but it was not my favorite procedure. It was up there with the EEG, where they scraped my scalp to connect wires and monitored my brain activity to see if I was brain dead.

For the MRI, first they x-rayed my face to see if I had any retained metal in my eyeballs. I think I'd know if I'd been in a blast and had a hunk of steel in my eye. Then I had to put on a hospital gown, for who knows what reason. I was there to get a picture of my brain not the other end. Next, I was told to lie perfectly still on a cold, hard table face up for thirty to forty minutes, not breathing half the time. The technician, who looked like the cousin of the patient care technician, ran out like he was escaping the bubonic plague. He would talk to me through a speaker. Breathe, don't breathe; think, don't think.

I can totally see how one could be claustrophobic in an MRI machine. The thing is inches from your face, no way out, very noisy. There was a report in the news a couple of years ago about someone who was accidentally left in the scanner overnight.

The MRI results finally came back. My parents and the doctor's office had to fight with the insurance company to get the MRI approved. The insurance company wanted me to be dragging a leg, drooling, and incontinent before they would approve it. Insurance companies totally suck; they're an evil empire. Thankfully, the results were normal. Maybe the insurance company will send us a note saying, "Told you so. Please send us the money back."

Fortunately, I have all my marbles. The doctor wanted to make sure there wasn't a tumor that could be precipitating a partial seizure. He showed us the pictures. It was strange to see the inside of my head. I didn't look too attractive without a face. Seeing my brain was a little bit fascinating, but also a little bit gross. I never realized what a large muscle the tongue is. I guess it needs to be with all the eating and talking that we do.

My parents were worried but relieved by this positive information. Even though the EEG was normal, the doctor still couldn't be certain that it wasn't a partial seizure. After all that, the neurologist threw his hands up and concluded that my brain appeared to be as normal as a teenager's brain could be. Not humorous. Apparently, I was cleared from a neurological perspective. My noodle was intact so the problem must be psychiatric. Therefore, I was turfed to psychiatry and was beginning to feel like I needed one. The neurologist's assistant kindly helped us make an appointment to see a shrink a few days later.

The psychiatrist's office ended up being just down the hall from the neurologist in a four-story modern medical office building next to the hospital. I wondered what they had said about me. Does that make me paranoid?

We learned from the first lovely experience with the neurologist when to leave home and where to park. I figured that if a person could drive a car and find the office, he or she didn't need a neurologist. Might as well save the copay and go shopping.

Even though it was a cute office, I don't have much faith in shrinks; maybe I get my skepticism from Father.

I noticed that the psychiatrist's assistant had a bowl of chocolates on her desk. "Help yourself—that's what they're for," she said with a smile.

I rummaged through them and picked out the dark chocolates with almonds.

The shrink had a really great office. The furniture was large and comfortable. The colors coordinated beautifully. They seemed warm, relaxing, and hippy retro with a touch of hipster. He must see mostly crazy kids like me, I thought. While waiting in this therapeutic milieu, I let my mind wander, and I had a few minutes to myself to relax and think.

When I get into one of my trancelike states, sometimes my mind seems to fuse with other people's minds. I can look at a stranger in a car stopped at a red light, and I think that person probably believes he or she is completely separate from me and everything else in the universe, but that can't be the case. Maybe our egos separate us from everything else and our true selves. I blame some of it on cars, computers, and TV. When I talk to my mom about it, she calls me an old soul. My friends say that I think too much.

The doctor, wearing a floral Hawaiian shirt, greeted me in the waiting room and escorted me back to his office.

"Hello, Katie. I'm Dr. Wilier. I'm going to ask you some questions today. Did you find the place okay? Feel free to ask me questions or stop me at any time as well. I want this to feel like a conversation."

Dr. Wilier seemed like he was around fifty. He wore frameless, silver, wire-rimmed glasses that sat low on his nose. He had a giant forehead and a thick mane of hair in back that was more salt then pepper. He looked like he hadn't been to the gym in a long time.

Wilier kept clicking his pen and taking notes on a yellow pad. His fingers were thick as sausages with neat, trim nails, but it was like there were no knuckles. The outline of a cell phone lit up and vibrated through the thin summer wool of his loose slacks. I could tell he thought about reaching for it but didn't.

He wanted to know if I felt sad, blue, or hopeless. Did I feel like killing myself or others? I thought about killing him immediately. How were my sleep and my appetite? I didn't have to ask about his appetite; his gut told the whole story.

"Do you hear voices telling you things or do you see things?"

In my head one of those voices chuckled. Hello, Sigmund, the committee in my brain is fully in session right now. All are present.

"Doesn't everyone hear a voice in their head?" I asked. "Kind of like a running commentary?" The pen clicked, more notes taken down.

I read somewhere that we all have that voice talking to us constantly. If only we could get it to shut the hell up, the world might be a better place. Sure, that voice can come in handy when whistling past the graveyard or dealing with day-to day-activities, but can you imagine if that incessant voice was a roommate constantly complaining? You'd shoot it within twenty-four hours.

"So, yes, damn it, I've got a voice talking to me that usually won't shut the heck up."

"Does that make you angry?" he asked.

I got up.

"Please, Katie, stay awhile. Please sit."

I stood instead and paced, my nostrils flared, my arms folded in front of me. He was probably noting that I was an agitated lunatic.

He wanted to know if I'd ever been abused or molested.

"No!"

I wanted to ask him if a gust of wind ever blew him right out of his plush-ass chair and out his fourth-floor window.

"Do you feel safe and secure at home?" he asked.

"I do get creeped out at night in our big squeaky house when my parents go out. I felt safer when we had our big dog." I spelled *creeped out* for him and noted that the term *sketched out* would also work.

He wanted me to tell him about my parents and life at home. Dr. Wilier delved into my dreams and thoughts. We talked about school, anxiety, and anything that was on my mind. After a little while, I sat down again. His body shifted into a less tense posture.

I was considering standing again just to freak him out. Up, down, up, down, randomly, maybe break into a few jumping jacks every time he clicked his pen. If I could sing, I would have.

He asked if my grades were slipping, which they weren't. I had taken the ACT during my junior year. The thought of taking the SAT as a senior gave me chest tightness—like I might have an asthma attack. So much rides on that one damned exam. The true measure of students' worth is not found in a standardized so-called aptitude test. I really wanted to do well and get into a decent college, but the prep courses seemed so overwhelming with everything else that was going on.

"Do your parents pressure you into achieving and getting good grades?"

"Well, not really." I shrugged.

The doctor asked with an inquisitive look. "Can you explain?"

"Sure, I guess. My parents don't pressure me to get good grades. They are constantly bragging and praising me. It's stupid already. 'Katie did this,' or 'Good job, Katie.' Yeah, go me. I could come home with a C, and they'd say it was okay as long as I did my best. I'm not three. I don't need to be praised for not pooping my pants. I feel like I grew up in the fantasy society where every kid is a winner and gets a trophy just for showing up.

"It's not going to be like that in college. I feel cheated in the sense that I've been so sheltered that I don't know if I really have what it takes to make it in the real world. So, there is this undercurrent, like, I need to know what it is I am really made of. I need to find out if in the sphere of my growing world there are others besides my parents who would say 'Yeah, you go, girl.' That is the pressure. That's why the SAT, the great equalizer, gives me chest tightness."

Dr. Wilier said, "You go, girl. I suspect that the big, bad, real world is going to receive you well. You are very bright and insightful.

"Katie, what brought you in today?"

At first I shut down again. I didn't want to retell my story.

"My parents and the neurologist told me I needed to see you, and I'm not eighteen yet."

"Can you please describe the events that have been troubling you and your parents? Take your time. Tell me anything that's on your mind. I'm going to stop writing and just listen. I might have a few questions or comments here or there."

After a few minutes of hearing about the sad tree and the rose, the doctor asked, "Do you experiment with drugs or alcohol?"

"No, Dr. Wilier, I've concluded all my experiments. I'm way past that stage. Seriously, I'm not a stoner, but I'm considering starting this afternoon."

He laughed.

Looking at the floor I asked, "Could these things that are happening to me be a coincidence, just in my mind, or some paranormal experiences? Like stuff I've been reading about online? Now that you asked, I can tell you that when I'm in one of my trance-like states, my mind is still. There are no other voices."

He brushed his hair back with his hand and sighed. "Tell me again, are you sure that you don't hear voices that tell you to do certain things?" Then he delved more into the things that I believe that I've been seeing.

I told him about the clouds and Josh. I was fairly insistent about what I thought had happened. I was sure; there was no question. "How did I end up soaking wet next to the tree? Ask the tuba player if the windstorm that I'm sure I created really happened out of nowhere on an otherwise perfectly calm day." Tears welled up. I began to feel very tiny and vulnerable.

"Answer me that, doctor."

His brow furrowed, like Dad's did. The doctor's eyes were more jovial and lighthearted now, like he didn't take life or himself too seriously. It made me feel a little better.

Dr. Wilier spent over an hour and a half with me. It was a very long ninety minutes. Wilier got up twice to adjust the air conditioning.

When it was over, the temperature in that room was still up ten degrees. I couldn't wait to get the heck out of there. I left the office and waited outside but overheard the doctor's entire conversation with my parents through a glass transom.

~~~~~~

"Mr. and Mrs. Jackson, I've completed my initial evaluation of your daughter, Kaye."

"Katie," my mother corrected.

"Yes, Katie. I'm sorry, ma'am. Your daughter is delightful. She's bright and articulate. She seems safe and secure. She is a bit anxious. Perhaps some rebellious tendencies? Her grades are still good. She's well nourished and well groomed, with good attention to hygiene. There are no signs of substance abuse." I'm glad he thought I didn't smell.

My dad asked in a confrontational tone, "What do you mean that her grades are still good?"

"Well, Mr. Jackson, I'm not sure. I don't think she's developing a thought disorder such as schizophrenia, or some other form of psychosis, though she is entering the right age group. She isn't depressed, but I'm afraid she might be delusional. I think that these unusual happenings she describes and insists on must have a logical explanation."

Wilier continued. "Isn't it quite possible that the gust of wind and the rain cloud were all coincidences?

"I'm a little bit more perplexed and worried about the rosebud and the cloud incidents. Those concern me. They might be nothing, or they could possibly represent visual hallucinations."

As though thinking out loud, the doctor announced, "This child is either highly disturbed or a paranormal advanced spiritual soul. I'm just not convinced or sure yet.

No. I am like so done with this crap, I thought. I'm going in that room. I don't like eaves dropping, but I wasn't going to stand there while they were all in there talking about me. It was like totally wrong. I knocked, more like pounded with one hand and simultaneously opened the door with the other. "Hello whats up?" My shoulders went up and I defiantly whipped a lock of hair out of my face. "Like if you have something to say about me I want to be present. It's my mind you're discussing."

Mother was taken aback. Dad's left eyebrow went up like he approved of my boldness.

The psychiatrist was totally chill. He didn't miss a step.

"Come in Katie. We were just starting to discuss your case."

"Yes, I know."

Wilier questioningly added. "No secrets here, correct and Mrs. Jackson?"

Dr. Scott, the neurologist, has concluded that the EEG brain waves are within normal limits. I suppose a partial temporal lobe seizure of some type is possible. When people hold on to a delusion that isn't validated, other things can happen, such as worsening anxiety, paranoia, or depression. In Katie's age group, we may see anorexia or poor grades."

"Tell me," the doctor asked my parents, "what was she like as a very small child? Was there anything unusual or traumatic? Any special friends?"

My mom adjusted her shoulder bag, twisted her hands, glanced at me and began to tell Dr. Wilier how when I was a toddler I had an imaginary friend that they never discouraged me from playing with. My friend was part bear part human as I used to describe her. I would try to draw her with a crayon.

"Wow mom remember that?"

The doctor interrupted. "What colors did you use Katie? Do you have any of those pictures? They might prove useful."

Mom answered. "Katie would talk to her friend, and she would answer. To Katie she was perfectly real."

My bear friend still comes to me in my dreams, and sometimes I can see her when the weather shifts or the seasons change.

My mother went on that at around the age of four I would tell her that when I used to be a grown-up, I was a strong or powerful chieftain of some kind. I don't recall that.

"My daughter is not crazy!" exclaimed Dad. "Okay, she's always been a bit eccentric, but she isn't sick."

"Thank you dad. Eccentric, really?"

Now both men frowned at each other. It was a Botox moment, a frown-off contest.

"Look, Mr. and Mrs. Jackson, I'm not saying Katie here is ill. You have to admit her claims are a bit extraordinary and not what we would describe as normal, correct?" Wilier's voice went up in tone and inflection at the end of the sentence.

Dad answered with a somewhat defeated tone that trailed down into a baritone. "Correct," he replied. "What are her, err, our options?"

"Doing nothing is one option, but that is not why you came here to see me today. We could try medications such as an antipsychotic like Respiradol, and something for anxiety like Ativan when needed.

"There is no way I'm taking that stuff."

But there is one other option," exclaimed Wilier.

"Yes?" said Dad expectantly. "Anything is better than drugging up our baby. She is nearly a straight A student and doesn't give us any trouble, well, usually."

"Let's assume she is not ill and is telling the truth."

I'm standing right here, not deaf and telling the truth. Are patients allowed to punch their doctors? I waved a pen like a baton.

Doctor Wonderful kept going. "Let's take it a step further. Let's just say she is on to something very important."

Now he got my attention. I cracked a smile.

"Here's what I'd like the three of you to do. Have Katie here show one of you, or me—someone, anyone—that these episodes are real. Then either everyone's nuts by proxy in some delusional folly, or something in the paranormal realm might be happening. I'd like you to contact someone I know and trust. I have done some research in the spiritual aspects of the so-called mind. I have been keenly interested in exploring the realm where science and the human spirit meet. Where, for example, is the mind? It's not a thing. And it does not sit exclusively within the brain, yet it interacts with the molecules of our body. As a fellow scientist, Mr. Jackson, you can appreciate that there is still much work to do and so much more that we can't explain." Dad perked up, feeling important. He needed a boost.

"All I'm saying is perhaps there are forces at play that are beyond our immediate grasp. The childhood entity she had as an imaginary friend might have been someone Katie has been connected to in the far distant past. If you keep an open mind, maybe even before this life."

My father raised his arms in a sign of objection.

Wilier put out his hand as if to gesture wait or stop, like a school crossing guard.

"Mr. Jackson, huge segments of humanity over millennia consider rebirth a fact of life. There have been reputable pediatric studies supporting this. The comment that Katie made as a child that she has memories of who she was when she used to be a grown-up are very suggestive. This invokes an Eastern concept called continuity of consciousness."

Mother clearly was buying into this stuff. She had a clear, intent gaze, or maybe the double latte had kicked in.

Dr. Wilier wrote a name, phone number, and e-mail address on his prescription pad and handed it over with a knowing look—a partial smile where one side of his mouth lifted. Something bordered on a wink.

Both Mom and Dad reached for it and almost tore the paper.

It said Professor Schlisselvasser.

Dr. Wilier continued. "Dr. S., as he goes by, has a PhD in anthropology. He studies special children with unusual abilities internationally. His expertise is indigenous cultures and their mystics. He has written extensively about topics such as spirituality and the human psyche. The power of the mind. He has worked with other gifted and/or troubled individuals in the past, depending on your point of view. Some of them have turned out to be well-known intuitives and those we might call psychics in the metaphysical sense. His knowledge is encyclopedic.

"If, after Katie has been unable to demonstrate these so-called abilities and Dr. S. thinks she's not the real deal, then I'll reexamine her, and we can talk about pills. In the meantime, keep a close watch over Katie."

We all got up and left the office, and I went to the girls' room.

When I got back, my parents were looking at each other like they weren't sure what had just happened. Then they looked at me like, it's okay, sweetie; we're here for you. I looked at them like, whatever.

Dad said to Mom, "Did you get that? Is he nuts? Is our daughter gifted—or crazy? They say there's a slim line between the two, but can we blur the line a little here?"

I was already down the hall, getting into the elevator just ahead of them. After the door closed, I banged and kicked the door. I hoped that this other Dr. S. could help me.

"Shush, John; she'll hear you," whispered Mom.

Dad whispered back loudly, "What did we just spend three hundred bucks for—a lesson in voodoo?"

"Well, John, maybe she's got a special gift."

"Oh, what, like your nutty family? Is she going to wiggle her nose or cast a spell?"

"John, don't start that again. My grandmother had some of these special spiritual traits. How do you know they weren't passed on to Katie? She even sort of looks like my grandmother did at Katie's age."

"You mean a woo-woo gene? I was hoping Katie got a math genius gene."

"Grandmother used to tell me when I was a little girl that she could look at people and see an aura of light and colors radiating around their bodies."

"Rena, it was probably her cataracts."

"Don't be so cynical. Did you listen to the doctor about all the things we don't know? Before some of the people grandmother knew got sick, she could see dark spots in their light."

I got out of the elevator ahead of them in the lobby and waited for them to get through bickering.

CHAPTER 3

AS KATIE and her parents drove away from Dr. Wilier's office, halfway around the world a terrorist nicknamed the Axe threw his arms up high, closed his eyes, and opened his stinking mouth revealing both yellow and gold teeth. The shaved head, straggly beard on his chin, and a mustache framed a brutal, downturned mouth. He had no neck. Massive pectoral muscles defined his torso. With tree trunks for legs and small boulders for biceps, he stood at six feet, two hundred pounds. A violent tapestry of battle scars painted his warrior body, and his back was a shimmering pink mass of keloids and proud flesh from beatings and various detainments. Another scar decorated the left side of his face.

The Axe's nickname referred to his favorite weapon for close combat. Likewise, it was his preferred negotiating tool when he needed to be persuasive. His exotic collection was worth a small fortune. Some were authentic pieces from antiquity. His favorite was one from Alexander the Great's conquests. They ranged from Danish axes to tomahawks. There were seventeenth-century bardiches and Yemeni jimbayas as well as ancient Roman pieces. He kept them all sharp, oiled, restored, and in perfect working order. They weren't wall queens. They were accessories to his outfits and moods.

In a secluded mountain cabin hidden somewhere in the forests of Eastern Europe, Axe peered at his inner circle of hired thugs with dead shark eyes. "We are so close," he told the ten of them in a dictatorial manner. Quivering with excitement and rubbing his arms to feel goose bumps, Axe went on. "Soon we will reveal our capabilities to the world. They will learn a painful lesson. But, we are all here to learn lessons, no? Learning is painful, yes? The American media and its current regime have already reported that weather and climatic change are the greatest potentially destabilizing threat to society, and their Pentagon is worried. Tell that to India and China." He laughed.

"Climate instability makes the usual brand of terrorism look like child's play. Weather is insidious. Think of it. We can capitalize and profit from a failing planet by making it fail harder and faster. It's like betting on a stock commodity or staple food like soybeans or rice that you know in advance will fail. We bet on it failing and get richer. After all, we are mercenary capitalists, opportunists. The time has come for us to reign."

His minions cheered halfheartedly, mostly out of fear and certainly not out of respect. One member of the team glanced around furtively without cheering.

The Axe meandered among his audience and asked for comments from his most prized group. His cabinet was a brain trust of computer experts, scientists, climatologists, and top-notch ex-military combatants for hire. *Hire* was the operative term. They were all paid exorbitantly scandalous sums for their allegiance. Some were paid in nonmonetary ways. A secret kept, blackmail, rescue from a tyrannical regime, perhaps a promise to keep the family back home safe if all went well.

No one raised a hand. Not even to go to the bathroom. Axe stopped when he reached Rav, a prior military commander from a dethroned regime who was now one of Axe's hired guns. This supposed team player did not cheer; Axe had a bad feeling about him and lately had become suspicious. Axe thought Rav might not be loyal to the cause because Rav was saying too many of the wrong things to the wrong people. Rav also exhibited a lackluster expression and an air of mistrust. Axe had learned to listen to his feelings. They had served him well and kept him alive, gotten him to where he was today. Plus, the sorcerous tattoo on Axe's forearm stung and tingled; he'd gotten the ink while visiting the Amazon. Today was no time to disobey these gnawing sensations. He looked at Rav as he walked, touching people. A friendly pat here, a squeeze of the shoulder or a wink there.

In the blink of an eye, Axe unsheathed his weapon with his right hand from the left side of his waist. With a backhanded swing, he wielded his axe and sliced through the top of Rav's shoulder. The blade pointed inward toward the neck and chest. It sliced through the muscles, smashed the clavicle bone, and split the large lung vessels and part of the brachial plexus of nerves like a melon. It was a gaping mortal wound.

Rav looked at Axe with a confused expression before he crumpled from his chair to the floor. The torn arm went limp and froth oozed from the wound before his body twitched like a caught fish.

As if he'd done nothing more than adjust his tie, Axe checked his Swiss chronometer to make sure he hadn't scratched the new rose-gold bezel or stained it with blood. He replaced the weapon in its sheath and continued. Scratching his watches really irritated him.

"Not a scratch. Okay, enough excitement for one day. Let's get down to business. The take-home message for today is that the cost of disloyalty is high." He barked an order and two militia guards with Kalashnikovs standing at the door ran over and dragged the lifeless husk away.

~~~~~~~~~

Axe had degenerated into the embodiment of evil. What made it all the more disturbing was the banality. He started out as a reasonably normal little boy. He was a bed wetter and scrawny. Later, he was picked on and bullied. He became withdrawn and isolated, not fitting into any clique. People around him would only say he was a quiet boy. He was biding his time to break out.

Born Uktam Sadyakov, Axe had been obsessed with knives and martial arts as a kid. He studied, practiced, and improvised into adulthood. Use of edged weapons or just about anything else he could get his hands on became applied improvised physics. Axe could use his own shirt to disarm a man.

Growing up in Uzbekistan was oppressive by US standards, albeit less so than before the collapse of the USSR. There were growing tensions between the religious world, which comprised 80 percent of the populace, and a government that considered itself to be secular. Paranoia about spies who turned people in for the language that they spoke or the God they worshipped threatened to create a failed state. Uktam and his parents were constantly living with this specter. One couldn't be sure that a newcomer wasn't going to turn a person in for his or her beliefs.

Sometimes at night young Uktam would sneak out and steal neighbors' eggs, vegetables, or whatever else he could find to supplement the family until a neighbor reported him. Local authorities caught him, held him down, and beat him with rubber hoses. He was bedridden for a week. He tried to find out who turned him in and exact revenge, but no one was talking.

Uktam's mother was threatened by loss of work or worse for their beliefs. Most people that he knew were not brave enough to resist persistent intimidation. Even journalists fled and sought asylum, feeling that their lives were in jeopardy. Going out for a movie was becoming a luxury.

~~~~~~

Axe's next major setback happened during the Uzbekistan unrest of 2005 when he was in his early twenties. His father, an antigovernment agitator, was arrested and never heard from again. It didn't take much to be arrested in the middle of a cold night, beaten, and convicted of terrorism, which meant a bullet if one was lucky, or years in hard labor. Fatherless, Uktam became another disenfranchised statistic in central Asia, an ever-growing problem for Mother Russia and the world.

An embittered, unravelling Uktam, had to find work whenever

he could get it. A few months after his father's abduction, Uktam was at his mother Madina's side when the antigovernment protests broke out over living conditions. Still newly widowed, she protested over basics, like clean water, electricity, resources, and equality.

He remembered the crowds, bodies, mounted soldiers on horses trying to control the fevered masses. His mother held his arm. With the others, she chanted cries, her fist flying in the air, wearing a scarf, no makeup. Her lips wrinkled beyond her years.

Tanks rolled in.

At first the noises seemed distant—scattered and unrelated popping sounds. They became closer, louder, and more organized, and soon they came in regular reports. It was like packs of firecrackers going off. He witnessed people around him falling. Others were running or dropping to the ground and covering their ears and faces. Mists of red sprayed around him. People stampeded and trampled others.

Then it was his mother who, in the middle of a passionate yell, screamed and let out a groan. The side of her head and throat had been ripped away. Gurgling, she let go of his arm and slumped down his side. He dropped with her and clutched her body. He sobbed as her life ebbed. Smeared with her blood, he saw the soldiers close in and heard the gunfire continue, growing louder and closer. Without thinking, he ran and never stopped. With each step along the way, he became more radicalized. He would never attain the wisdom and kindness that can grow out of hardship but instead became just the opposite. The world would pay for what it did to him. As he raged against the universe, the universe raged back at him.

CHAPTER 4

AXE'S GANG continued to hatch its ongoing plan in the cold damp country cabin. After dark, long into the night, howling northern winds found every vacant drafty crevice in the old thinly lit structure. Axe provided hot food and coffee, which was no substitute for warmth.

The windows were covered by blackout shades for privacy. Armed security set an outside perimeter in the frosty, moonless night so dark they couldn't even see their own breath. To help keep warm, guards rubbed and breathed into their gloved hands as they paced.

"Global warming? A very sweet notion." Axe preached to his audience, smacking the table with his palm. "That's nothing compared to what's in store. We will not be, and cannot be, stopped in our quest. Let's get a status report on our latest weapon, please."

His lead scientist stood up, scraping his chair on the floor. The newest, smallest, multistage nuclear bomb they were completing for this mission was a technological marvel. It was designed to simulate a megavolcano. "We are rating the potential explosion to be somewhere between the Mount Tambora eruption of 1815 and the Yellowstone Caldera some six hundred thousand years ago. These eruptions in the past have caused climate change, extinctions, acid rain that burned people, and destruction of civilizations. We do not have the capacity to test these devices since we do not have a testing ground."

Axe said, "We will do a live test soon enough. It had better work."

The staff laughed nervously remembering Rav.

The scientist continued, "As a multistage bomb, its design allows each successive stage to amplify forces exponentially. The first blast deep from within a mountain would blow downward, farther compressing the unbearable shock wave. The mountain itself would then serve as a secondary device, like an engine's cylinder, to accelerate and intensify the final gush.

"We have the tools to drill ten miles down. Some oil companies and research institutes are experimenting with similar drills. These diamond and alloy drill bits along with the specialized lubricants have to be changed every fifty to sixty hours because the heat, friction, and rock wear them down that quickly.

"The secondary blast thousands of feet below ground will intensely heat everything in its path. Pressure will boil over like a super pressure cooker beyond a critical threshold, leading to a violent massive plume of toxic cloud debris.

"This fusion reaction will be the closest thing to the sun's temperature this side of the solar system," continued the scientist. "It is like shooting a two-stage rocket down instead of up from the earth's surface."

Earlier in the developmental stages, Axe had considered Yellowstone as a potential site for the detonation but decided against it because security was too tight. Other than the security issues, it would have been an ideal place to create a catastrophic volcano and associated weather changes. Best of all, doing his dirty deed at a national park would create true terror.

The combined effect of all this destruction and mayhem would yield a six- to nine-month blockage of sunlight from above and several feet of dust and debris on the ground, causing the surface of the planet from parts of California west through Texas and down into Mexico to become incompatible with life.

As far back as 1784, Benjamin Franklin made the connection between volcanic eruptions and climate change. Ash clouds also have dangerous levels of gas such as sulfur dioxide, hydrogen chloride, and hydrogen fluoride. When mixed into the atmosphere, these gases can lead to acid rains, further destroying crops and killing livestock.

Death from radiation would result, too—not only on the planet's surface, but also from the destruction of the underground water table. For Axe, radiation poisoning was an insignificant side effect. It bored him to think of radiation killing people and animals. Any terrorist with a dirty bomb could do it that way. It had become passé. What excited him was the elegance of having the planet wither and starve slowly like a dying fig tree because of the debilitating effect on the climate after the explosions. From his twisted perspective, the human race was slowly killing earth anyway. He would just hasten the process.

In his misguided, misanthropic brain, he believed that humans were merely cancer cells inhabiting what could have been an otherwise great planet. He decided that he would be the earth's surgical oncologist. Here by divine providence to wipe out the cancerous cells, he would teach the world a lesson. He scoffed at religious zealots' belief that man was created in God's image. No. He insisted that humans on this planet were an error in the grand scheme—a temporary blip on the radar that crawled out of pond scum.

Soon after these detonations, the western United States would have no food or water. Everyone would be living in the dark, eating and breathing toxic dust. Crisp fresh air would be a distant memory. There would be such social upheaval that looting and chaos would quickly take over. Fresh water would be gold, food worth more than diamonds. The simple pleasure of watching a puppy and a small child reveling in the grass would be impossible. Desperate and starving, people en masse would attempt to migrate east over the following weeks to months.

If his monetary demand of a huge billion-dollar ransom from the US Treasury was not met (not to mention betting on destabilizing markets), the same type of explosion would occur at a second site within the Rocky Mountains, which would render useless the breadbasket of middle America and part of Canada.

"Any questions or comments?" yelled Axe, foamy white spittle forming in the corners of his mouth. "Some of you have wondered what we hope to get out of this exercise. Now I think that you understand the huge fortune we can make by threatening to do this again, and we can and will. My main motive is pleasure. I'm a sadist and a sociopath; don't forget."

Vuuv, the scientist who had presented and Axe's chief techie, asked, "Why the United States, boss?"

"That's a great question. I suppose ultimately it's because I can. And frankly they deserve their comeuppance. England, Germany, France, and Italy are no better. The Middle East is far worse. Russia and China are horrid, and Pakistan—well, let's not go there. Really. We are not going there.

"Yet, when you attack a gang, always take out the biggest threat first. The rest will usually scatter like scared little children."

It was three in the morning, and Axe stared menacingly at his exhausted team.

"That's why the United States. Taking down America is something no one has been able to do until us now. I prefer to be feared rather than loved. I am an equal opportunity hater, as long as there is money to be made."

Axe smiled. Reflexively, the others did too.

"Americans and their greedy allies have opted to falsely believe that they can help curb the climate changes they supposedly created through excessive consumption. So let them. I will be their new climate broker. As their enemy, I will change the climate now. They will look at me and see a dark reflection of themselves.

"Think about it. These stupid carbon rules and new taxes they'll impose will do nothing more than divert trillions from the haves to the have-nots. Better the money should come to us through terrorism, correct?

A few in the audience, some now standing around a coffee pot in the rustic cabin, hooted, clapped, or yelled yes.

"Do they now think after deforesting a continent and building their empire that they can continue to wage war under a banner of freedom? They send their youth into battle for oil, corporate greed, and control of resources. They disgust me, and yet they are after my own heart. I could not have done better. But I shall soon. Consuming, gluttonous slobs."

Now Axe was in a tirade that was decreasing in lucidity as his agitation increased.

Screaming his oration, the terrorist proclaimed, "Let there be no light. Let them call me the servant of darkness, the prince of chaos. When there is nothing left to eat on their lands, they will eat each other. I swear I will watch them devour themselves. They will eat their own waste on their backyard grills."

Axe had holdings in global commodities outside North America whose prices would skyrocket to astronomical levels after he laid waste to parts of the United States. With his insider knowledge of what was about to happen, he had placed orders in stock exchanges betting that the supplies of food and other commodities would be scarce and that prices would rise. This knowledge alone would create vast wealth. He encouraged his team to invest along with him and reap the rewards of sick amounts of money beyond anyone's dreams.

As a follow-up question, Vuuv, who had been on a need-to-know basis like the rest of Axe's team asked, "Boss, where next?"

Axe replied, "You're one step ahead of me, Vuuv. That's why I pay you the big bucks. Our base in Arizona is now fully operational and lies deep within a mountainous range called the Santa Catalinas. It is in the northern part of their county called Pima. This range is poorly patrolled and has very little security. It does have some potential security threats for us, which we have a great deal of intelligence about. The population in that county totals approximately one million unfortunate souls."

Vuuv listened with an intent expression. Everyone in the room was silent.

"Besides the usual local law enforcement, there are border patrol agents, park rangers, national guard, and a large air-force base to the south. By the time they scramble jets to the area, detonation would have occurred, and we will be long gone. The nearest army base is approximately ninety minutes away by car at Fort Huachuca in the town of Sierra Vista. They have one major interstate highway and poor public transportation. Pedestrian traffic is nearly nonexistent except for downtown during business hours.

"The health-care system there is stretched thin and can barely handle a bad flu outbreak, let alone something of this magnitude. They are close to the Mexican border. Many survivors will try to escape heading south of the border. Their local civilian population is said to be fairly well armed—mostly side arms, shotguns, and hunting rifles. This is a result of American Western culture and their constitutional Second Amendment as it is currently interpreted. Combined, these forces are not to be underestimated. However, I believe that the guns of the people will turn on each other and their officials within weeks of the devastation. We leave for the American State of Arizona in three days at zero four hundred hours."

CHAPTER 5

THE SQUEAKY door slowly opened.

"Time to get up, dear," Mom whispered.

"What time is it, Mom?"

"Five after."

"Five after what?"

"Seven."

"Five more minutes, Mom. Please." I rolled back over in bed. As I adjusted my pillow, a ray of sunlight hit my eyes.

"What would you like for breakfast, Katie?" Mom asked.

I put the pillow over my head.

"We have bagels and pancakes, or I can make you some eggs or cereal."

"Nothing, Mom."

"You have a history exam today. You need energy," she said as she gathered up some laundry and opened the shades.

"Mother."

I put the pillow over my head again.

"Rise and shine."

I tossed the pillow onto a chair. "Mom, every muscle in my body hurts. I have aches in places where I didn't know that I had muscles. They're torturing me in PE. I'm about to rage. PE is so stupid. It's like total crap. They're grading us on it. Some kids can hardly even do the exercises. It's not fair. I have to jog two miles today. Then I'm all gross and sweaty for the next class." I crawled out of bed.

"You can jog a mile, Katie."

"Two, Mom. Two. Not one. You never listen. I walk some and jog some. I am so pissed off. We are getting a quiz on yoga poses, too. How stupid is that?"

"Do you know downward dog? I can show you."

"Seriously, Mother?"

Against my explicit wishes, there was Mother in the middle of my room doing downward dog.

"They're killing me at that high school. PE is the stupidest thing ever invented."

"Well, dear, you know you can't graduate without PE."

"I guess. I'll have a bagel. Toasted light with butter. Not too much butter. You know, the way I like it, all melted."

"It'll be ready in five minutes, *mijita.*"

I am five foot two and weigh 105 pounds dressed and wet, including my sneakers, according to the scale last week. My hair is dark brown, waist length, and wavy. I part it in the middle. If I look down just a little, you can barely see my face, which is just the way I like it. When I sit on a stool, my dad teases me and says I look like Cousin It from behind. I never saw *The Addams Family.* I googled it once and Facebooked my friends about it. Ancient history. My dad is so immature.

Father entered the kitchen to get a cup of coffee. He was fresh and zippy and eager to get to work.

We have one of those espresso makers that does one capsule at a time. I love the way it smells and the hissing noise it makes when it lets off steam. During the weekends while I sleep in, I can smell the coffee aroma licking and wafting in between dreams. Dad gets annoyed when he's the one who gets caught with the coffee waste-basket full of used capsules. He has to empty it before he can make a brew.

I don't like the taste of coffee. I prefer tea, and passion fruit tea is my favorite.

I walked down the stairs in my T-shirt and pajama bottoms.

"Morning, kitten." Dad's been calling me that my whole life.

"Hi, Dad."

"Ready for your test?"

"I guess."

"Did you study hard, feel ready?"

"It's no big deal, Dad. Okay?"

My parents slip a little look at each other as if I didn't notice. "What's gotten into her? She must have gotten up on the wrong side of the bed," they telegraph via eye contact.

As far as I'm concerned, when I get woken out of a dead sleep, both sides of the bed are wrong. I stayed awake until midnight studying. A bit of a cram.

I love history.

My dad doesn't get it.

He thinks it's strange to dwell on the past. He asks why I love history so much if we already know how it always ends and never changes.

Some of my friends' parents have told their kids that unless they major in engineering, premed, or prelaw their parents won't pay for college.

My dad has always said that I should follow my heart and do what I love. Choose any crazy major I want to pursue. I'm good at math and science but don't like them. The thought of blood is gross—too many germs and diseases going around. My father can't stand lawyers. He's always going on and on about how they have ruined this country.

In between a swig of coffee and a bite of toast, Dad announced, "Katie, this week we have that meeting at the professor's house. I think that you will like him—at least I hope so. He's an anthropologist. That sure ties into history. Doesn't it sound interesting, kitten? I'm looking forward to it."

"Okay, Dad." I was texting and listening to music. I barely heard a word that he said.

I drive now. I feel like I practically grew up in my parents' car. Now I'm in the driver's seat. My parents try to get me to chauffeur them around. I'll have no part of that. No one in my family loves to drive, including me. Maybe it's genetic.

My dad gave me his old Ford. He offered to buy me a car that he wanted, but I preferred his Ford. No drama. It brings back good memories and makes me feel safe. Our family has done a lot of stuff in that car. We have driven to San Diego a bunch of times. I really like the sand dunes outside of Yuma. We almost ran out of gas in Jacumba once. That has got to be the windiest little town I've ever seen; I could probably have some fun with that bluster.

I recently went to a great deal of trouble to get a parking sticker at school so that I could park on the high-school campus. When I got to school that day, someone was parked in my spot again. I hate that, and I didn't want to be late. My first-period class was the history exam for which I stayed up late, was woken early, got up on the wrong side of the bed, and was force-fed a bagel lightly toasted with melted butter. I was in no mood and had no choice but to park in someone else's spot.

The last time this happened, after I parked in the wrong spot and ran into class, the person who was illegally parked in my spot without a sticker left. To the security guard who was making his rounds later that morning, it appeared that no one was in my spot, yet I was illegally parked. I got a school summons or citation or whatever security calls it. They can be obnoxious and very annoying.

By that point, I didn't know whose car was parked in my spot and didn't care. I was fuming. As my emotions began to boil over, I stared down at the ground where the car was parked in my spot. And then it happened.

My hair fell over my face. With my head tilted forward and right, I squinted while my breathing became very deep and slow. I went into that unfocused thousand-yard stare, and it was on an exhale that the ground beneath the errant car split with a bang, like someone's too tight pants when they bend over. At first it was just an innocent crack, and then it looked like a little pothole. Some people stopped and stared, but I ran to history class.

Later on that morning at my locker, I heard more. Kids were talking. They called what happened in the parking lot a sinkhole. School officials and my buddies in security found it very mysterious.

After they heard the blaring alarm horn, they found that little BMW vertical and front down in a hole. Outstanding, I thought.

Josh Ryan looked aghast at his new but lightly used metallic black BMW's trunk stuck vertically out of the ground showing the new temporary plates. He had just gotten it. I had never seen it and didn't know whose it was. I don't hang around with him or his friends. I was even more excited when I learned it was Josh's. There's no shortage of kids with fancy BMWs around here.

He was a senior and a jock, an enviable combination. Rumor had it that booze was a bit too important to him. His wealthy parents were pushy troublemakers. His mom was especially annoying.

She was one of those PTA ladies. She always looked like she just blew in off the tennis court with her ponytail sticking out the back of her cap, full makeup over collagen implants, diamond earring studs, shirt collar up, and driving a big ugly German SUV. I thought she was a little too chunky in the thighs to be prancing about in the tennis skirt. But I'm just saying.

Within five minutes of being within twenty feet of her, everyone in earshot would know about their summer condo in La Jolla, the winter trips to Aspen, or about her successful lawyer hubby, all of which was secret speech for "don't mess with me; I'm just way too important." Josh's dad had a similar streak—very showy about his bling. Sometimes when he parted company with someone, instead of saying, I'll be seeing you, he would say, "I'll be suing you." One of his worst attributes was the way he used his church to gain position in the community and get business. He was less spiritual than the car he drove and the diamond his-and-her watches he and his wife wore.

Josh's mom got involved at the school for one reason: to gain better advantages for her precious son, who didn't need her help. We weren't convinced that she wasn't a cougar as well. My mom called her *volada*, which in Spanish means a flirt, and not in a kindly way.

Josh Ryan, the trust-fund baby, was born with a golf club protruding from one of his orifices. Even though he's a good-looking, tall, rich jock, he is not a complete idiot. I began to worry that he suspected me. Maybe I was overthinking it. He noticed me running away when the gust of wind smashed him into a wall. Lately when he saw me, he would call me freaky. I was afraid he knew something.

In any case, I felt prepared for this morning's exam. I nervously chewed wild cherry gum, and my stomach rumbled and churned as the papers were handed out. It was mostly multiple choice and essays. I could do this. Fifteen minutes into it, I started to calm down. My gum had lost its taste, and I wasn't sure what to do with it. I seriously considered sticking it under the desk, but I had a tissue stuffed deep in my pocket; I was hesitant to start fishing for it, though, because I didn't want my teacher, who is the absolute greatest person on the planet, to think that I was cheating or something.

I was already dreading my next class, which was PE.

I kept getting anxious about these so-called powers that I might have. I tried to focus on the essay about the Henry Dawes Act of 1887. My mind drifted again wondering what this Professor S. was going to be like.

I finally got into a groove and wrote a killer essay.

After the exam, which I felt good about, I hurried to the locker room to change into gym clothes. I had just bought some cute new gym shorts. School rules prohibited them from being too short or tight, which I'm good with, especially today since it's that time of the month.

Lately, I had noticed another interesting change in my body. When I have my period, I feel a certain pull. It seems to correlate with a pulse that is within my body. In my mind it's a connection with what is happening with the moon's cycle and its pull on the earth. Even though we live a few hundred miles from the coast in California, I can sense the ocean's pull and tides along with the wind and rain associated with it. The ocean's pull at the shore as the tide goes out is similar to what happens monthly deep within my body. The ocean is magnificent. I worry about her. I can feel that she is not well; her tides have been more painful, and it saddens me. The ocean to me is like a life force, and we are all the waves peeking out at each other thinking we are separate but all the while connected by the power of the ocean's depths.

~~~~~~~

After a brief lecture and a pep talk by our gym teacher, Mr. Shapiro, we did some warm-up exercises and stretches. This included push-ups and sit-ups, which are totally lame. He would call out get warm, stretch what you need to. Kids had necks craning and shoulders twirling. Torsos twisted like wrung-out towels. Spines contorted and arched like mad cats, and then there was the downward dog and child's pose.

We had to jog those two damned miles. More like run a little, sweat a little, walk a lot. Don't want to get too sweaty, not cool.

I'm petite, but my appetite is huge. I don't know where I put it all. I don't exercise. I'm not in shape, especially cardio.

We headed out to the football field to do laps—four to a mile, to be exact. To get down to the field, we have to walk down a few wide short stairs. It overlooks the valley. At night kids like to sit around and watch the crystal city lights below. Parents go on and on about how when they were in high school, they never had facilities like this and how lucky we were to have such a grand sports facility. It looked more like a junior college campus than a high school. Whatever. When they were kids, students weren't shooting each other at school and bullying each other to death on social media.

To us our high school was all we knew. And I still had to do laps.

I had the great misfortune of running into Josh. Here I was, sweating slightly too much. It was running down my cheek and the back of my neck. Huffing with a beet-red face, I watched as he effortlessly glided by, his muscles rippling.

Admittedly, he looked great, and he knew it.

He was wearing those ultralight orange-and-yellow running sneakers that showed each toe and silver-colored running shorts. Not that I was staring or anything—it's just that I noticed as he passed me for the second time, smelling great. I got a whiff of him. I wasn't sure if it was shampoo, sunscreen, or cologne mixed with his pheromones, but the scent caused a mildly intoxicating tingle. This was my idea of high-school chemistry. Suddenly a cool breeze developed at my back. Clouds gathered overhead, and blocked the sky's creamy blues.

I noticed that he looked smooth and didn't have any body hair. He was more hairless than me, including arms and legs. I don't think it was all cosmetic. I later found out that he was trying to become more aerodynamic.

Apparently, his true athletic prowess was road cycling. His ability as a cyclist was sick. He was barely eighteen and already a very highly ranked rider in the elite Peloton of El Tour de Tucson. The tour was coming around again soon. He didn't need a sponsor and already had an impressive fleet of pricy bicycles. Josh didn't dope his blood with steroids. He had no need to. Energy drinks and beer were his drugs of choice.

If he stopped partying so much, his physical capability would be scary.

The third time he was about to pass me on the track, I noticed that his skin had developed a fine sheen of sweat. He slowed down, or maybe I sped up. It might have been that time itself warped. I cannot say with any certainty. He walked alongside of me and called to me, "Hey, freaky."

I looked at his face.

"Hey."

His lips were a bit more on the thin side than I would have liked. He was also a bit on the toothy side, but I could forgive that.

He asked, "How come whenever I see you, you seem to be running from something? Now you can barely do a twelve-minute mile."

I told him, "I'm tired of running right now. I'm cooling down and walking instead. Sometimes I run if I'm late to class, or if I'm just plain happy, I like to skip. So what?" He didn't appreciate me being sassy.

Still seeming suspicious of me, Josh said, "I'm going to keep an eye on you. You had better watch it."

I took it as a compliment.

I smiled and said while panting from near exhaustion and mild stimulation from being two inches away from Josh Ryan's half-naked body, "I thought the same thing about keeping an eye on and watching you." As I considered asking eye-candy boy if he'd like to go get tea sometime, he sprinted away.

"Bye, freaky Katie."

I wished I could create another hole in the ground for me to fall into. What was I friggin' thinking? Bastard.

My girlfriend Sara sped up next to me. She never ran so fast in her life.

"Oh my God. That was Josh Ryan. He is so freakin' hot. What'd he say, girl? I'm dying over here. He is, like, totally gorgeous. I can't believe he was talking to you. Well, that didn't come out right. It's not like a hot guy wouldn't talk to you. You know what I mean. What did you say?"

"I told him he needs a cold shower."

CHAPTER 6

AS I pulled out of the school parking lot to go home, I saw that the area around Josh's spot had yellow crime tape around it. A crane was arriving to remove the wreckage that was once his BMW from the sinkhole that I facilitated into being. The only sounds left in the aftermath were the beeping noise of the crane backing up into position and the sickening scratch of paint and fenders dragging across rock.

I got home somewhere between three thirty and four o'clock. My mom was home.

She said, "Hi, *mijita*. You look exhausted. How was school and that test? I just made some fresh tamales. Nona and Chella dropped off some fresh salsa for you. They wanted to wait and see you but couldn't. Don't forget to call and thank them."

My mother is Mexican American—Rena Gonzalez. My dad is the token gringo in the family. We have a large extended Mexican family on Mom's side. They mostly live up in Catalina, not far from the state park. When I was a kid, we used to swim in the natural pools and go horseback riding along the fifty-year trail where hikers, mountain bikers, and horseback riders try to get along. Occasionally, it doesn't work out that way. Bikers complain that the horse people leave manure behind. The horseback riders argue that the bicyclists spook the horses and carve up the trails. Hikers don't care for either group. One time we rode up there on mountain bikes, and some hiker yelled and told us to leave.

Grandpa practically grew up on that land and lamented that

cowboys have traded their horses for bicycles, ATVs, and dirt bikes. He was an old-time retired copper miner and cowboy who fathered my mother when he was around fifty. My mom has a pile of brothers and sisters. Sometimes I think that every Mexican north of Catalina is a cousin of ours. Abuelo's rotund yet taut gut hung over his hip huggers and cowboy belt with a big silver buckle and a bull carved on it. Sometimes his boxer shorts stuck out in the back. When he squatted, he had plumber's butt. He wore a cowboy hat, bifocals, and boots. Gramps still drove his 1971 Buick Riviera. The trunk lock broke awhile back so he rigged it with a chain and combination lock. He was the only one who knew the secret combination. They say the old *codo* tightwad kept a wad of bills hidden in the trunk. Besides the trunk and various patches of bondo, it looked like the thing was held together with bail wire and duct tape.

The blue paint was dull, and the vinyl roof was peeling. But nothing rusts out here. The engine worked great except for a little blue smoke now and again. You had to finesse it while idling sometimes. One day I'm going to restore it to its former glory.

Gramps always had a toothpick twirling from his mouth. It could be six in the morning, and I swear that man had the toothpick. He must have slept with the damn thing. I'd ask him why he needed one at that hour if he hadn't eaten yet. He would mumble something about breakfast, while he jiggled the loose change in his pocket. Excuse me, isn't that what a toothbrush is for? In Gramps's defense, they say a toothpick is almost as good as flossing. I floss constantly. Abuelo did have a great set of choppers and a smile to go with it. They were all his except for the one he lost in a rodeo accident according to him. Grandmother says it was a fight that broke out after the rodeo when another handsome cowboy smiled at her the wrong way. My grandparents argue about it to this day. The toothpick protruded from the space where his bottom incisor used to live. It was the perfect toothpick holder.

His hygiene was impeccable. All his clothes were perfectly pressed.

I think it was my grandmother who ironed for him. She is a traditional wife. I would never iron a macho husband's clothes, assuming I ever even have one.

~~~~~~

Axe looked down at the watch of the day, a platinum Rolex Yacht-Master II. They were making good time in his exclusively appointed Gulfstream G650. Not all the upgrades were cosmetic. This beauty was capable of defending herself if the need arose. The twin 16,500 IBF Rolls Royce engines were humming at thirty-four thousand feet.

This private jet had a range of seven thousand nautical miles. They wouldn't need to consume that much fuel to make it to their destination outside Nogales, Mexico. The private luxury airplane was known for its ability to fly globally at speeds of mach 0.9. It was capable of landing at fairly small airports to keep the uberrich away from the proletariat, plebs, and the hustle of large international airports, not to mention prying eyes. It could carry two pilots and up to eighteen passengers and was equipped with bathroom facilities, a full bar, and deluxe provisions. Besides the two pilots, he had his entourage of security and technical assistants.

CHAPTER 7

DOCTOR S. agreed to meet my dad and me on Saturday morning at his home near the university. My dad said it was very good of him to give us some time on the weekend. I thought it was even better of me to show up anywhere before noon on a Saturday morning. I mean, really, Dad. Hello.

My dad is a weapons engineer. He's a rocket scientist, no joke. He works with pilots and the big brass at the air-force base. Dad jokes that if he told me what he did, then he'd have to kill me. Apparently, he has high-level clearance only given to certain fully equipped geeks and nerds. You can be a geek without being a nerd. He buys Hagar slacks at the PX. That's nerdy. At night he has his nose in different engineering journals. Boring. My mom tries to dress him, but it's no use. Sometimes he still uses a slide rule for fun. I asked him why he uses the equivalent of an abacus. His left brain is on overdrive, and unless it turns out proof positive by some Newtonian or Cartesian method that there is a very specific scientific reason for my weirdness, he will not get it, buy it, or otherwise cooperate.

He belonged to a scientific skeptic society until my mom made him quit. She has a more spiritual, somewhat metaphysical side to her. She's not a scientist but has enough smarts to realize that human beings are not simply machines and that quantum mechanics opens up a new world for the marriage of science and the spirit.

The professor had the coolest little house off Eighteenth Street downtown. Rows of old pueblo adobes or rammed-earth casitas lined the street punctuated by meandering alleyways. Each house had a different color scheme ranging from purple to mustard. Many of the massively thick-walled homes looked like they had been there for a hundred years of tender loving care. The buildings settled this way or that, making some of the ancient-looking, brightly painted, distressed doors and shutters not fit perfectly. Some had metal roofs. Together it was a spectrum of color. The street was like a magical impressionist painting.

My dad explained how people pay big bucks to get new houses to take on the authentic look that these had acquired. It's like jeans. People pay extra to have them look shredded and worn out and have holes in just the right places.

Sure, there were problems downtown, just like there were in any city. Yet, this neighborhood represented a simpler time of community in a neighborhood. I couldn't help myself. I got this intense feeling of love—love as a state, a condition, like being hungry, tired, or happy. I was, for the moment, love. The trance began, in front of my dad. An arising unstoppable, levitating force.

Dad yelled, "Katie, kitten, are you okay? Oh my God."

Despite my best efforts, I couldn't control it. I couldn't hear my dad. His voice became one tiny sparkle of energy in the din of the universe. I melted into space in my mind. Nothingness.

The *it* I'm referring to was one of my spells. The doctors think it's a partial seizure. My breathing slowed and temporarily almost stopped. My head spun, my knees buckled. It was embarrassing for this to happen in front of my father. It kind of felt like the time he walked into the bathroom and found me on the toilet, or like trying to control a sneeze in a quiet room.

From the ground I stopped and stared that thousand-yard stare down the alleyway between the professor's house and his neighbor's. My eyes squinted, and I looked down and cocked my head right. There was an almost dead calm in the alley. A feral cat stared at us wide-eyed, spooked. A dog barked. That I could hear. Little critters sunned themselves on rocks. A dead bougainvillea plant languished about twenty feet ahead. The barking dog came around the corner toward us followed by a mangy-looking guy with a ruddy complexion and a big stick. It was obvious that the dog was attempting an escape from an abusive person.

A large hawk swooped and screamed above ushering in a gorgeous and transformative gust of wind that blew through the alley followed by a cool mist of tiny, bursting clouds. The dog, a forty-pound blond mutt with big drooping ears, was malnourished, a dull, filthy coat. It ran behind me, sat down, and panted, heavily stressed and thirsty. I stood and dusted myself off.

Within minutes the plant up ahead fully blossomed as the flowers became a bright red. Before father's eyes, the alley shone, and a rainbow appeared. I'm not even sure if I was the only one who noticed the change. "Dad, did you see . . ."

"Katie, did you do . . ."

The curmudgeon approached and said, "Get out of my way. Give me my dog." I started to say something, and my dad stepped forward in front of me.

"Sir, we haven't taken your dog. She's off leash and just sitting here. She doesn't have a collar and looks to be in a state of severe neglect." The man came closer, and the dog cowered. As he approached closer, the reek of booze, cigarettes, grease, and sweat rolled off him. There was a single file now of dog, me, Dad, and creepster. He sidestepped Dad and raised his stick with his dirty hand.

In the blink of an eye, I raised my hand and pushed the air, and like a punch to the midsection, it knocked him back. The hawk flew down onto his head while the cat attacked, not even giving my dad the opportunity to try the judo flip he was getting into position to do, that he supposedly learned in the air force during the last century.

After the man scrambled to get away, my dad yelled at him to get lost and not come back or else we would call the police. "If we see you again, I'll sic my daughter on you."

Muttering, he hobbled away. I chuckled, rubbing my wrist.

The front door of the professor's house squeaked open tentatively, and he greeted us with a look of consternation, holding a big sweating glass of iced tea in his left hand. "I'm terribly sorry this

happened; are you all okay? Anyway, welcome. Please do come in."
He gestured us in like he was trying to gather us. His body language
suggested someone who felt a bit foolish for just standing there not
sure what to do next. He offered his right hand to my dad who nervously shook it so hard that it made the ice cubes in the professor's
glass jingle. We began to calm down as the adrenaline receded, and
our breathing relaxed. The shock was over. Professor S. gave the dog
a bowl of water and offered it a treat. He said that he had seen that
guy hanging around here.

The professor's house was totally awesome—man-cave dark, yet
not gloomy. A respite from the desert sun. Mom wouldn't approve.
Books and artifacts lined every available space. Unusual artwork from
around the world was displayed.

Not too messy. Not neat. I love the smell of books combined with
wood and clean rugs. It smelled and felt like a temple or a shrine.

We followed him into his kitchen. He said for us to please sit. He
was steeping a dark aromatic tea and asked if we would like any.

"Yes, please," I said.

My dad said, "Sure." He was clearly out of his element.

The professor's kitchen window faced the alleyway where my
dad and I had been standing moments ago. I stared out the window
at the now radiant plant that was nearly dead only moments ago. I
glanced up in the professor's direction with a sheepish and questioning expression, wrinkling my nose somewhere between a smile, mild
pain, and a faint odor in the air.

The professor said, "Yes, I saw the whole thing."

CHAPTER 8

AXE'S JET successfully landed in Mexico. The crew and equipment disgorged, and soon they were headed for the US border.

The last thing Axe wanted was trouble that interested authorities. He wanted neutrality during this part of the operation. Once across, he'd have no trouble reaching his final destination in the mountainous region north of Tucson.

Axe and his group casually blended in and coalesced like oil droplets in a puddle at a Nogales border crossing near Calle Pesquiera near the Farmacia San Francisco unarmed and looking like a knot of tourists who had drunk one too many margaritas.

A few birds bathed and drank from the fountain. Men called out to tourists looking for half-priced Ambien and Lipitor. "Amigo, please, come in; our pharmacy is cheaper. If you don't have a legitimate prescription, no problem. Our doctor will write you one on the spot. Diet pills for a skinny woman? Sure. Twenty bucks."

Within a matter of minutes, the temperature dropped twenty degrees. It hailed and poured for twenty minutes emptying out a gray sky. Everyone took cover under the awning in the alley behind the stores that led to the border crossing. The deluge gushed through the streets overwhelming the sewers, which backed up. The air was heavy, smelling of sewage and car fumes. A long line of people and cars waited to cross what appeared to be an arbitrary line in the earth.

Lights flickered, and the power went out. Annoyed storekeepers had to add everything on a calculator or with a pencil.

The fence outlined the landscape into the hills.

When the weather let up and the power returned, a color-coordinated mariachi band played on outside a laser dental clinic. Armed beneath their uniforms, and not with violins, these were paid musical hit men on Axe's payroll. They weren't bad musicians either. But hopefully they were better shots than they were performers. They took requests from the tourists. Love songs, "La Bamba," anything at all.

Jovial and carrying souvenirs, Axe and his friends bantered and joked around. Axe donned his new straw Mexican hat and bought candy from one of the vendors.

The candy vendor's wagon was a riot of color with ornaments for sale hanging everywhere flanking a giant umbrella. The wagon was a shiny, riveted-aluminum affair with two spoked wheels and a handle. The vendor was listening to his little radio. He handed Axe his change and said *gracias* as he stared at Axe's scar, making a positive identification. The vendor's gaze held just a second too long for Axe's comfort. Axe stepped away and studied the man, his stance, posture, frame, facial features, and skin. The details were burned into his memory. Axe never forgot a face. Now the demoniac tattoo on Axe's forearm undulated like a bag of worms. He turned his arm over to observe its writhing shape as he recalled another face he would never forget, the reason for the tattoo. Professor Schlisselvaser.

It's true that many people see Axe and are taken aback by his appearance and scarred face. It's usually the children that stare. Most sensible grown men and women look away, not making eye contact.

Axe nodded to the band and walked away, humming and eating candy. He sent a brief hand signal to the mariachi band by touching his ear and squeezing his nose like a baseball coach signaling that a player should wait or steal third base.

Multitudes walked into the alley behind the row of stores and waited in line at the US border crossing near Morley Avenue. It was prison-like, a fortress, similar to a metropolitan subway turnstile system. It controlled human movement with guards, sets of revolving metal doors, and heavy gates making people feel like they were behind bars for crossing. Veteran shoppers looked like they had been doing this by foot for years.

Axe's team easily spotted the troublemakers that were hired to divert attention away from Axe. Local, hard-working drug dealers and gangbangers were also present. The majority of the people milling about were tourists. US border agents watched.

The border patrol agent checking people through began to ask the standard questions. Axe took off his hat, smiled, and said hello with a mouthful of chocolate, handing over his perfect US passport.

The patrol agent cordially replied and joked with the people, "How was your visit in Mexico? What did you purchase today?" Border patrol officers were very interested in making sure people didn't bring back drugs without a prescription or go over allowed dollar amounts. They kept an eye out for contraband.

Axe showed him the plastic shopping bag of useless souvenirs.

The agent responded, "Welcome back. Next."

Axe walked across the turnstile into the United States of America.

So did the rest of his group one at a time.

~~~~~~~~

The candy vendor's bladder was full. Duty called. A men's room pit stop was way overdue—too much coffee; it went right through him. The mariachi band had decided to take a break, too. Two of them apparently had to go to the bathroom at the same time.

Shane Weaver, the candy vendor with the full bladder who just sold Axe his candy and watched him cross the border, noticed the mariachi band members following him also. Oh boy, he thought, everyone seems to need the bathroom. Maybe it's the water.

He pushed open the metal door to the men's room. The concrete floor was wet and cold. There was a sink with no hot water and a small, polished, metal mirror with graffiti scratched into it. Two urinals, two stalls. Close quarters. Everything was white or green and smelled of disinfectant.

Weaver walked to the urinal. His back was to the door, and as he started to unzip his pants, a man came quietly through the door. In the academy he was taught to not get caught with his pants down.

As Weaver began urinating, he thought this is one of the most underrated pleasures of life. His eyes teared up a bit. He looked up at the yellowing stained ceiling. He was not touching himself, though from the rear it looked like he was, with his hands in front of his groin. Instead, he had his hands on his Glock.

Weaver heard the rasping heavy metal door open behind him; two more feet entered. He counted them. The door closed.

"Hey, amigo. Where's Jose, the regular candy vendor who is here every day?" a husky voice demanded with a thick accent.

Weaver turned around, letting it all hang out, and peed on the guy's fancy mariachi pants and cowboy boots.

As mariachi number one looked down, Weaver said, "He took a vacation," and kicked the guy in the nuts. Next, using his free hand Weaver jabbed the man hard in the throat with the ridge formed by his thumb and second finger. The man starting clawing at his own neck as his face turned red then blue. Weaver hit the man hard three more times—jabs to the face with the barrel of his gun. In two seconds, mariachi one was done. Mariachi two had a tentative yet shocked expression that lasted a millisecond too long.

His left hand held the brim of his large hat concealing something in his right hand.

Weaver didn't want to make any unnecessary noise and wasted no time.

Rapidly closing the distance by hopping off his left steel-toed boot in a diagonal direction, Weaver delivered a sharp low thrust kick to the guy's shin. As Weaver's boot came down to the floor he scraped hard along the shin and finished with a stomp to the foot. Now that he was up close and personal, he asked the second mariachi, "Having a good day?"

Breathing more heavily, Shane then asked, "Care to show me what's under the hat?"

Without waiting for a reply, he grabbed the man's right wrist with his left hand and pushed it down and into the man's abdomen, driving him back. Weaver could not tell what weapon the man was going for. Simultaneously, Weaver head-butted the mariachi's nose, breaking it instantly. As the assailant's head snapped backward and his arms grew weak, Weaver delivered a similarly hard blow to the trachea and then swung the flailing opponent around. The enemy's semiautomatic pistol skipped across the floor. The musician easily yielded to Weaver, who methodically placed the perpetrator's jugular in the crook of his own powerful right elbow while the palm of his left hand applied a forward and downward pressure. Weaver asked him if he'd kindly tell him who he was working for and if he was done sparring for the day. Unfortunately, the man was no longer in any condition to have a conversation or socialize with Weaver, who applied continued pressure in the choke hold and cut off the blood supply to the attacker's brain. The mariachi sank to the floor. Weaver squatted and let the unconscious man down more easily than he should have.

Shane Weaver tried to rouse the men to find out who put them up to this, although he already strongly suspected the correct answer. He rifled through their pockets and took whatever identification he could find. He then tried zipping his pants, but the zipper had broken during the altercation. It took longer to fiddle with the zipper than the whole altercation. Embarrassed, he had to leave the men's room without zipping his fly.

As he left, Shane smiled to himself and was glad that he recently attended the refresher seminar on silent resolution to close-quarter combat scenarios. His instinct and sometimes weakness was to just to blast his way through the shortest distance from point A to point B. It was just the marine still in him. He was tempted to simply put a double tap in each of the musicians' faces even if he did like their music. The first guy wasn't a half-bad violinist.

Shane Weaver made the call he was instructed to make and informed his superiors that to the best of his knowledge Uktam Sadyakov, a.k.a. the Axe, had reentered the United States. Two local casualties. He casually walked toward the US entry point past the

Mexican Federales and flashed his badge to a border patrol agent who became very deferential as Weaver walked on home to the United States of America. The subordinate border agent debated whether to tell Weaver about his open fly but thought better of it.

CHAPTER 9

THE EMPTY tea cups and saucers clinked loudly as the professor placed them in a big white porcelain sink. He drank more tea while sucking on a brown sugar cube, an old European trick I had never seen but wanted to try, though I was too shy to ask.

He had asked many questions and listened for a long time. His tone was kind and soothing; the line of questioning was in a sense clinical, the questions of a scientist, yet they were not medical.

It seemed as though he wasn't quite sure where to begin, and I got the feeling he would have been more comfortable without my dad there. He scratched and pulled at his beard. His fingernails were bitten but spotless. "Katie, Mr. Jackson." He stared at us and then looked down at the palms of his hands as if he were reading from some invisible book or the creases of his palm. "Have you ever heard of mystics? Now, I know you're an engineer, John. May I call you John?" He didn't wait for an answer or permission and continued.

I shook my head no. The dog was asleep under my chair.

"Some people in our culture have called them spirit travelers."

"Now, come on here—" exclaimed my dad. His shoulders, which were rolled forward, straightened, and his chest puffed out. "I'd sooner buy that my daughter has partial seizures or is nuts and needs a shrink."

I glared at Dad.

"John, your daughter is a gifted intuitive communicator. You saw what happened outside with your own eyes. Or did you both just stage that for my entertainment?"

Dad had no comment.

"Now, hear me out."

The wooden chair grated against stone tile as Dad stood up. "Is this some kinda circus? Let's go, Katie."

"No, Dad, I'm not leaving. This was your and Mom's idea."

Professor S. made a gesture with his hands. His palms turned up. "Please stay, Mr. Jackson."

My dad stared at me, his little girl. It seemed to me that all he saw were the big eyes, tiny nose, and freckles of a little girl who yesterday was three years old and not the seventeen-year-old sitting in front of him. Dad sat back down anyway.

The professor continued. "I am not saying that she is a shaman or mystic, or might soon develop into one. However, given everything I've heard and what the doctors have told you, it is a valid theory, just a label. It's the best way to try to explain the evidence of these paranormal phenomenon.

"Shamanism is as old as human civilization. Nearly every indigenous population has had this phenomenon. It is believed to be the practice of an individual who attains an altered state of consciousness. In so doing, the shaman is able to contact the so-called spirit world. Some would call these individuals mystics, mediums, or intuitive healers. Loosely translated, the term means 'one who came from the heavens.'"

I looked up at the professor, sideways at first then straight on. Me? Was he referring to me? I thought, shifting uncomfortably in my seat. My hip was a bit sore from where I fell.

"The shaman is thought to be a messenger who enters dimensions that we mortals cannot yet perceive. As an engineer, John, you can appreciate that modern quantum physics has described that there may be many dimensions, or other universes, on planes we have yet to describe or understand. It's as if the more science explains to us, the more it helps prove and reveal what the ancients already knew."

Although Professor S. spoke authoritatively, my father, as usual, appeared skeptical. I glanced at Dad. He caught me looking and forced a smiled.

Dr. S. stood and struck the casual pose of a lecturer, with one leg out in front of the other and a hand in his pocket.

"One possible explanation for these apparent aberrations may be an energetic web called the zero-point field that connects all matter and wave forms. It cannot be ignored. Some believe that gifted individuals are probably tapping into this cosmic energy field. I respect what you do, John, but this ain't rocket science."

I asked, "Is this stuff legal?"

We all laughed a bit falsely, but the comic relief was needed to cut the building fog of tension. The dog awoke, yawned, drank water, drooled, walked in a circle, plopped back down, and dozed off, probably feeling the safest she'd ever felt in her life. Dog snored gently.

Doc S. walked over to pet her. I began to like him even if everything he just explained went right over my head. I felt clueless.

"Dad, you taking notes? I'm not understanding any of this science stuff."

"Pseudoscience, Katie, pseudoscience. I need data, numbers, proof."

Even so, Dad loosened up a bit.

"John, have a little faith," said Dr. S. "You, too, Katie."

"Huh? What? Sorry you lost me."

Dad said, "You're not alone."

"I must have dozed a minute; I'm kind of tired after what happened outside earlier. The sound of the dog snoring made me sleepy."

"I'm sorry, young lady. We won't be much longer.

"Did you know that if you took this table"—he knocked on wood—"and stretched its fiber so that as we looked deeper and deeper into its molecules and atoms, eventually all we would see is an energy field or waves that have previously been written off as empty space? Space is alive, aware, and conscious, vibrating with a frequency-emitting light. There is no apparent separation from where it ends and you begin."

I responded, "Sure, I guess, but science is not my best subject. What does all of this have to do with what has been happening to me? The one thing I get is that when I have one of my trances, I do feel the sense of connection, like the lines between where I end and where the table starts, to use your example, get blurred. Professor, are you saying that I'm not sick and that what I'm going through is a mystical alteration of my mind of some kind?"

"Excellent, Katie. That's exactly what I'm saying. You don't need doctors or drugs, and I will tell that to Dr. Wilier. But know this: we are all connected by this energy field. We are the field."

The professor winked at me and addressed my dad. "Your daughter over here may have a rare gift. If what I'm thinking is accurate, while Mother Nature can gouge through a rock in a thousand years with wind and water, Katie could do it in milliseconds. It would be like harnessing the power of the sun through a magnifying glass and being able to set a piece of paper on fire with it.

"These unusual practices can help heal souls and correct imbalances in the elements and in communities. Many tribes throughout history have used their spiritually gifted ones in ecological management.

"There are records of some practices that have altered the migratory patterns of wildlife and weather patterns to assist hunting and survival of indigenous tribes." The professor absentmindedly waved at a wall full of books.

"Often, the spiritual communicator enters what we may call an ecstatic state, during which the mystic has greatly reduced awareness of her external surroundings as she turns within, leading to expanded interior mental and spiritual awareness, which can be associated with physical occurrences in the external world."

"Hey, Dad, this sounds a lot like what I've been going through." I beamed hopefully.

Dad slumped again and said, "Heady stuff for a high schooler, kitten."

Doc added, "Yes, stick with me here—it's important. There was a time when these gifted individuals were called witches and were hunted down. They are still often mocked. Granted, many charlatans are selling snake oil. They can put on a great show. In some circles these spiritual individuals are still considered a threat. It's a controversial and polarizing subject."

Now Doc took on a dark, annoyed expression leveled at father. "Just consider your reaction today. You're an engineer in the military munitions industrial complex."

That statement made my dad bristle.

"Even the Soviet and American military have or had programs using seers and their talents. These individuals sometimes assist law enforcement as well. This talent may be inherited. From interviewing your daughter, I'm seeing a potential genetic link here. Apparently, your wife's grandmother was born along the Amazon River in South America, which is fertile territory for indigenous mystical peoples. I have personally spent a great deal of time studying plants and herbal medications in South America. From what Katie says your wife told her, Katie's grandmother gathered herbs, some with mind-expanding properties, and went into trances.

"Her grandmother then migrated to Mexico where she met and married Katie's grandfather. Additionally, in the Latin American–Mexican front there were groups called *mestizo* who had some mystical qualities. I found it interesting and important that when Katie was a toddler she had an imaginary friend that she spoke to. It was very wise of you and her mom, your wife, not to interfere with or extinguish this pattern of behavior."

My dad added, "Before my wife Rena's grandmother passed away, she talked a lot about the importance of not suppressing and rather fostering Katie's vivid imagination."

The doctor added, "The imaginary friend who was part human, part animal may become helpful, as this is often an archetypal spiritual guide attempting to call a spiritual warrior into training. It may be her time, whether we like it or not, and for reasons we may not yet understand. In Katie's case, it sounds like she is being called into practice to in some way alter or impact the environment or ecologic balance around her, using nature's elements. There may be more signs coming, like those we witnessed this morning.

"According to historical documents, some of the most challenging cases are ones where an only child is called to action at a very young age, with resistant parents. This can lead to great stress and even illness in the child. There have been reported cases of individuals sweating blood until they came to terms with their fate. Others have roamed the countryside sleeping most of the time until their ultimate awakening. Budding medicine men or women who start early on in life often become the most powerful.

"Early in a mystic's career, the initial mind-bending states can be quite scary. They can feel like a lucid nightmare. The only option is to learn to relax, release, get behind it, and let go. Common experiences can include the feeling of leaving your body and hovering. This can be accompanied by a feeling of being constricted or squeezed initially before the sense of freedom and travel begins." Doc S. got up and began to collect some books and references. "Any questions so far, either of you?"

"Yes, please, Professor. I just have to tell you that I have had many of these lucid dreams and nightmares. I don't want to get sick over turning away from a heavy responsibility. But I'm just a regular kid. I can't handle all this stuff. I'm getting very weirded out. After meeting with you, though, I've never felt better. Like someone gets it, like I'm not nuts. Now you're saying that if I don't go with it, I could be wandering around ill and sweating blood."

Dad was pale, sweat glistening on the nape of his creased neck. His shoulders hunched and sagged again. The professor had left him feeling deflated. He looked like someone had told him I had just been arrested and was pregnant and on crack.

I tried to say something light and fluffy. "Hey, Dad, I might be a mystic or something. Cool, huh?"

"Katie, even though you probably have this talent or gift, it is something that requires training," said the professor.

He went on with a parental knowing look. "For one thing, you've already pointed out that you have no real control over this power. When it happens, it takes over quickly like anger or joy. This is a skill that can be cultivated. It requires practice. Dedication. It should come as no surprise that this power cannot solely be emotionally driven.

"You must commit to using this power with great caution and responsibility and for the good of humanity. After all, one of the reasons we are here is to elevate our spirit and help repair the fallen world we inhabit. It's easy to lose discernment and slip into the dark side. Once it's been identified that a person has these powers, there will be opposing forces. The war of good versus evil will become stronger both within your soul and here in the earthly plane. Do you understand this? Beware."

I think I barely nodded, but my wide-open eyes said it all.

All the professor said was, "Good. Usually the intensity into which the state is entered is roughly proportional to the power that is tapped into. Also, across all of humanity, it is agreed that developing the ability to meditate in one form or another, sometimes using herbs, chanting, or other paraphernalia, assists in the process. Breathing properly is paramount. You've already discovered intuitively to slow down your breathing and execute your power on an exhale."

The professor got up and sauntered across the house to his library, leaving Dad and me staring at each other awkwardly. He pulled some old editions off his shelves and returned with an armful of books, blowing dust off the spines. He showed us pictures of drums, instruments, feathers, and dances used by these ancient healers. The pictures he presented of indigenous men and women of varying ages had expressions and facial distortions similar to what happens to me when I get in the zone. Some say that eye color can change when the sessions are taking place. No one has looked at me that closely yet.

My father was totally stymied. He thought that his daughter was a character in a Carlos Castaneda book. All he could say was, "Can Katie get a scholarship for this stuff to pay for college?"

The professor laughed. "Maybe in Northern California." The tension in the room began to let up. "Katie, if you have the true desire and your parents are willing, we can teach you. You will need to learn about the elements, see an acupuncturist that I know, and learn how to meditate. Occasionally, we use a form of hypnosis called regression therapy. It may help a person go back, very far back, in his or her memory banks and remember things that might help explain what you are experiencing now."

I spoke up. "When I get these spells, it seems like my mind changes or bends. Things seem to come apart into smaller and smaller pieces." I looked up. Father and professor were staring at me intently. The room was silent.

Putting my fingers together like they had been glued, I continued.

"Normally when I think about something, I tend to believe that what I think is right, real. When I'm in the place you are describing, it's different. Ordinarily, when I look at a tree, or even a person, I see a thing."

I pointed to my father who looked offended and made a little ticking sound with his mouth over being compared a thing or a tree.

"When I get into the zone—I don't know what else to call it—I see forms and patterns of color, sound, and swirling waves combining and rising. Everything seems related or connected. Professor, sometimes I see solid objects as shimmering energy waves. Solid matter unfrozen free to move."

The professor sat quietly and smiled at me. He said that I was on my way. Where, I did not know. Eventually, he stood up in a way that let us know the meeting was now officially over. It was a comfortable ending.

I stood up, too. There was some dust and dirt on the professor's chair from my pants where I fell. I began to wipe it with my hand.

"No need, Katie, but thank you. Saturday chores await," he said as we walked the way we came in. "Got to get to the store. I'll try to do a better job of tending to the bougainvillea that you did CPR on. What about the pooch?"

Dad and I looked at each other. We both lit up and knew what the right thing to do was, even though I was upset with him over his reactions to my morning of feeling normal, valid, and legit. We were worried that Mom might say no to a stray. Dad said he would talk to

JUST WATCH ME   69

her and that we could get the dog to the vet next week and make sure that she was all right. I think he wanted her more than I did. He's a big kid with a big heart who loves animals. I could just see him asking Mom to keep the dog. No dog will ever replace the one who died, but I love animals, and this girl desperately needs a good home.

We said our farewells, and when Dad opened the car door, the dog did a running leap into the backseat and slid into the armrest. The car was a million degrees inside after sitting in the Arizona sun for a couple of hours. It was too hot to even touch the steering wheel. Dad blasted the air conditioner, and we were off. All my dad could say when we got back in the car was why couldn't I have taken up debating or steel drums.

"Now, listen here, young lady, if you so much as blow some-one's house away in a storm or anything like that, you are grounded. Understood?"

"If someone ever calls me a witch, I will destroy them, just watch me."

Dad ignored my comment. Men. I couldn't tell if he wasn't paying attention, or glossing over it. "You hungry, kitten? Maybe you won't feel like destroying anyone after a good lunch. First, we have to get our new friend home and situated. We don't know if she's housebro-ken."

"Whatever."

"Whatever what? Is everything whatever to you?"

"Yes, Father. Are you saying I'm a witch? Or do you think I'm still a kid and that I'm just hungry and cranky?"

"No. But I'm starving. Wanna drive?"

"No."

I sat in the back with dog.

"Can you call Mom and see what she's up to?"

I dialed my mom. "Mom, Dad is so mean."

"Ay. What happened, sweetie?"

My dad said over his right shoulder, "Put that thing on speaker. I have a right to defend myself."

"Well, the professor said I was mystical. Dad said he would have been happier if I was having seizures and that I should have joined a debate team or steel-drum band. I didn't choose to be this way, Mom. He's so mean. That boy Josh Ryan is right. I am a freak."

"John, what did you say to your daughter?"

I continued talking as my dad got a beleaguered expression.

Then the dog barked.

"John, was that a dog? What is going on?"

"Mom, the professor wants to teach me stuff, and Dad freaked out and practically stormed out."

Dad said, "I didn't freak or storm out or anything of the kind. Kate, you are exaggerating. Rena, I said nothing wrong."

Dad only called me Kate when he was getting upset.

Mom said, "I'm completely lost. Someone better explain what the heck is going on." She addressed me and asked tenderly, "Will you be all right, Katie? You are not a freak. Do you hear me?" It was the tone of voice a mother uses when it's time to gang up on Dad.

"See you soon, Mom. Love you," I said as I shot my dad a piercing look and told him, "I am so never talking to you again."

He gave me that lovable dad look and said, "Never?"

"Not ever."

"How about one week of the silent treatment?"

"No."

"Ten days?"

"Yeah, right."

"E-mail?"

"Not even."

"Skype?"

"Nope."

"Text me? You gotta admit, kitten, that this is all a bit weird especially for a hard-boiled rocket-science person like me. I'm just an engineer. Either it flies or it doesn't. If there isn't hard-core data that appeals to my left brain, it's a stretch of my very limited imagination. I need time to digest this stuff. Work with me. I'll get used to it and get the hang of what's going on here."

I let a little smile slip out of the corner of my mouth. We were stuck at the downtown train-crossing red light when it started up again. Sounds faded, but in the distance I could still hear the clanging train tracks, the bell, and the train's loud horn as it passed through town. My head tilted down and right. I squinted and stared. My breathing changed. I was mumbling and could no longer hear Father talking. Every cell in my body felt squeezed tight. My body wasn't mine, and I wasn't sure who or what I was. I couldn't breathe, sure that I was dying on the spot and very scared. It only lasted a moment.

Soon I was letting go just like the professor said. I don't think that I was breathing or even had a need to. It was more like the body in the backseat of Dad's car was breathing itself. I saw and felt the presence of my childhood friend. She was a bear and yet somewhat human. The apparition stood on hind legs. She had human eyes and black human hair that flowed forever. The face was vaguely familiar. Like family, but I could not place it. She was waiting for me to follow her, but I couldn't move. Bear threw me on her back, and we descended deep into the earth.

At the same time, I was in the back of my dad's Volvo wagon. I looked at myself before the bear and I ventured off. The dog stared at me with her head cocked sideways and her ears up and back. She pawed me and let out a little whimper.

I was effectively in two places.

On Bear's back I felt invincible. No. I *was* invincible. She ran with the speed of light as I held on to her incredible mane. I became truly ecstatic. Momentarily it felt like I was nothing more than a point in space composed of pure consciousness that was everywhere at once. Time was meaningless. I was never so happy and did not want to return. Even though we were going deeper underground, I could see the entire sky above and everything below us. I saw Finger Rock, a landmark outcropping north of town. She turned to me and smiled. I began to cry tears of joy. We didn't speak but communicated through our thoughts. She was taking me somewhere I needed to be. There was something I needed to know. But what?

Little was revealed. Deep tunnels, an underground river, Finger Rock. An evil man. Somehow I knew of this man. I can't say when or how but not in this life. We were enemies once before. A karmic debt would need to be paid. I saw the spirit of two explorers far beneath Finger Rock. They shared a strong bond of love.

A yellow rail lifted allowing traffic to flow again. The train had finally passed, and it seemed like a century had gone by. A furious dust devil came up out of the ground and forced my dad to pull over. He was already annoyed by the delay from the train and now he had to stop for this thing. "Katie, do you see that huge dust devil?"

Suddenly I awoke and was back.

"You okay, kitten?"

"I guess so, Dad." I dried the tears on my face with my sleeve. "I must have fallen asleep. I was having a dream."

"Hope it was a sweet one. Rest now. It's been a tough morning. I'll wake you when we get home."

My parents wanted to eat lunch so that we could talk. But first we introduced the dog to Mom. "Dog, Mom. Mom, dog. Okay, let's eat." Mom thought the dog was adorable but stinky and suggested— no, ordered—us to pull out the old crate we used to keep our prior dog in.

"Mom, can't we do this after lunch?"

"No. We cannot give this girl the run of the house yet, especially considering that she was living on the streets with that *cabron*."

"Mother." My face got hot. I think I blushed listening to Mom cuss. She was pissed.

"Any man who could be mean to an animal deserves worse," she countered. "We should find him and stuff him in a crate for good."

We didn't want to leave her in the backyard without a collar on for fear she might bolt. We did have a little dog run, but the walls weren't that high. We had to decide on the dog run or the crate. Mom voted for the crate, Dad for the run. It was up to me. Mom said, "She's your dog. What will you name her?"

For now I was just calling her Dog.

We tried crating her, but first she tried to get away, and then she began to howl, cry, and paw at the bars. After a few minutes, she pulled at the bars with her teeth and pushed with her legs. She began to bend the bars, at which point I said, "No way. I vote for the dog run." I opened the crate, the dog rushed in to my arms, and we headed out to the old dog run and set it up with our old dog's bowl, now dusty with an abandoned spider web. A few toys and the dog settled down after I threw the ball with her awhile.

"Lunch now, anyone? Hello?"

CHAPTER 10

SEVERAL VEHICLES were waiting as Axe and his squad regrouped in the four-dollar parking lot, which was the one that allowed drivers in and out with a yellow token near the McDonald's next to the pedestrian walkway on the US side of Nogales, Arizona.

Axe threw the remainder of his candy into the scrub behind the car where beer cans, broken bottles, and a few condoms littered the ground. He fixed his belt, spit, and got into the Range Rover. They were FAVs—fully armored vehicles. Poor on gas mileage. Not green.

The group organized and adhered to standard convoy security formation with Axe in the middle vehicle and then headed for I-19 toward Tucson past the K-nine checkpoint. When they got onto I-10 heading west, Axe pointed to the haboob in the distance to his right. "Look over there," he said to Vuuv as he casually backhanded his shoulder pointing to a dust storm. "I've heard about these here in the desert. They are usually harmless minitornadoes."

Vuuv said, "That is really cool looking. It reminds me of a big grizzly bear on its hind legs."

Axe retorted, "You take too many drugs." They both laughed.

They stayed on the interstate and got off at the Ina Road exit. It was a little slow going due to construction, and there were sheriff's deputies moving traffic along. Axe's jaw and shoulders tensed up, but he cruised along, not too slow, not too fast. They headed east toward Skyline Drive and then north on Alvernon Road. His vehicle and the others who joined stopped at the electric access to his compound near the Finger Rock trailhead parking lot.

<center>~~~~~~~</center>

The Southern Pacific railroad came to Tucson in 1880. Soon after construction of the train depot, Wyatt Earp and Doc Holiday had a shootout with Frank Stilwell on the tracks at the west end of the depot. Maynard Flood, the local railroad icon, and Maynard Dixon, an artist who painted historic images, were the namesakes of the restaurant called Maynards that my parents and I were finally sitting down to eat in.

After a lengthy discussion about what to order, my parents decided on a salad. How boring.

We brought Mom up to speed on what happened with the professor.

"Ay, my little mystic. It's wonderful. John, why do you look so sad? You're acting like she went away to college or drove off a cliff."

"Rena, I'm not sure which is worse at this point."

Mom hit Dad playfully, which cheered everyone up. "I always wanted some type of doctor in the family. I wasn't expecting this. Maybe a pediatrician?"

Dad laughed.

"Anyway, it's something to celebrate. Right? We will get a big family dinner together. Maybe we should all go up to Sedona and have a party near those vortexes where all the crystal people hang out."

Here we go again, I thought. My family always looked for a reason to make a big dinner and throw a party. "Mom, this is no time to joke."

"You know," she said, "my grandmother was a little different, too. They say she could help heal people and do things." Mom did this thing with her hands and wiggled her fingers to convey the doing of things.

"Katie, look, I have something to show you. You are practically the spitting image of my abuela when she was your age and living near the Amazon before they moved to Mexico."

Mother handed me an old black-and-white, five-by-seven photo that was yellowed to a sepia color. The edges were scalloped, and the photo had been crinkled and folded so that white lines crisscrossed the scene of my great grandmother. It was spooky. She looked just like me except with black hair. It was the face I thought I recognized in Bear. Great grandmother was a native girl with braided hair standing in the Amazon rain forest, wearing local peasant clothing and holding a plant or bark I didn't recognize.

"Mom, I'm not that different, am I?" I was beginning to accept it. Now it was a matter of degree.

"I'm sorry, baby. We are all different. We all have unique gifts and traits." She paused and continued, "Like the professor said, maybe it runs in the family."

"Mother, I'm no longer speaking with either of you."

Dad smiled slightly, seemingly vindicated. I presume he was enjoying the company of mother in the doghouse now that both parental units were outcasts in teenage exile. Father proceeded to tell the story about the time he was at a business dinner with one of his colleagues who brought a date. They made the usual introductions and exchanged pleasantries. She asked him what his job was. Then he asked her the same.

She told Dad that she was a fairy.

"Excuse me?"

"Yes, I am a fairy. I live in Sedona. We have a serious fairy organization there."

"I see," commented Dad who had little patience for this sort of thing. He asked if she had specialized in something like tooth.

Mom cracks up every time Dad tells this story.

Fairy didn't speak to Father the rest of the evening, which was a good decision in my estimation.

She's a wise woman my mother. During that lunch she told me that my life would be special and extraordinary. Not always in an easy way. That I would be tested. She told me how she always suspected this day would come.

Mom said, "When I was pregnant with you, my love, I had strange dreams."

Mother described how she blew them off at the time with a shrug. I could understand why.

"Watching you grow, my daughter," Mom said, stroking my hair and smiling, "it became apparent to me that you were a very special child, here for a purpose. I couldn't quite comprehend it at the time. But now I know." Mom was a little anxious as she told me all of this because some of her dreams were of great danger. She would have preferred a much gentler, easier road for me. I hugged myself, and tears began to flow. "All the same, Katie, it is a cause to live life, celebrate, and give thanks." Mom's eyes welled up, and her mascara ran. "I don't want to lose you, kitten. You're growing so fast and strong."

"Mom, why didn't you tell the psychiatrist?" I asked.

"He didn't ask." Mom laughed through her tears. "I didn't want to share these stories with the doctors. Maybe I wanted it to be our secret until the time was right. Your time has come."

She said that when she was a girl they had a cat. She was sick but still purred every day. My grandpa would tell her that we shouldn't put the cat down because she still enjoyed life. Enjoy every purr, Grandpa told her. Dad put his arm around her. He misted up, too. They both looked at me from across the table like it was our last meal together. I asked my mother if they were planning to put me down if I stopped purring. Mom nearly spit out her coffee.

Later that night, my parents were getting ready for bed. It was the nightly ritual of getting into comfy shorts and T-shirts, brushing teeth, listening to music, and dimming the lights. The end-of-day bedroom talk between a married couple. Mom had this whole skin routine that made her look iridescent and slick. I was walking to the living room to get my favorite scented candle and overheard them. Again, I don't normally eavesdrop.

Mom said, "John, I can't handle it."

"Why, what's the matter?"

"What's the matter? Are you crazy to ask me that question? Katie, our daughter, is what's the matter."

"At lunch you sounded like it was great honor and that we were going to celebrate that our daughter is wacked—err, I mean, gifted—with a big fairy party in Sedona waiting for bliss to arrive."

Mom rambled on. "I didn't want to upset Katie more than she already is."

"This is for real?"

"My poor girl. We need to do something. Maybe talk to a preacher. I love her."

Mom started bawling uncontrollably. I could hear the muffled sobs now as I snuck back to my room. I felt terrible. I knew it was about me. When I was little, whenever I heard loud noises and conversation coming from my parents' room, and believe me they were no strangers to loudness, both good and bad, I would silently sneak over and eavesdrop. Tonight I didn't need to because I could hear quite well.

Dad gently consoled her and said, "What you said before is true. She didn't get hurt. She's not sick. She didn't leave home. I must admit I can hardly believe the scene I witnessed outside the professor's. And that dust devil out of nowhere could have been a coincidence. Like Dr. S. explained, no one said any of these theories are for certain. If it is true, then it's a gift she seems to possess. It's not an illness to the best of our knowledge. He feels it can be cultivated into something very useful. I was shocked, too. Look, as a family we have been through a lot together. We will face this and deal with it as well. You'll see. I promise."

"How can you be so sure? She could be in danger."

"I'm not. All I know is we have each other. Katie seems genuinely excited to pursue this. We have always supported her endeavors within reason except the time she wanted to cliff dive in Mexico at the age of twelve. Yes, this is intense and otherworldly, but we will see it through. You look exhausted. Why don't you go lie down? I'll rub your back."

CHAPTER 11

AXE AND his gang arrived at their compound in the northern Tucson foothills. His mansion sat on the middle of the acreage. Pristine Sonoran Desert. The saguaro cacti with their huge strong arms had been there in a delicate balancing act soaking up the sun and reaching toward the heavens for two hundred years. Their shallow root system formed tentacles communicating with the earth below, revealing a miracle of nature that they could even stand upright at all. Mesquite trees provided some shady respite for the desert floor below. The wildlife stood still and silent when the humans arrived.

Bobcats and coyotes had lots to eat. Quail and rabbits were plentiful. Javelena lounged in the shade, which was twenty degrees cooler than being in the sun. The entire desert was their smorgasbord—cacti stickers and all. A curious deer peeked out from behind a paloverde tree as an odiferous skunk roamed. She took ownership of her domain. It wasn't hot enough for the snakes to come out and sun themselves yet. They rested beneath the surface.

The house was over fourteen thousand square feet of pure decadence that belied its nefarious purpose. Northern views encompassed the Catalina Mountains beneath Finger Rock, while southern views revealed the glittering city night lights of the valley floor. The most important feature of the building was underneath it

After losing his mother in Uzbekistan, Axe wandered angry through the shadowy underbelly of Central Asia. Hard men ruled. Trouble was easy to find but harder to spot.

Still in his twenties, Axe travelled overland from his hometown trying to avoid capture, arrest and deportation. That would have been a fatal error for him.

He made it to the Caspian Sea, had enough money left to get a visa, buy a ticket, and boarded an old ferry to Chechnya.

After sea sickness exhaustion and a dangerous trek to Grozny, someone approached Axe with an opportunity for survival. Axe the green newcomer had dropped thirty pounds. Desperate, he was offered a hot meal ticket, a bath, and a bed if he would deliver a certain package to a certain place. "Hey, kid, wanna make a few bucks?" Hungrily he agreed.

Axe was warned not to open the package or ask any questions. Drop the goods and leave. Don't look back; if he managed that, he was promised there would be more work with greater rewards to follow. If not the punishment would be swift.

Instead, being the adventurous and all-too-curious type, he opened the package, and it contained heroin and cocaine.

Axe showed up at the designated place, did the drop and walked away as instructed. He didn't look back, hid and watched instead. The package was picked up by another new loser just like himself who was also looking for life's necessities. Axe felt a little sorry for the guy.

The pickup guy was younger and smaller than Axe, an easy target. The boy seemed very nervous, pasty, and jittery; his clear eyes darted here and there. Axe observed from a dark shadowy doorway in an alley. At the opportune moment, Axe delivered a swift kick and quickly made off with the package. The younger, malnourished man gave chase, which surprised Axe. The youth had a knife and was yelling and cursing through the streets because his life depended on it. Axe ran as fast as he could, holding the package like a football. The young man chasing him was fast, so he managed to close the gap and throw the knife at Axe's spine, but it missed completely. Axe might as well have killed the dude himself because when he showed up empty-handed, this guy was going to be dead meat anyway. The clang of the knife bouncing off the brick wall made Axe realize the young man just threw what he had. Took his best shot. Axe stopped running and turned, impressed that he and the stranger had something in common—knives. Axe picked up the knife and pursued the man, who did an about-face and tore off. Axe would never have caught him had the guy not reached a dead end and tried to scramble and climb over a wall.

Axe yelled, "You idiot, fool, wait, wait." Axe finally tackled the male, who wasn't much more than a boy. He wasn't sure where this would go, had no plan and nothing to lose. Axe smacked the guy, rifled his pockets, found a little money, some power bars, a cell phone, and some identification. Axe asked questions at knifepoint and soon realized the kid was indeed a new arrival being used like a pawn to do drops and pickups like Axe was doing.

Axe made the punk an offer. "If I let you go, they will kill you because I will not return the drugs. If you fight me, I will kill you. Yes, I looked in the package, and the stuff is worth good money. Or you can help me sell these drugs, and I'll split it with you seventy-thirty." The boy wanted fifty-fifty, but as the knife pressed harder against his jugular, the deal seemed more attractive to him. The boy's name was Vuuv. He couldn't have been more than twenty or so, but looked sixteen.

The two miscreants peddled the drugs while looking over their shoulders. One watched, and one dealt. Altercations ensued. Twice someone grabbed the little yellow bag of coke and ran. Vuuv caught one, but the other was too fast.

Sharing woeful tales of how they ended up here, Axe and Vuuv were still able to laugh at their pathos. Vuuv was hesitant about laughter. Axe quickly became alpha dog. He was boisterous and grandiose about the future and how they would make it big. Part of the big talk and bravado was Axe putting some of the profits up his over-sized nose.

In dark alleyways, double-crossers that they were, the two youths felt that their luck had turned. Things were looking up. They had pocket cash, food, and drugs, which meant women came around and paid attention to them. The girls were similar to Axe and Vuuv— hungry, tired, green, young, and looking for some action. They thought gangsters who were moving up might be a winning ticket. The ultimate genetic selection process. The way of the world, a force of nature to be reckoned with. No better, no worse than opportunis- tic male hyenas.

But the Russian owners of the package heard about it and did catch up with Axe. It was somewhere in the devastated Mikrorayon market section of Grozny, where grey streets rotted with a smell to match. Amid poor economic conditions and high unemployment, the pristine black Bentley coupe rolled smoothly, lazily, to a halt. The rise of new Eastern European money. Axe couldn't give a rat's ass about Russian gangsters though he was fast becoming one and loving every minute of it. He was hungry, mean, and tasted blood. He wanted what they had, with their deals, drugs, people smuggling, and weapons.

Vuuv had gone in search of coffee. The encounter in the market was how Axe got his nickname and a few of his scars, along with the street credibility that went with it, letting others know a formidable player was on the move.

There were two of them, the driver and his passenger, who looked like police or military. It was getting progressively more difficult to tell the difference between the mafia and the police. The driver looked like he had been eating too much steak and caviar, washing it down with vodka. He was lumpy with rheumy eyes. Lids thick and low. The nose was full of burst capillaries.

Their clothes were perfectly laundered and pressed. The only thing Axe wished to launder was their money. The two Russians walked toward him. The overfed one lit a cigarette, while the other reached inside his coat, producing a gun.

Caviar man was the mouthpiece. "You have my package."

Axe said, "You call that an icebreaker? Is that anyway to greet a newcomer to your fine country? I thought you had a housewarming gift for me."

"Where is it, *mudak*?"

"If you're nice, I'll tell you." The man with the gun took a step closer, which is exactly what Axe was hoping for—using words as bait to lure him in for the kill.

Axe took a step back. Military man drew his gun but stayed about a foot away from Axe's skull.

Axe pretended to be placating. "Okay, all right, I'll give you what you want. Please. You can't blame a kid for trying. You were young once. You must have made your mark somehow, some way. Give me a chance."

Military man said in a heavy Russian accent, "I count to two, and then your head removed by gun."

"It's right over there," Axe said as he feigned a look then did a snapping, inside out block deflecting the barrel an inch or two, just enough to put his brains out of the line of fire. A shot did get off, grazing his ear and leaving it deaf and ringing for ten days. Out of nowhere, with blinding speed, Axe hit the gunman's wrist with a small hatchet leaving the hand dangling and squirming by a few glistening, sinewy tendons. Military man was tough—pale with shock, but tough. He regrouped and applied a tourniquet while Axe negotiated with caviar man.

Axe, now a fully grown young man near his prime, had a little more fun with him since he hadn't practiced kicking drills in a long time. An old favorite was a cross behind hook to the ribs with the right leg, step pivot, follow through with a left roundhouse, and then keep turning and finish with a turning hook to the man's temple. A choreographic pirouette. As he kicked, Axe informed steak belly that he was a filthy pig and that he sold all his dope. Meanwhile, with caviar man down as a result of the kicking assault, military man had slowed his bleeding with his belt and didn't look well but kept coming. Axe pulled the car keys, wallet, and gun away from the downed man, who reeked of booze and tobacco, and ran.

Axe barely got to the car. Military man pulled a small revolver out of a leg holster with his intact arm and unloaded uselessly since the Bentley was bullet proof. Before passing out, the hit man tried to shoot out a tire and failed.

Axe hooted and hollered at his victory and sped down the street in the newly confiscated vehicle. Two blocks away he saw Vuuv drinking coffee with one hand and carrying another back to Axe, who screeched to a halt, opened the window, and yelled, "Hurry. Get in." Vuuv looked stunned, recognized Axe, and cocked his head inquisitively.

"Get in. There's no time to explain," Axe urged.

Vuuv hopped in and before both legs were in the car and the door was closed, Axe was off. The coffee nearly fell over, and some spilled on the seats. Axe said, "Careful! Watch it—these are fine, leather, hand-stitched seats."

They drove the car but soon ditched it.

Instead of snorting all the profits, drinking booze, and woman-izing more than absolutely necessary by their low standards, Axe and Vuuv reinvested most of their money. Axe bought more drugs, more guns, and hired help. He became a ruthless dealer. At one point the nickname Hacker was given to him. It didn't stick since it conjured up images of a Chinese computer geek. Vuuv was more the hacker type. He had been a sharp engineering student keenly interested in computers before the floor fell out from under him.

As Axe's growing empire became more sophisticated, it morally devolved and included international, Asian, and Russian human smuggling that preyed on fear, poverty, and drug-addicted girls with low self-esteem. Axe's debauchery would have made the Roman emperor Tiberius jealous. He considered dabbling in piracy for a short time but again became seasick and gave up. Maritime crime was not his gig. As a result he decided not to acquire the obligatory status megayacht.

Instead, in his free time he travelled, seeking new avenues of power and control. Vuuv advised that the future would be mind control via chipping the brain. In the meantime the best investment would be to capitalize on hallucinogenic herbs that can control the mind and foster black magic.

Axe laundered tens if not hundreds of millions of dollars and parlayed his growing fortune into currency speculation and commodities. He was a high-risk, high-reward, high-rolling, adrenaline junkie. His accounts in the Caymans and Switzerland grew like weeds. There was no shortage of questionable money exchanges that asked very few questions globally.

Overall, he was proud to be a one-stop shop for all nefarious needs. A spa day with Axe's clients could include cocaine, free mimosas, a rocket-propelled grenade from the former Soviet Union to play with, and an escort. He was able to capitalize on modern-day warfare that can easily be committed by lone wolves and nonstate actors with huge profits selling plutonium and other fissionable materials. He hoarded these for his own devices under the property he now occupied. After a while, selling RPGs became boring, like selling firecrackers on the Fourth of July.

~~~~~~

There are numerous caves in and around the Tucson foothills. Axe chose his Arizona property because of a particular cave under it. He and two hired experts went spelunking at the time he was considering buying the land. Being curious and energetic, he decided to explore the cave with his hired guides. That way he could keep an eye on things and see for himself.

The cave's entrance had southwestern petroglyphs on the walls, including one of a ferocious bear with a hawk perched on her shoulder. The three ventured on, but the novelty quickly waned for Axe. Stale air. A progressively narrowing and darkened passage like a constricted bronchial tube. Claustrophobia. Axe decided to turn back partway into the expedition. Panic and agitation gripped him from all sides when he realized that he couldn't turn back. He could not turn at all. There was barely enough room to take a deep breath without the cave walls restricting his ribs, leaving him feeling entombed and gasping for air. The only way out was to slither backward in a semistretched position. He forced his breathing to slow.

On his way out, a tarantula crawled across his face. He tried to bite it, blow on it, anything to make it more scared than he was. The sound of a rattlesnake warned him that maybe his being there wasn't a good idea. He screamed ahead to his guides. It was a sound of muted terror disguised as an order to continue without him and report the findings when they got back.

The hired pair was experienced and well equipped with helmets, lights, harnesses, ropes, food, water, and music. They were a physically flexible couple that knew how to make themselves small and could just as easily have joined the circus as acrobats or clowns that pile into a tiny car by the dozen.

After about another hour of inching along, the cavers negotiated a sharp turn to the right that Axe never would have been able to get around. It opened up into a moderately sized cavern. The guides hadn't been able to stand up straight for some time, and it felt great just to do so and stretch.

Bat guano and urine stained the cave walls and floor. The smell was strong and distinct. Pungent burnt orange and corn flour.

Stalactites and stalagmites revealed that this was an ancient cave system. Sounds of running water came from below. A tinkling drip and a large whoosh lower down. This room was over a thousand square feet. It dropped down twenty feet. From floor to ceiling, it must have been thirty-five feet tall.

When these two got to the floor, there was another descent of at least a hundred feet down with a fifty- or sixty-degree slope that opened into a cavern twice the size of the first. Getting down there was almost more of an underground mountain climbers' descent than caving. After resting, eating, drinking, and checking their equipment, the two continued on in awe of this discovery. Strewn along the way was evidence that they were not the first human visitors. There were ancient artifacts that included pottery, arrowheads, and human skulls. A sacred burial ground or tomb of some sort.

To accumulate the data required, the team decided to descend into the lower cavern and spend the night. They had enough provisions to easily do so. The humidity was 98 percent, the temperature cool. This was a wet living cave ecosystem beneath the property. A treasure for the world. The couple enjoyed their night of exploration, secrecy, seclusion, and discovery. They had brought plenty of powerful batteries and chemical camping lights. They did not smell gas but weren't going to light candles or start a fire. They relished the find and were delighted that they would be paid handsomely in cash.

They descended to depths greater than 175 feet where they sat by a lake of unspoiled, cold, clear underground water fed by a stream. They yelled into the walls with joy that echoed back with a cry and a laugh. The two made love. Their only witness was the spirit bear, the earliest inhabitant of this place in time.

To Axe the two guides were nothing more than canaries in the mine shaft. Had he made it all the way in with them and had the courage to get back out alone, he would have terminated them himself deep inside the cave.

Axe did not plan to have them eliminated if all they had found was a useless dead end. Then he would have paid them with a smile and a handshake, good luck and good riddance. But that was not the case. This find was too substantial, which made Axe salivate. No way these two could keep it a secret. No one could. So, unfortunately, he had no choice. No one could know about the cave system unless they were on a need-to-know basis, which he alone controlled.

The cavers returned jubilant and briefed Axe about the amazing passageways, archaeological treasures, and water that they had found. They couldn't wait to share the news with colleagues. This would never happen. In Axe's hands, the explorers became yet another sad statistic about the dangers of caving. According to the paperwork trail and the news, the story was that improper equipment led to disastrous consequences. After months of police investigation, the bodies were never found.

After acquiring the property, Axe filed county permits for building the house. Everything was done to code for the most part. Permitting included the design of a basement level. In Arizona it is atypical to dig a basement in the granite common to mountainous regions, which made for a hard dig. Some luxury homes do have various rooms and structures carved into the hills at different elevations, which sometimes include a basement.

The structure built remained an exterior shell for the longest time to hide what was happening below. It raised no eyebrows or suspicion. Equipment was sent down through the growing cave system piecemeal during the dark of night. The engineering and construction crew that Axe handpicked designed it so that the most superficial part of the cave lay directly beneath the enormous master-bedroom closet, which itself was a crib that would be the envy of any fashionista or celebrity. Behind his rack of suits, cowboy boots, and shoes was a floor-to-ceiling, one-of-a-kind mirror. Its handmade frame was studded with blown glass and crystal that seemed to drip into the edges of the mirror. Turning a watch winder on the dresser in the closet released a mechanism that caused the piece to recede electronically. The watch collection, display, and winders were museum-quality pieces. There was a time-out mechanism so that if the winder wasn't handled in an allotted period, the sequence would have to be repeated. If the sequence was not successful after two tries, the system shut down and required manual override with a code that only Axe knew. Some would say this was over the top; others attributed it to paranoia, for which he had good reason. Someone trying to destroy a continent might not be too popular. Behind the mirror was an elevator that descended to the caverns below.

Axe thought about how his team implanted the technological marvel that would be the catalyst for one the largest terrorist disasters in history secretly by night. Surviving governments and military experts would try to comprehend this mystery for years to come.

How did he get the fissionable materials into the country? Was it one suitcase at a time, an inside job? Axe wanted military historians to look back on it as a permanent marker that once again changed the way society conducted itself, further tightening controls and limiting freedoms.

The underground bunker system was not impenetrable. Axe's

system could be taken out by United States Massive Ordinance Penetrator Bombs, or something like the MOAB, mother of all bombs. However, this bunker lay beneath an affluent, heavily populated civilian area that was next to a public trailhead frequented by tourists. This would make the use of drones challenging as well. A drone attack used on domestic soil would create an outcry that would make Congress members wet themselves. Its location and secrecy alone were a good defense. The underground cave system design was deep and narrow with a simulated vent deep enough so that when the blast went off it would trigger a cataclysmic eruption.

Tucson, Arizona, sits in a valley between the Santa Catalina Mountains to the north and the Tucson Mountains to the west. The Tucson Mountains, once the top of a large volcano, sat atop the Catalina range. After the top volcanically blew off, it slid twenty miles west beginning the Tucson Mountain range. This created the basin called a caldera, which has a fault system containing probably five thousand feet of sediment that could be tapped into.

Naturally, Axe could care less that radioactive materials would seep into the water table below.

CHAPTER 12

SHANE WEAVER stepped out of the hot shower, a shimmering muscular ripple emerging from a puff of steam. The watery imprint left on the floor revealed a strong high arch.

He used his hand to clear enough condensation off the mirror with a circular motion so he could see his face to shave. It was a good, strong face with an honest, bold, wide chin. The face of a warrior. The complexion was a bronzed coffee color. The short Afro was high and tight, buzzed around the sides. The hairline around the temples was receding just enough to lend Shane a dignified appearance. With a big bath towel draped around his shoulders so he could wipe off the excess shaving cream, he scraped that face with a razor but couldn't stop thinking about Axe as he cut himself.

"Damn."

He washed off the excess shaving cream. Blood-tinged water swirled down the drain. He swigged his coffee as he tried to figure out what he was going to do about this adversary. He shut the water off, except when he was rinsing off his razor, and put a piece of toilet paper on his razor cut while it clotted. Leaving the water running during the entire shave like some guys did was a pet peeve of his. He hated wasting water like that, especially in the desert.

He stood six foot three and was 185 pounds of steel cable. Weaver was freakishly strong, like an ant that could lift and drag several times its weight. His arms and legs were long, and his torso was shaped a bit like a comma when viewed from the side.

He had a mild curvature to his back called kyphosis that he used effectively to his advantage in close combat. It never stopped him from doing anything and just made him more lethal. His posture magnified his ability to scoop his body and turn his torso to deflect blows. In the marines his nickname was Scoop.

Originally from the East Flatbush section of Brooklyn, the son of a Puerto Rican mother and a Haitian American father, Weaver joined the marines after two years of community college.

Now that he lived in Arizona, he realized that growing up in New York City was a very unique experience. It truly was a world city. He was from a tough, inner-city, hardworking neighborhood and had not led a privileged life. Brooklyn was now becoming a gentrified, desirable place to live with more strollers and babies than bums on the streets. East Flatbush was a middle-class, predominantly black neighborhood. It seemed like every cab driver and mass transit worker lived there. They moved millions of people around daily.

Growing up, Shane had lived in a redbrick walk-up apartment building that had been built in the early twentieth century. Neighbors could get noisy. At night there were yelping sirens mixed with loud music. Shane and his family lived on the fourth floor. Hauling groceries up the stairs was a hassle, especially after his mom had a heart attack. Shane took those stairs three at a time, especially when he was late or realized that he had forgotten something and had to run back up. In the summer, he would hang out on the fire escape or retreat to the roof tar beach on balmy nights, taking in the cacophony in all its glory. The landlord didn't like it when people went up there. The roof was getting on in years and was bubbled in spots. The landlord was tired of fixing leaks. Shane liked to jump rope on the roof. Neighbors complained. He found a spot that wasn't over anyone's apartment or exercised when he knew no one would be home. He also developed a technique of jumping rope in such a way that he landed on the balls of his feet very gently, like a cat.

In the city it was always landlord versus tenant. The rules were stacked in favor of the tenants. In the winter old folks would call city housing and complain. More heat. Young men would complain it was too hot and open the window. The old boiler coils in the basement would sometimes blow, or the oil delivery trucks would be late. The price of oil kept going up, but that didn't mean the landlord could raise the rent in the rent-controlled apartments or some of the Section Eight apartments.

That old basement was terrifying. Dark and rank. Rats and feral cats. Low-hanging pipes with asbestos. Storage rooms filled with junk from the age of the flood. A lurking super who looked like he ate people's young in a dungeon.

The building needed new windows. Most of them had rusted chains and counterweights. In summer the windows were pocked with air conditioners and fans. Comforters were aired out. Fuses blew. Tenant tempers shortened. Most people had compact closet washer/dryers, but some still had clotheslines hanging high above the courtyard that waved like ship flags and kites of underwear and jeans in the sky. In winter jeans froze on the line and were placed on softly hissing radiator steam pipes to thaw.

The bricks needed to be pointed, which allowed moisture to seep in. Inside, the apartment walls were hand-lathed plaster that bellied in places. Ceilings were a generous nine feet high. Rooms were of a good size.

The fragrance of some of the most delicious food on earth would waft from apartment to apartment through open windows. Weaver's dad would comment, "Looks like they're arguing and having a roast tonight across the courtyard in apartment D5." Everybody knew everyone else's business. Living in an apartment made privacy difficult.

His mom, a licensed practical nurse, worked at a nursing home. She was grateful that it was close enough so that she didn't need to commute by subway. When she wasn't hurting too bad, she waddled to work. Some days it was a short bus ride. All the heavy patient care and lifting took its toll on her skeleton. It didn't help that she was carrying an extra eighty pounds in her belly, hips, and butt. Sometimes she would see the doctor to get cortisone shots for her spine, but she kept working because the kids depended on her. She never complained. Shane, her oldest, knew, and he deeply admired her for it.

Shane's father was a New York cab driver for a while. He didn't like it; he said people were too crazy. People were saying the same thing about New York cabbies. He put in for a job at mass transit on the advice of a neighbor. He didn't want to be a bus driver; that would be worse. He preferred work in the subway as if that was any better.

Shane never had a car growing up. He too depended on buses and trains. In the city one could get anywhere anytime that way. There was nothing like jumping onto an air-conditioned bus on a sweltering summer day and heading for Coney Island beach.

That famous historical Brooklyn boardwalk had made quite the comeback. Up through the 1950s, Coney Island was a summer haven where people didn't lock their doors at night. By the late sixties and early seventies, it was dangerous to go out to get a gallon of milk. The early 2000s heralded an influx of artists, musicians, and Eastern Europeans. The rents were comparatively low by New York standards, and to the city's credit, the train terminal was magnificent.

The boardwalk bustled with Russian vendors selling everything in a bazaar-like environment. A visitor couldn't walk two feet without encountering the aroma of a hero, pizza, or knish. Some of the rides were gone, destroyed by the hurricane or torn down to build condos backed by investors who lived in Seagate. In an empty lot there was a paintball game called Shoot the Freak. The object of the live carnival game was to shoot a paintball gun at a guy dressed like a freak. He tried his best to avoid the bullets by dodging, running, and hiding behind obstacles. If he hid too long, the owner would replace him with a more courageous freak.

Almost no one could hit the freak. He was fast and would roll furiously on the ground from barrel to boulder like in an old western movie. Like other carnival games, this one usually took a person's money. The operator knew just how long to keep the freak out and how far apart to place the hiding spots. Weaver quickly studied the jerky rhythm of movement and kept taking the freak out, two in the chest, one in the butt, three in the back. Even got off a head shot.

People were howling with laughter. It was sick modern-day version of watching a gladiator. Police looked on. This was a daily sideshow.

Shane was a natural, walking away with the two biggest stuffed animals they had. He could barely see where he was going as he walked onto the beach. In the background he could hear the operator yelling. "Five bucks here, shoot the freak."

The beach was packed with scantily clad girls and hot-looking guys. Gangs in their colors would clash on the sand. Cops broke it up. Shane's idea of good gang colors was light-green camouflage military uniforms.

Weaver confidently walked over to the girl he thought was the most gorgeous on the whole beach, the entire world, and told her so. He gave her the stuffed animals for being the most stunning woman he had ever laid eyes on.

A passionate explosive chemistry was sparked. Six months later he married Lana.

Weaver's parents beat hard work into him. Stay in school. Make something of himself. For them the American dream was still alive. They had patriotic fervor not often seen in modern immigrants. As a result Shane saw the military and law enforcement as the path for him.

His Puerto Rican mom talked about the complex relationship between the United States and her homeland and why she came here in search of a better life. She grew up in an environment of high unemployment and stagnation. The middle class had shriveled. It was mostly rich or poor with little opportunity for advancement. She missed the lush tropics but wanted more than being a maid in a hotel. Occasionally, the old debate about Puerto Rico becoming a state and the evils of big corporations would catch fire.

After joining the marines, Shane deployed twice to the Middle East, spent time at Taqaddum forward operating base in Iraq, and sent pictures home of him hitting golf balls off the top of a helicopter to cheer up his worried family. His lonely, twenty-something-year-old wife, Lana, wasn't amused, nor did she find it cute. At first she missed him terribly, crying and hugging herself to sleep with soft sobs into a pillow. But sadness soon turned into resentment and hard feelings. The long separation took its toll. Skyping stopped; e-mails became less frequent. Packages and phone calls slowed to a trickle. Lana's self-esteem deteriorated. She became depressed and lost. Feeling like a trapped bird in a cage staring up at a grandfather clock, she listened when her friends urged to come out with them. Have a few drinks, dance. How could it hurt? In time she went out earlier, stayed out later, more often coming home after the sun was up to change and go to work. She eventually found most of what she missed in the arms of another man.

Afghanistan wasn't nearly as pleasant for Weaver as Iraq. He lost close buddies, had a close call, and lost his wife. The Dear John letter from Lana was a devastating blow to his morale and ego. She didn't even include in the letter that she was going to have someone else's baby. He wished night after night that the roadside IED had taken his life. Shane decided not to make the military a career after his last deployment.

Five years ago after leaving the military, Shane joined Homeland Security. It was an expanding bureaucracy, seemed like a decent day job, and offered a chance to rebuild his life with a bit more normalcy, he thought. Good benefits.

He started off in border patrol. Soon he missed the adrenaline. He still missed Lana. There was no one to answer to now. When the opportunity presented itself, Shane applied for BORTAC, the Border Patrol Tactical Unit, which is the special ops division of border patrol. Its mission was to use covert operations to defend the US homeland against foreign and domestic terrorists.

Current assignments included the Arizona joint field command that was gathering intelligence and surveilling a terrorist gang leader called Axe.

Axe was smooth; they'd give him that. They had nothing firm on him so far. Weaver's agency believed that he was connected to various smuggling operations, and he had become an individual of great interest, currently in the United States.

CHAPTER 13

I SLEPT fitfully that night, icy feet and a warm head, the opposite of what a good night's sleep calls for. I wasn't sick and didn't have a fever. Every few moments I'd flip over and refluff my pillows. I tried turning on a fan and using a white noise application on my phone. I was tempted to read or go online, but I just couldn't get motivated. Maybe TV? Nah. Count sheep, count boys, Josh. Midnight snack?

Finally at two thirty in the morning, the sweetness of sleep enveloped me; like a popping bubble, it released me from daily tensions. Lucid dreaming happens someplace between being awake and falling asleep. The shrink calls it a hypnagogic state. They say sleep is one-sixtieth of death, a time for the soul to go and play but remain tethered to the body only to return again fully upon awakening. In some cultures dreaming is considered closer to reality than the awake state. It is felt that dreams inform us about what to do in daily life.

During one of those in-between states, I thought that I was really awake. I drifted above myself and observed Katie's body, which was my body, in the bed below. I was in both places as I saw her/me sleeping quite peacefully below in the bed, unable to move no matter how hard I tried. There I was, a hovering entity. It felt magnificently light, energetic. This time, unlike when I was a child, it was no nightmare.

My old childhood friend Walking Bear appeared to me. Her eyes, ancient, crinkled, and brown, smiled. It seemed like her fur was lighter and more colorful than I remembered. Reds, ambers, and twists of brown. We both floated and danced in my room, just like we used to when I was very young. I held a paw, she nuzzled my neck. I'd sit on her back like a cub. She would lay on her back or side, and we cuddled. It was like floating in a pool of cotton and pudding, free but supportive. Everything was bathed in a clear, golden light. It all seemed perfectly normal and exactly how it should be. She asked me if I remembered all the times we used to play together when I was a little girl. Of course I did. How could I forget? She said that her favorites were the pretend picnics and tea parties. "Katie, do you recall the place in your heart and mind we used to go for those picnics?"

"Yes," I said. In a flash we were there.

We moved together down the old familiar verdant hill to the water. It wasn't walking but more like sailing on land. An orange ferry boat twinkled with purple, green, and red jeweled facets. Without a driver or motor, it magically took us to a park. To access this park, we flew low over the land in our ferry boat together. The ferry then turned into a rowboat that Bear paddled through the air to our final destination. Then we sat at our favorite bench gazing at magnificent urban and sculptural structures with impossible geometry. Nothing seemed to hold them up. Across the garden, I poured the tea as I always had before.

I started by asking Bear her name. I mean, all those years I called her everything but never got her real name.

"The first human natives here referred to me as Hania Aponivi. I am the free spirit warrior where the great wind blows into the great abyss. Those that are allowed to summon me, such as yourself, call upon me by chanting Honon. You have demonstrated powers over the wind and elements, young one. Soon it will be time for you to emerge. I have been here from the beginning, my love. You and I have known each other for a very long time in many forms and in many ways. Can you remember?"

"No, not really."

"That's fine. In time you may recall everything."

She explained to me that when our essential spiritual energy, or soul, embodies the human form, for a period of time, we retain the knowledge and memory of what occurred in utero, and before that. We remain an open vessel to the past, present, and possibly even the future until a veil of maturity and ego formation closes its curtain on recollections. A forgetting begins in early childhood. She was very hesitant to call the connection to our spirit before this life, the past. She could make no real distinction of time arising in a linear trajectory. The notion that the past leads to the present, which then ushers in the future, was untrue in her realm. Instead, time was part of a greater field of energy, a medium allowing forms and tendencies to come and go. But there was really no other human form of communication or expression she could summon that would be comprehensible to my level of understanding.

For my purposes at this juncture, Honon's spirit had been awoken from hibernation.

"Why now, and what does this have to do with me?" I asked, gazing at her lovingly.

"My child, and I call you my child because you are,"—Honon's face again resembled my great-grandmother's for a flash—"it is my nature to protect and defend as a mother bear with her cubs. I will defend freedom. I will help to heal and protect these sacred lands."

"Am I in danger? Is this land in danger?"

"You are not yet in danger, and yes, this land is in grave danger. Your visions of me in the past have been as a bear on my hind legs dancing gratefully in the golden rays of sun. Now I stand up for a different reason. I stand up with courage and power from all that is above and below. I stand for what we know to be universal truths. It is with confidence that we shall win a great victory and protect our sacred mountains. We call for harmony and balance."

"Who is *we*?"

"The great spirit masters and ancestors."

This whole time-space continuum confused me. I have had schoolteachers in the past who have told me that when you don't understand something, just memorize and hope that eventually it will make sense.

"The Honon spirit is by nature peaceful. When provoked, it

becomes unpredictable and ferocious. It is a furious storm beneath the surface. Remember that little dust storm when you were in the car with your father?"

I felt ablaze from within, joyous to be in her presence.

"Remember this, kitten."

"Wow, my dad calls me that."

"I know. Your father is a good man, and your mother a good woman. You chose your parents well. It is a great blessing."

"I chose them? I don't understand."

"You will, my love. Your spirit entered into an arrangement with the one master over souls before you entered this plane for a great purpose. It required the parents, the location, and the life that you now temporarily occupy. Cause and effect are always at work."

"You mean, like, it was preordained or meant to be?"

"Something along those lines. I can also share with you that we two have been intertwined many times before. My kitten now grows into a lioness. Remember that nature will communicate her intent to you."

"Honon, what am I supposed to do? I still don't understand."

"You possess an earthly gift that you must learn to understand. You will learn to bridge our two worlds in trance walking. It will require reverence and discipline. Operate from a position of love and compassion, not fear. You must never forget that while your earthly form is unstable and temporary your spirit is eternal. You are loved and never alone. Be patient, but right now it is time to return."

She flung me on her great neck. It was powerful and strong yet gentle. I held on tightly with my arms and legs, and we flew underground. Nevertheless, I could see everything up to the mountain tops. Space didn't seem to follow the usual rules. On the way back, she made sure to revisit and point out Finger Rock mountain peak again. With her mind she turned my full attention to a vast compound. A miserable chilling blackness that was palpable emanated from there. I could smell it, and it was sickening. I would not forget that feeling. She communicated without words that what I was feeling was the presence of a bad man named Axe who was a great threat to the world. This was the evil man Honon began to explain during my dream at the railroad crossing.

"Will I die?"

"The opposite of birth is death, yet life has no opposite."

Then it was morning. I woke up with an awful headache but feeling strong and remembering every detail of my so-called dream.

~~~~~~~

Lunch.

It's usually my favorite period. I sat on one of the benches outside the school cafeteria and looked at the mountains. I thought about what I had learned last night. My stomach growled, and my headache subsided. Maybe food? Let's see. I opened my backpack. My mom packs a lunch for me every day. As seniors with cars, we're still not supposed to leave campus to get lunch, but kids do anyway. I just wasn't in the mood.

Hmm, peanut butter and jelly sandwich. Yuck, not today. Some days I like peanut butter and jelly, especially the crunchy kind with apricot jam and thick slabs of fresh, homemade bread. In summer, Abuela gathers the prickly pear cactus fruit with gloves on. She scrapes off the stickers and makes a wonderful homemade jam; with the rest she makes calabacitas. She swears it helps Grandpa's sugar and his big old prostate that makes him get up to go to the bathroom ten times a night.

I noticed a kid walk by pulling a gooey piece of hot cheese off of a slice of pizza. It smelled great. Some of the local vendors have set up shop in the school cafeteria so we can buy stuff. I got on the pizza line. I was hungrier than usual after my dreamy adventure last night. I looked at my phone. Sara was late, and I wondered where she was. I had texted her, checked my mail, and started to play an app game on the phone when Josh Ryan got behind me in line. I looked forward and down.

"Hi, freaky Katie. How are you today?" he asked.

I totally ignored him, so he gently put his fingertips on my shoulder. I could not believe that he actually touched me. The nerve. What the heck? His hand brushed against my hair. I turned around and looked at him. Part of me melted like the cheese, and the other part became hardened, crusty. I couldn't tell one part from the other as the butterflies churned inside. I finally uttered, "Listen, Jock, or is it Josh, my name is Katie, not freaky."

"Okay." He sort of chuckled nervously.

I now held my pizza triumphantly ready to throw it at him if need be. It was hot, and the melted mozzarella cheese was stringy. The oil and red sauce seeped into the paper plate turning it soggy and a translucent orange-yellow. I was starving but was not planning to dig into the extra cheese slice in front of him. I pulled a piece of cheese off with my hand and ate it as I headed back outside.

"Wait, um, Katie?" Josh caught up and walked with me. "Look, I'm sorry for calling you freaky." He followed me to my seat. The metal benches were warm from the sun. "Mind if I sit?" he asked.

"Huh? Sure, whatever," was all I could come up with.

He sat opposite me. My pizza was getting cold, and I was planning ten different ways to kill Sara if she ever showed up. He wasn't much of a conversationalist. The best he could come up with was, "So, uh, what's up? Um, how's PE coming for you?"

"Hate it. Did you follow me just to say what's up?"

Crap, I thought to myself. Do you have to be so negative?

"Well," Josh said, "you're looking good out there. Getting stronger, I mean, at track." He became physically animated, struck a runner's pose, made a muscle with his arm.

"Thank you."

Awkward pregnant pause.

Deflated, he tried again and looking down said, "So, how's it goin'?"

"Good. How's it goin' for you?"

"Good," he uttered and looked at his phone. Picking up a phone has become everyone's default nervous habit. My smart phone was tightly lodged in my back pocket.

Finally, he said something useful. "Did you watch the recent episode of *Crushed* on TV?" His head popped, perked up like a stallion.

"Yes, I love that show."

"Wow. Me too, Katie." Oh, that smile.

"No way."

"Hey, I like how you decorated your notebook. It's awesome," he continued. "Tells a story."

"Yup." I'm Katie One Word today.

We got onto the subject of teachers. Josh started imitating some of our teachers and making fun of them, which had me cracking up, especially when he starting making fun of the principal and walking like him. The next thing I knew, I was eating my pizza. I just need to calm down. This is good stuff. Josh and a slice go well together.

"Um, Katie, I think the way you laugh is totally adorable. The way you cover your mouth, and your eyes sparkle as if you are keeping some big secret that you want nobody to know. I guess the formal is in a couple of weeks. You going?"

Oh. My. God. Josh Ryan is flirting with me. I am turning crimson red. Sara better just not show up at all now.

"I was thinking about going with my girlfriends."

"Yeah, me too. Not with your girlfriends, I mean." He laughed at his own slip. I caught his lingering stare now, and I liked it.

Did I mention he's so totally adorable that I can't stand it?

To move the conversation forward, I mistakenly asked, "How's your car?"

I shouldn't have brought it up. On the other hand, the sinkhole destroying a car was the big campus-wide news. So, why not? Just be chill about it I figured.

"Still in the shop," he announced disappointedly with an exhale.

With concern and empathy, I wanted to touch his arm or shoulder but stopped myself. "Will it be all right? I mean, can it be fixed?"

"Good as new they say. Katie, why were you running away from the scene that day?"

"I was late for class, I guess. The loud noise freaked me out. Gotta do a lot of running, you know. Get in shape." I made this exercising motion with my arms now that he didn't buy for a second. He just gave me a peculiar look.

"Hey, isn't Bryan in your English class?"

"Yeah. The teacher, Mr. K., is totally chill." Then I added, "Bryan is totally hysterical."

"He's my best friend." I guess Josh wanted me to know this for some reason.

"I think he's really into Carla," he mentioned very casually like he was talking about nothing of importance. "They're going to the formal together."

"Wow. Great." I'm such a wonderful conversationalist.

"Katie? How about if we go to the formal together?"

The bomb. He hit the send key and lit me on fire.

My face was hot, and the rest of me was not far behind. I hate it when my face gets red and blotchy. It's not a uniform pink. I seriously thought that I had a bladder that I could not even handle. This was an epiphany moment. Someone take me to the school nurse now, please. Suddenly the metal benches were too hot to sit on. I thought of Honon and stood up, feeling personally responsible for global warming. The air around us was electrified and smelled like ozone.

The only sound that chirped out of my face was, "Sure," as I twisted my right shoulder over my right hip, combed my hair back off my face with my fingers, dropped my right shoulder, and slightly arched my back." I was posturing and telegraphing a sensuous receptivity that I had seen models do in a magazine. My bad for trying to puff up for Josh.

I cannot believe that Josh Ryan just asked me to the formal, and all I had to do was smash him into a wall and drop his car into a sinkhole.

"Cool. Awesome." He flashed me a genuinely gorgeous smile. His eyes beamed and glittered. "So, like, some of us are planning to meet for dinner first and then go to the formal. I can pick you up around six? Um, if my car is ready by then."

We both laughed. I told him, "If it's not, I'll come and get you."

CHAPTER 14

ABOUT A week or two later, Dr. S. had arranged for my acupuncture session after school, and Mom came along. She had always wanted to try acupuncture; I was going to be her guinea pig. I didn't know what to expect. Perhaps a dark shack with incense and canvas sacks full of herbs.

Instead, the place looked like a regular doctor's office. Maybe that was to draw people in. It was a little too cozy. The adobe brick walls and beamed ceilings gave the office an earthy, southwestern ambience. On the wall there was a picture of a generic human. No gender, no race, not Asian or Caucasian, not exactly male or female. How politically correct, I thought, so metro. Lines were drawn on the body. They ran up and down, mostly vertical in orientation. Some started in the foot and went up the back to the skull. The sign underneath it said it was a map of the meridians.

"Interesting, isn't it?" asked a little voice behind me. "They represent subtle energetic pathways that run throughout the body." Merna Lee, licensed acupuncturist, went on, "You must be Katie. I'm your acupuncturist." She shook my hand. "Ready to come on back?"

My mom said, "Yes, we are."

"Good. Walk this way, please."

She wore a white coat and looked clean and professional. She wore her black hair pulled back tightly and a little eye makeup.

We followed through the labyrinth to her inner sanctum. My mom signed papers.

The treatment room was even cuter. No fluorescent lights bulbs, just incandescents and candles, more like a massage spa. A delicious aroma wafted in the breeze while the sound of flutes and chimes subtly filled the room, coming from hidden speakers.

"Oh boy," my mother whispered. "This is probably going to be expensive."

"Mom," I whispered raspily.

Merna Lee told us how Dr. Schlisselvasser wanted an evaluation of my energetic patterning and structural biopsycho-type. She started asking peculiar questions like what my favorite color was. What type of foods I like. Do I prefer dark chocolate or milk chocolate, spicy or salty foods? Sweets? How I would react to certain situations.

After the third degree, she checked my pulse—though not the way the regular doctor does. She had three or four fingers on my pulse for a very long time. She would occasionally let out "ah hah," or "I see." The woman was communing with my artery, having this intimate conversation with my wrist.

I asked, "Do you want to let me in on it?"

My mother said, "Shush."

Merna took notes. She made me stick my tongue out.

At my primary doctor's office, this is a three-second affair. Ah. Shine the light, stick the wooden tongue depressor in. Make me gag. Done. Here it felt like my tongue was hanging out to dry. She grabbed it with a piece of gauze and looked at it forever. Very attractive. All she said was, "Too much yang," and wrote it down.

Next, she placed this electric meter along different points on my body, including my ears, that corresponded to meridian lines, which I recognized from the poster, and she made some recordings. Finally, she asked me to hold vials of different substances in one hand and an electrode in the other. She would withdraw sample vials from a well-worn suitcase and then test my strength with and without various vials in my hand. They were all numerically ordered and had Chinese characters written on them. If my dad were here, he'd probably flip out.

I had been asked to wear loose shorts and a T-shirt for today's visit so I would be ready when it was time for the needles. She told us that my five elements were out of balance. My wind was far too yang, and my triple heater was off the chart or something. Please, I know my wind can be excessive but too yang?

Mom asked how a point between my first and second toes could have something to do with my liver. LR3 Merna called this spot.

Merna explained that the liver as an organ in Western physical terms is sitting in the abdominal cavity. "However, as a vital organ, it influences the function of cells throughout the body everywhere. From a traditional Chinese medicine perspective, the liver is more than an organ in physiological terms. It has a life-giving chi giving it an energetic sphere of influence that contributes to one's total life force.

"In a sense this is similar to the mind, which is present throughout your body," Mother said. "Like a mind body connection."

Clever mother, I thought. Merna Lee ignored Mom. She kept on going as if singing from Doc's songbook. "From a tissue point of view, on a cellular level, groups of liver cells are held together by loose connective tissue. The organ has lobes that are encapsulated and tethered in places to the abdominal cavity and muscular diaphragm, which is connected to other parts of the neuromusculoskeletal system and then finally becomes more superficial, exiting at the skin. To think that the skin and muscles don't communicate with something as vital as the liver is foolish. Just look at a middle-aged woman's hands for liver spots, or the color of someone's skin and eyes who has liver disease."

My mom looked at her hands, and Lee smiled at her reassuringly.

"So the ancients tapped into the energy of the liver's sphere of influence from the skin and superficial muscles, outside working backward." I was yawning.

My mother found it fascinating but was probably sorry she asked.

I was hungry and cranky, and I had homework to do. I hadn't even had the chance to tell Mom that I had a date for the formal.

Lee had me lay facedown with my head in a cradle and a pillow under my ankles, plus another one under my hips for good measure. She used ultrafine, disposable, sterile needles ensheathed in plastic tubing. Merna, as she liked to be called, examined the points, squeezed, and kneaded my muscles. With her left hand she held the plastic tube pushed up tight against my skin at those magical points. Her first two fingers held the sheath in a pincer-like grip. The other three fingers were secured against my body. With her right index finger she firmly and deftly tapped the needle, which entered my skin so quickly I could hardly feel a thing.

Merna then delicately handled the needle between her right thumb and index finger. She gently pushed and twisted the needle. My muscle twitched. I felt a warm heavy ache at the area. She knew when to let go of the needle and said, "Ah, chi."

"Bless you," I replied. She giggled infectiously and stated that she had reached my energy using the input of this needle.

She repeated this procedure with needles to my feet, hands, arms, legs, back, and ears. Finally, she lit up an incense cigar. It smelled kind of, well, like pot. Now, I do not smoke pot, so let's get that straight. Some kids at school smoke behind the apartment complex near school. I know pot when I smell it. I'm just saying.

She took the tip of the glowing hot incense stick and warmed up some of the needles, which felt like a warm liquid spreading relaxation. Then she would retwist other needles, which got my attention quickly. She quietly left the room.

I felt wonderful. I wondered if it was legal to feel this good.

It was like a floaty, balanced feeling. Well-being. Lack of dis-ease. I didn't have a care in the world. My only problem was that lying facedown made my nose stuffy and drippy. A tickling little drop formed at the tip of my nose, and I asked Mom for a tissue. I must have fallen asleep because Bear came to me. She was laughing at me.

"And what, may I ask, is so amusing?" I protested.

"Are you having fun?" she asked.

"Well, I'm doing what the doctor and my parents said to do."

"Good, good, but there is much work to be done, not to mention keeping up with your studies."

"You sound like my father."

"Why, thank you. This woman is good with the needles, but this nonsense is not helping us right now. She needs to be firing up that windy yang of yours, not trying to equilibrate and dilute your energy by quieting it down. Your wind has been yang since the beginning of time, which is now. That's the way you are, my dearest.

"Anyway, she doesn't have a clue about the forces she is dealing with. She is not a true healer. She was a great student and is very competent, but this is not the time for a spa vacation. I've known some truly gifted medicine men and women over the centuries, let me tell you."

"What if I don't want to do any of this work that you want me to do? Who put you in charge? You're not the boss of me. I think I'll come here and get my yang popped every day for as long as Mom's credit card holds out if it pleases me."

"Katie, you have been designed with free will, and it is your choice as well as it is my hope that in time you will wish to do the work you were sent here to do. It is your destiny."

"Now you sound like my mother laying on a guilt trip."

"Oh, forgive me. I forget that you're a teenager, which is a test, even for me. Let me tell you a story since your acupuncturist will be back in a minute. There is an ancient legend of a great spiritual master who emerged from the ocean. You might say that he's my boss or supervisor. He is the archetypal force associated with the weather. Her feminine aspect is the keeper of the wind. You, my child, embody a spark that was given by the masters. So yes, your wind element energy is so yang that it is very much unbalanced, but in a good and powerful way."

Merna Lee touched my back and gently told me we were through and that she would remove the needles. As Bear departed, she said, "Go out with that boy, and don't forget to tell your mother and father about him."

When I got off the table, my head was foggy, and my knees were weak. Merna Lee said not to worry and placed a firm hand on my shoulder. I was experiencing the natural endorphins that acupuncture stimulates in the brain.

"In the business," she said, "we call it *being dorphed out*." She smiled. "It's advisable to drink plenty of fluids, eat lightly, no vigorous exercise today, and get a good night's sleep."

"Doc, can I get a note to skip PE for a week?"

"Oh, stop it," Mother said. "How do you feel, Katie?"

I explained to her my sense of well-being, floating, balance.

Merna Lee would send her results to Dr. S.

I felt well in a wet rag sort of way. I don't think I could have blown up a balloon. I wanted a nap.

Stoked by the whole experience, Mom scheduled acupuncture appointments for herself on the way out. Little did I know then that I would have precious little time left to devote to further training.

~~~~~~

Scoop Weaver walked down the center aisle of the meeting room with his coffee cup perched on a donut in one hand, papers in the other, and his car keys in his mouth. The room was a large, nondescript, white rectangle downtown in the federal building. Tightly woven synthetic commercial carpet with a swirly maroon-and-brown design would hide the thousandth coffee spill that was about to happen. The ceiling was large industrial white square tiles. The exits were well demarcated with obnoxious red signs that the fire inspectors get crazy about. The air conditioner blew refrigerated air so that no one could become lethargic. The room was windowless.

There was nowhere to hide beneath the overhead fluorescents. Up front was a podium that said Tucson Sector Border Patrol Tactical BORTAC Unit. Everyone had been instructed to pick up a packet from the table in the back of the room on the way to his or her seat. Weaver negotiated his way into an uncomfortable fold-up seat in the fourth row. He purposely stepped on some guy's toes, who promptly gave him a friendly elbow and said, "Scooper, what up, dude?" After putting his keys in his pocket, Scoop licked his thumb and sipped off the top of the white coffee lid that had popped off while he was monkeying around.

He settled in, and the guy behind him said, "Hey, Scoop, way to go at the border," and reached over Weaver's shoulder so they could shake hands. He nodded to another team member across the room and got a thumbs-up.

About to get started was the multiagency task force meeting of local, state, and federal law enforcement officials. The topic was Axe.

Axe originally became a person of interest to federal authorities after the spelunkers went missing. The last they were heard from was before going near Axe's acreage. He was already a suspect in multiple international crimes. If only they could find something to charge him with. If only some evidence about the missing explorers could lead to a search or an arrest. Soon after that murder Axe began a public relations campaign to create positive local buzz about himself and defuse mounting rumors. He became mildly but noticeably philanthropic, showing up at charity events with sizable checks. He had his picture taken at orphanages, homeless shelters, and food drives. Axe allowed his right-sided profile to be photographed, hiding facial scars from the cameras, his hideousness from the world. This behavior, developing a sympathetic image, is not uncommon among crooks and certain CEOs to make it more difficult for the criminal justice system to find impartial jurors.

Recent satellite surveillance hadn't yielded much data about Uktam, a.k.a. the Axe.

At the BORTAC meeting, it was discussed that Axe's counterintelligence was good, even though his e-mails, calls, and visits to the bathroom were being monitored in a data dragnet.

The Axe problem was not limited to surveillance issues. All strategic, operational, and tactical options were on the table. No authority could make anything stick. He was on his own property and hadn't been caught breaking the law. Scoop volunteered to inspect the area alone at night.

His commander was reluctant to send him out alone. He wouldn't agree to the plan unless necessary assets were available. He insisted that Scoop have appropriate communication. Backup would include other agents on a designated perimeter with the availability of helicopter extraction and night-vision technology. From his military training, Scoop felt that it was imperative to pursue silent nighttime entry if he was to learn anything valuable. He had expertise in silent entry and extraction. If Axe had security and intelligence, he would see all the feds coming a mile away. Weaver wanted to do simple, quiet, old-fashioned, detective work. He liked working alone.

<center>~~~~~~~</center>

Axe moved swiftly out of his two-story garage filled with exotic and muscle sports cars through his sumptuous mansion. As he passed he tinkled the keys on his Steinway and straightened a priceless painting. He skipped down the stairs to the wine cellar. Taking a specific bottle off the shelves, he placed his thumb on a certain spot and lifted the bottle to his right eye; the bottle scanned his finger print and retina. He'd recently read in the paper that soon companies were hoping to do away with passwords and go to retina scans. Glad they're catching up, he thought with a dismissive shoulder shrug.

The massive wooden table shifted. Then there was a wooden creak and a gear-tumbling sound. The floor hesitated. Finally, with a protest and a grind, it parted. A transparent human-sized capsule that looked much like tubes at the bank drive-through rose up from the floor.

Axe entered the capsule, one of three designated entrances to his world below ground. It descended with a vacuum suctioning sound as the floor swallowed him down into the caves. He was going to check on Vuuv. Detonation was rapidly becoming imminent. They had crossed the red line.

Vuuv didn't look well. Living underground in a dark damp cave didn't agree with him. Pale and sticky was his baseline, but now he was even more so. Except for a thick, greasy clump matted to his forehead, his hair pointed straight up. Skinny and fluorescent white, he was jacked up on energy drinks. The workstation was littered with empty pizza boxes and Chinese food containers. He would fit right in in Silicon Valley. If it weren't for the lack of hygiene and shabby loose clothes, he could have passed for hipster. Vuuv had also developed a pungent, gamy odor and hadn't shaved in days. He was overripe.

Surrounded by an array of blinking screens, humming consoles, and computer towers, he had an eerie tinge. Red lights reflected off his oversized eyeglasses, which hung low off his shiny, chiseled nose.

Vuuv noticed Axe and then gasped and swallowed. His huge Adam's apple moved up and down like some ancient reptile. "Boss, you scared the hell out of me. There are bats down here."

"Vuuv. It'll be over soon, yes?"

"Yes, sir. We are on schedule."

"Good man. Go up and get some rest now in the house. Hot shower; a real, hot homemade meal; soak in the hot tub. Feel free to choose any bottle of wine and a cigar in the cellar. After that a warm, dry bed, as opposed to this cave. It will do you some good. I'll keep watch down here. We've come a long way from the streets and back alleys of central Asia, huh? Soon, soon we will be done here." Axe grabbed Vuuv's face and then applied a few gentle affectionate taps on his friend's neck, face, and shoulder.

"I'm wired, boss; don't know if I can rest, but that sure sounds generous. Thank you."

CHAPTER 15

I THOUGHT about what my parents said when I'd told them I'd be going to the dance with Josh Ryan. Mom was cool and excited for me that I got asked out. Soon she started giving unsolicited advice. She explained how to behave and when to breathe. It was a fifteen-minute finishing school. I tried to be kind because she was happy for me. So was I. When she digressed into her first love and date, I was all, "No, eww, Mom, too much information."

Her eyes welled and lit up as she held my hands. She looked at me and said, "Look at you growing up. When did my girl grow up?"

Dad, on the other hand, wasn't too keen. He mumbled stuff like, "I trust you, but not him. I was that age once; I know what goes on at these parties." Okay, Dad, what happened to true love?

Later, I decided to take a little walk. Ambling down the street at dusk and kicking up sand next to a dry wash, I thought about Josh. The sky was a thin pink.

What to wear to the formal? Maybe I shouldn't wear combat boots after all, I don't know. Heels or flats? I hate dancing in heels. I'll just end up taking them off. What if my feet smell? Heels are so uncomfortable. They do look good, though, and I'm kind of shrimpy. Still, I'm not used to them. When I walk in high heels, I look clumsy, not provocative or coquettish. It sucks, but I should look girly. A sleeveless dress might be right, but my arms are scrawny. I took a few more steps, thinking about my parents' reactions.

Next to the wash there are well-worn trails made by human

activity. People walk, and kids ride mountain bikes in the single track. Grownups might yell at cyclists, "Be more careful; slow down." Neighborhood youths dug berms so they could catch air on their bikes.

The last rut at the bottom of the hill was at the edge of a twisty residential street. Neighbors complained, usually the same ones who did most of the yelling. No one listened, and I didn't know the little neighbor boy who was riding.

He rode down hard. Fast and fearless, he took the first two bumps well, good timing, looking serious with his helmet off center, cute outfit, and aviator sunglasses. Pure fun. Watching him whip around cacti, hit his rear brake, drop a foot, skid out, and accelerate again made me think about getting a bike, but only for a second.

On the last bump, something went terribly wrong. Time slowed. My strange sensations returned. If I were a migraine patient, they'd call it an aura. If I had been a seizure patient, it would be called a prodrome. Whatever it is that I possess, the human form has only so many biologic means of expression. Fish swim; birds fly; I do this bizarre stuff.

The kid on his bike was airborne, but his front tire was turned too far left, and his body was too far right. I'm no physics expert when it comes to one's center of gravity, but this was plainly bad. In midair he looked like one of those stunt riders in a magazine, but he was just an inexperienced little boy, and when he hit the ground, the front shock thumped and rebounded fast. He flipped over his handle bars and landed facedown in the road just as a yellow Mustang came zooming around the corner.

It seemed like I had all the time in the world. Time warped and stood still, but I didn't. His mother was on a rusty chained hybrid with a bell, which made for slow going, so she was coming along from far behind huffing and puffing. When she saw her son flip, she jumped off her bike and fell too. With bloodied knees she ran with all her might.

I looked at her and looked at him. I moved out into the street between the downed child and the oncoming car.

The Mustang hit the brakes. The mother screamed a primal ago-
nizing howl that started in the pit of her soul and exited through her
lungs. She yelled his name. "Andyyy!"

There was loose gravel on the twisty road. It was too late for the
car to stop, so I stopped it. How? As I've tried to explain a zillion
times to police, reporters, my parents, the boy's parents, and even Dr.
S., I do not know.

All I could say was that I saw the horse design in that Mustang's
grill inches away, felt the heat of the radiator on my face, caught the
oily smell of the engine. It was a very sweet-looking grill, I might
add. I made eye contact with the driver. I squinted and breathed once
or twice at most. I didn't have all day. On my exhale I squatted. My
right hand was on the boy and my left was outstretched. There was a
sense of compressed warmth between my left outstretched palm and
the right bumper of the car, which by the way was destroyed along
with the hot-looking grill even though it didn't hit anything but air.

Dr. S. later explained that I had tapped into a force that he called
the zero-point field and used it as a burning gust that pushed the car
hard left, causing it to miss Andy and me. It charred the fender in the
process.

The sound that I emitted was a mixture of a screeching hawk, a
roar, and then a booming explosion. The light was blue white and
electric. The power of the recoil was like ten shotguns and knocked
me back a few feet.

I lay there for a moment winded. Smoke darkened my face and
my hair floated out sideways from the static electricity. My arm was
scratched up from road rash, my shoulder sore.

I didn't think I'd need the services of a shrink after that episode,
just urgent care to pick cactus stickers and gravel out of my arm,
which had a small patch that looked like a blood pudding. To top it
off my phone cracked which really irked me.

After finding out about this event, Dr. S., who had become very
protective, totally freaked out. He wanted a new panel of tests.

Unfortunately, the whole world found out about my secret talent.
Within twenty-four to forty-eight hours, our local newspaper called

me a new teen superhero. I was mortified. The cable stations played the shaky homemade video caught by a passerby on a cell phone. It was on YouTube and went viral over the next week. Once that happened, my dad started standing outside the house, talking to reporters. Our front yard attracted paranormal groups and worshippers. Deputies arrived because of the disturbance. Down the street, vendors sold crystals claiming our street sat on a mystical portal, an energy vortex.

I don't like reporters. They remind me of fleas who mostly like to hear themselves talk and preen for the camera. I preferred to avoid them, but it became more difficult daily. They were at school, in front of the house, and in front of Doc S.'s house and office, since they had seen me frequenting his places. They asked stupid questions: "How does it feel?" "What will you do next?" "Who's Dr. Schlisselvasser, Katie?"

As I exited the professor's office, I answered, "I am going home to do my homework, eat, and take a nap. I have a math quiz tomorrow."

They laughed. They asked my dad what it was like to have a daughter who is a superhero.

He said that I was always his hero. One point for Dad.

My biggest challenge at the moment was not blowing reporters away. They just kept coming back. The news media televised the brief interaction.

I feel like the world has become a place where everything we do is recorded constantly. If it isn't the media, it's the government. If it isn't the government, it's the universe. Honestly, I do not know how celebrities tolerate the paparazzi without raging.

The media claims to be an objective mirror of ourselves, but they are not. Journalism has become entertainment, spin, ratings, and commercialized sensationalism. Another symptom of cultural collapse. I cannot tell if they are a cause or a result. It sickens me to hear about incessant scandals and murder trials when my parents watch the news and then see it cut to a commercial with a little jingle about burgers, chips, or beer, or a safe, cute baby in the back of a new sedan. I'd rather listen to music or read a book. Some journalists are brilliant, but most sell out first chance they get. Guess they're just human. Remind me not to major in journalism.

My mother was still angry with me. She yelled at me for two days about how I could have been killed by that car. I told her to chill and that she just didn't understand. I didn't think this was the right time to discuss a phone upgrade.

By the way, the driver of the Mustang got a ticket for failure to control the vehicle, and Dad told me we're being sued for destroying the car by some pathetic ambulance chaser. I never touched the car.

We don't know any lawyers who represent superheroes. We are looking into superhero malpractice insurance for such occasions. The driver's defense was that he was in complete control until I came along. The insurance company is calling it an act of God.

Grandmother crossed herself, fainted, and had to be revived when she heard the news. As the daughter of my great grandmother the mystic from the Amazon, grandmother rebelled against the paranormal stuff. She felt it was all the work of the devil and ran from it rubbing rosary beads. Her beliefs were very traditional. Whenever conversations turned to the mystical, she said a prayer to expunge the blasphemy. Her daughter, my mother Rena, was much more open to other ways. She felt that just because you couldn't sense something and had no scientific explanation, that didn't mean it isn't there. Me? Looks like I'm picking up where great grandmother Isibella left off.

At school the day after the Mustang affair, I walked to my table at lunch, which was very awkward since I could feel people talking behind my back. Yet my walk was confident and slow because I now talked the walk. I very much appreciated administration not letting reporters on campus. Suddenly I was "oh so special."

I don't have a double life or wear a mask and tights. I'm just plain Katie.

Since all of this excitement, Josh seems to like me more and acts real sweet. I think he's just nervous that I'll kick his ass.

"Good evening, Jim. Erica Mann here reporting live at the scene in the foothills section of Tucson. She's being called a hometown superhero tonight. Some neighbors are calling it a miracle. Local high-school student Katie Jackson saved a little boy from being hit by a car when she dove in between an oncoming car and an injured child who fell off his bike. Investigators are still evaluating what happened.

"The boy's mother told reporters that her son Andy was riding his bike off Territory Drive and lost control, crashing into the residential street when a car came around the curve. A young woman stepped into the road and crouched between the boy and the car. All the mother could say was, 'The girl put out her arms and hands, there was a deafening screech. I'm not sure if the car swerved or was pushed out of the way. The next thing I knew, there was an explosion and smoke. I don't know, but I am just so grateful.'"

The reporter continued, "The driver claims he swerved of his own accord. Police have indicated that there is nothing yet to explain the damage to the vehicle since it didn't hit anything.

"Parents and residents are angry today. Emotions are flying high all around. One group claims that they have been trying to have that trail shut down and a traffic light installed. A neighbor who declined giving her name commented that something like this was inevitable. 'Does someone have to get killed around here before we do something about it? If it wasn't for that girl, whoever she is, we'd be telling a different story tonight.' Miss Jackson and her parents have declined comment so far. Katie Jackson, a local high-school student, has also been visiting regularly with a local college professor. We have tried to contact him to ask about the nature of their dealings. We wanted to know if he was tutoring her, if she was studying advanced college work, or if he would speak to what has happened. He has declined comment so far.

"A local caught the whole thing on video. Have a look, Jim."

"Hey, boss, you watching this on TV?" Vuuv asked.

"Yes," said Axe. He turned to Vuuv. "How could I miss it? Probably a hoax or a big publicity stunt."

Vuuv laughed. "Yeah, she is a little hottie. They say she has special powers. She's being called a superhero."

Axe's tattoo again itched like crazy; the creams had stopped helping of late now that he was close to detonation—and close to Dr. S. He found the superhero girl strangely fascinating and muttered under his breath. "Schlisselvasser is involved, another good reason to be in Arizona." He looked closely at the girl's image on TV and didn't see a tattoo but noticed the good luck charm she was wearing, which resembled his tattoo.

Vuuv said, "You say something, boss?"

"Oh, just that we should get to know her better, no? Perhaps she could come work for us."

CHAPTER 16

THE NIGHT of the formal arrived, and Josh was getting ready. He had considered bagging the whole thing since the local TV news about Katie kept repeating.

It was cool that she was heroic, Josh thought, but this was so strange. Josh read an article in a men's online magazine about how some guys get intimidated by powerful women who earn more money than the guy, but this was too much. If I try to kiss her, she might literally toast me, he thought. When I see her, should I shake her hand or kiss her?

At least I'm not a total idiot, Josh nodded to himself. I knew it all along. Katie was behind screwing up my car and smashing me into a wall when I harassed that stupid weasel. I have a good mind to break up with her before we even go out.

Wow, I need to tell her that I confronted that kid in the school-yard because I caught him cheating and picking on other kids, not because I'm a bully. I want Katie to trust me, to like me, because I'm nuts about her even if she is scary and odd. I love a challenge, an adventure. Live a little dangerously.

She probably thinks that I sleep around. She'd probably freak if she knew the truth was the exact opposite. Yes, I like beer. No, I love beer. Problem? Not yet. Could it be in the future? I don't know and don't care at the moment.

I guess I'll wear my plaid suit and a bow tie tonight. I'll have to review YouTube on how to tie one because the one I like needs tying.

The other one is a clip on, and it's not great. Deodorant, cologne, mouthwash twice, plus chewing gum. Moisturizer, mousse. Bring a condom? Too presumptuous. I think I'm going to be sick. I'll just call and cancel. Sweating, wear a T-shirt. More deodorant. My hands feel clammy.

She's so beautiful. Her smile and stare light up a room. I can't move, feel paralyzed and hot. The thought of her is arousing; guess I'll go through with it.

Josh looked in the mirror.

Crap a pimple. Now what? I'm running out of time. Squeeze. It's the only thing she will notice. Damn. It will do the talking for me. I know, I'll draw a circle around it and call it the bull's eye as a joke. Making her laugh is my favorite thing on earth to do.

〜〜〜〜〜

Sara drove up and pulled in. She had an adorable lime-green VW beetle with white and green floral designer wheels. I'm glad that she got rid of the lame flower in the dashboard. She and I were going to be getting ready for the dance together at my house.

She brought enough stuff to move in for a week. We were planning a sleepover after the event, which was to be held at the swanky Esperrero Canyon Country Club and Resort ballroom. The club had a nationally ranked thirty-six-hole golf course. It was set in the high desert foothills of Tucson.

Sara and I got busy.

"Sara, what are you doing?" She was making sure each eye lash was perfect. It takes me like two minutes to put on makeup.

Sara said it takes her thirty.

It took a while to blow-dry our hair as we talked loudly above the music and hair dryer, laughing mostly. The bathroom was hot and noisy. We decided that she would sit next to me, and Josh across from me. Then again maybe she should sit next to Josh so I could make eye contact with her. But if I'm Josh's date, shouldn't I be sitting next to him?

Seating arrangements at dinner tables are very confusing. I'll ask Mother. She's very picky about that. Drives Father mad. He will just plop down anywhere and then have to play musical chairs.

My mom yelled something from the kitchen.

"What, Mom?"

"Do you girls need any help?"

"No, we got it."

"Your dress is hanging in the laundry room."

"I know, Mom."

"Which shoes are you wearing?"

"Mom, I don't know where to sit."

"What? Your dress doesn't fit?"

"Never mind."

My mom later said in a hurt tone, "Where did the time go? You two are beautiful young ladies. You don't need me anymore."

Her expression indicated that she was clearly fishing for us to say that we still needed her. I didn't encourage Mother, but Sara said, "We will always need you, Mrs. Jackson."

"Aww, you're a good one, Sara." Mom smiled.

We were running out of time and hurriedly applied makeup together in front of the mirror.

"You look great, Sara."

"Thanks, so do you, Katie."

I tried out my new uncomfortable shiny black high heels that Mom ordered for me online. I felt like I was on stilts and kept tripping and rolling my feet, almost spraining my ankle. I walked like a drunken bow-legged cowboy. I couldn't comprehend how girls walked in these things looking sexy. They felt too loose. My dad had an extra pair of tongue pads that he gave me. I ended up choosing the flats. I guess if Josh tries to kiss me I'll have to stand on my tippy toes.

What should I do with my cell phone? I wondered.

I turned toward Sara. "I'll just leave my cell in your car. My dress has no pockets. I could leave it in my purse, but then what will I do with my purse? I'll be so pissed off if I bring it in with me and it gets lost or stolen. I don't care if my parents are pissed off that I don't have my phone on me. Are you bringing a camera?"

I turned my back to Sara and said over my shoulder, "Can you help me zip my dress?"

Then we were ready to have some fun.

My parents had to take pictures before we left. They told us to call, carry our phones, and stay safe. They hugged us, which messed my hair a little. Annoying.

My parents told us how gorgeous we were. My mother got choked up, and Dad snapped away with his camera. Sara told my parents how sweet they were, that this was her second family, and that she loved them. To me she said, "Now let us proceed to party, sister."

Dad told us to call him on his cell if we needed anything. "Anything at all." He made sure that Sara also had his cell number just in case. He'd be there in a flash he called out as we spilled out the front door giggling.

~~~~~~~

Stepping out of the desert heat into the restaurant, I was hit by a blast of cold air from the AC. The aroma of red sauce made me hungry as I waited with Sara in the entryway of Cusamano's Trattoria for Josh.

At first we stood attentively. It lapsed into hanging around and finally we sat on the padded entry benches. I began to nibble at my cuticle; Sara encouraged me to stop before I ruined my manicure. Relax. She assured me that I looked great.

I'm a stickler for punctuality; I get that from my mom. She and I tend to show up for things ten minutes early. Not my dad. He cuts it to the last second and is into the whole fashionably late thing.

Eventually everyone arrived. We occupied a long table for twenty in the middle of the restaurant. Josh entered. It was an athletic walk, not confident, a bit tentative. Looking around, he saw our growing group, and he saw me. We both smiled. He had on a charcoal-gray plaid suit. The fine plaid pattern was black with tiny strands of blue silk. The wool fell perfectly on his frame. His shirt was a light sky blue. He had on a red silk bow tie that gave him an air of intelligence, something he needed. His hair had the cutest little curl near his ears, and a thick lock fell over his forehead. The silver cufflinks and black, dress, lace-up, plain-toe blucher shoes with pant cuffs that broke perfectly completed the ensemble. Wow.

My hormones gushed from somewhere deep in my brain showering me like a fire hose from within and obliterating my hunger for food. I think I might have gasped lightly as my hand came up to my throat and my toes curled. Someone please put out the fire. The temperature in the restaurant inexplicably went up to over eighty degrees despite the air conditioner blasting. Patrons complained, lights flickered, and my legs grew rubbery. As he approached, I put out my hand; he took it, but then, with his other arm, he embraced me. He bent his neck and torso. I could feel how firm and taut he was. He kissed me on the cheek and not just a tiny peck. His breath was sweet like a freshly peeled apple. He smelled so good. I don't know what fragrance he had on—maybe death by pheromone? I noticed that he had a pimple, but in the context of things, who the hell cares?

Damn photographers appeared out of nowhere. Oh, look, the freaky superdork has a date. They approached, talking into their mikes, yelling. "Katie what's it like? Who's the lucky fella? How'd you do it? What's your secret?"

Finally, after I answered their questions and threw a few crumbs, the vultures seemed satisfied.

Oh, the warm bread was delicious—chewy on the inside, crusty on the outside. I went with the chicken parmesan. The sauce was made fresh by none other than Mrs. Cusamano.

There was background conversation, and classical music floated from flush-mounted ceiling speakers. Before long several different conversations were going on simultaneously at our table. I couldn't tell what was being said fourteen people down, but it was like waves that start at two ends, collide, and splash in the middle. Something would be said at one end of the table, and by the time it reached the other in a flurry of words, it had evolved into something that vaguely resembled what was initially said. Back and forth this went, words dangling on the end of a spoon or a tinkling glass, some whispered in an ear, others yelled out. Words were punctuated by contagious laughter that erupted every other minute for ninety minutes straight. Everything and anything seemed cheerful tonight. The slightest turn of phrase became a reason for rowdy boys to randomly leap from their seats, crack up, and high five each other. Neckties loosened, shirt tails hung out of their pants. All this and we weren't even of drinking age. But we were young, invincible, incorrigible, and this was our night.

Yet the words between Josh and me were clipped and terse. A thinly veiled tension existed. Not in a bad way. We were like an awkward package that you keep turning over and over trying to figure out how to open it up—where to pull the wrapper and slit the seal. We were just beginning a new jigsaw puzzle. We were looking at it and laying out the pieces.

At one point in the evening, he reached over me to the left to tap the guy's shoulder next to us and say something. Of course, more laughter erupted. He had his arm around me and touched my hair for a minute, and it felt good. Then later while he was talking and making hand gestures, he placed his warm hand on my hand, which was sitting in my lap, and covered it. His hands are long and slender like he is. My initial reaction was to pull my hand away, but I didn't. Instead, we locked eyes and smiled. The tension melted. The seal was broken.

We had broken the ice once before at school, but that had been only a hairline crack, not a first date. A brief introduction if not developed is quickly forgotten. That was two kids talking in school, this was different. I wondered if my nose might be dripping as a result of the very spicy food. He took a selfie of us with his phone.

I found out that he was looking forward to the upcoming bike race called a criterium. He couldn't stop talking about how he's a competitive cyclist. If he didn't ride his bike for a week, he felt as fat as the butcher's dog.

"Fat as the butcher's dog?" I asked.

"Yes," he smirked. "It's an old cowboy saying I heard."

He found out very little he didn't already know about me.

"Katie, I liked you from the first moment I saw you. I was nervous asking you to the formal. I was sure that you would say no."

I was really turned on by his natural honesty. This was a fresh, genuine side to him I had no idea about. I thought he was arrogant and full of himself.

"Well, Josh, when I first met you, I thought that your ego needed its own zip code. Now I see that I was wrong, but your smile sure lights up a room. I mean, you could have any girl at school."

"I don't want just any girl; I want Katie Jackson. You may not be the fastest girl runner on the field, but you sure are the best looking. It's adorable how you run like a duck. I like running behind you. Don't your knees get sore?" I blushed and slapped his thigh.

"How is it an amazing girl like you doesn't have a boyfriend?" We held hands.

"I was wondering the same about you, or will I be your latest conquest?"

He looked at me and said, "After what I've seen about you on TV, there will be no one conquering you."

"You better believe it. Stay in line or else."

"Or else what?"

He brought his right hand up to my cheek, swept my hair off my cheek, and kissed me tenderly on my neck. He smelled so male. I reached over and hugged him, feeling very aroused.

The neck? That's it? I wondered. Is that good? Bad? Maybe he doesn't like me? Where's Sara? Maybe he's just being a gentleman here at the restaurant. I was ready to pass out. By the end of the night, we would get to know each other better than we had hoped for.

～～～～～

At the dance, the lights were low, and the music was loud. Some people were dancing and grinding, and others were hanging around. The place got hot and moist. We took off our shoes. Josh undid his tie and loosened his shirt. After a while we got something to drink.

Chaperones and faculty appeared nonchalant and mostly talked to each other.

"Let's get out of here," Josh said.

"What?" I couldn't hear him over the music.

"Let's go somewhere," he shouted.

"Like where?"

"There's almost a full moon tonight. Let's go for a walk. It's getting so hot and noisy here."

"Well, I'm not going without Sara."

"No, of course not. I meant the three of us, even though I would love to be alone with you."

I was amazed and thrilled. I could hardly handle it. I blushed, but luckily it was dark. "Well, okay then."

"Let's head over to the Finger Rock hiking trail. It's gorgeous and cool up there at night. I know a secret cave that I haven't been to in a while. Do you have a flashlight app on your phone?"

"Sure, let me find Sara. I left my phone in her car."

The two of us slid and bumped our way through the crowded dance floor, lights flashing. At times my hands went up over my head moving to the beat as I looked out for Sara. We eventually found her dancing with a group of kids.

"Sara, I need you to come with me to the bathroom right this instant."

"What?"

Again too loud. I did not want to scream out loud that we had to go pee, so I just dragged her off the dance floor. In the bathroom I told her about Josh's proposal that we go hiking. All she could say was, "Cool. Have a great time."

"No, not Josh and I, we as in the three of us."

Sara was brushing her hair while I washed my hands.

"Oh, what am I, your chaperone now? Bring a teacher. I don't want to be a third wheel on your romantic moonlight walk." She laughed and started to hug herself, kiss the air, and look in the mirror. "Oh, Josh."

"Sara, don't be an idiot. You look like you are about to break into a verse of 'I Feel Pretty' from *West Side Story* where you played Maria in the school play."

We both laughed.

"You have to come," I told her. "First, you and I promised that we would come and go together. This is considered leaving. Second, I'm not comfortable going up there alone with him. I barely know him. Third, if you don't come with me, I will have to kill you."

"Pushy! All right, okay, let's go. Let me just say bye to some friends. I'll meet you outside in five minutes, and we can drive up together."

We got into Sara's car. I made sure Josh sat in the back. The back of the beetle is roomy enough. I wanted to sit with Sara. It would have been awkward for Josh and me to be on a date in the proverbial backseat of a car while Sara drove since I practically had to drag her out. I also thought that it would be awkward to have Josh and Sara up front with me alone in the back. Was I feeling slightly possessive?

We headed back out onto Skyline Drive. Traffic was light. The car felt sure and firm in a Germanic way.

Finger Rock trail was two minutes away. Heading north on Alvernon, Sara pulled into the parking lot off the crunchy road and shut down the engine, which made those pinging sounds after it was turned off. I always wondered what that noise was. We got our stuff and headed up the hill. In places the ledges were narrow and the drop-offs steep.

It was truly a sparkling night. Desert breeze, moonlight, good friends. The trail was well worn, and the crystal stars were like a billion unanswered questions. We stopped along the way sitting on boulders, telling jokes, and taking pictures of each other.

Sara said, "Are we there yet?"

Josh answered, "About ten more minutes."

"That's what you said thirty minutes ago," I said.

CHAPTER 17

EARLIER THAT day, Scoop Weaver headed up the mountain like any other fun-loving hiker. He set up camp in the foothills beneath Finger Rock, high enough above Axe's compound to disappear into the scenery. There, he found a small stone ridge shelf that dipped down three feet and backed up against a cliff creating some shelter that protected his back. He could nestle against the rocks and gain cover from the elements. The scraggly brush provided some cover and a little shade in daytime. This was where he was planning to spend the night and possibly live for a while. It would be a good old-fashioned stakeout combined with a camping trip. Watchful waiting and ample boredom. He could commune with nature and think.

It was less than an hour's steady hoof to his car, twenty minutes if he ran the trail hard. He could drive home when he needed to, or head straight to work smelling, which wouldn't even be noticed.

Several times over the past week, he had hiked up to his secluded spot and added materials that included turkey jerky, pretzels, dried fruit, nuts, water, vacuum-packed meals, and first aid supplies.

Within the space of a few days, he accumulated sufficient provisions. This last time up he hauled ammo, weapons, charges, and night-vision goggles. This time he wasn't planning to leave until he was good and ready, meaning he'd gotten what he came for—some definitive information on Axe and the compound. He had the gift of patience from his years in the military and was able to be agonizingly still, listening to his breathing and heartbeat. He could attend to the breeze all day long, note minor changes, and stalk his quarry. There were times during mideast deployments when he would lie on a thorn or a rock and be still for hours. A few inches of movement or a tiny reflection off sweaty skin could alert a sniper a mile away. Sure, he felt pain, but he was able to accept it.

The night revealed stars, moon, and a hooting owl.

There was activity at Axe's compound. Large unmarked trucks came and went through what looked like a sally port with two sets of ornate steel gates. The second, inner one opened after the first one closed upon entering. This increased security by serving as a pen and a checkpoint for entering traffic.

No reason to be taking deliveries at 11:00 PM, he thought. Weaver could make out several men with his night-vision goggles. Equipment of some kind was being delivered. Some of the cargo had the international sign for radiation. He could make out some writing, and letters on other boxes looked like Russian and Arabic. Every time a piece of equipment left a truck, it was accompanied by two armed men with AK-47s. Not very neighborly.

Deciding to get a closer look, Weaver ducked behind large boulders and crawled on elbows and knees facedown in the dirt over a cholla cactus. He picked up some stickers the size of a small dog. They were barbed and couldn't be pulled out by hand. Luckily, he came prepared. Getting stuck with cactus in this environment was not uncommon. A simple large comb in his back pocket did the trick. One quick sweep of the comb close to his pants, and the barbs pulled away. His bigger concern was getting a venomous bite, and he knew that if Axe's men found him there would be a fire fight. It was going to be a long night. He needed to stay focused, hydrated. He opened a pack of gel that contained caffeine, carbs, electrolytes and vitamins. He squeezed it into his mouth then stopped in his tracks and held his breath as three people came around the corner out of nowhere and approached laughing. Two females, one male. Young, maybe teens. Dressed in formal clothing. Not hikers, not Axe's people. Friendlies carrying flashlights, laughing, having fun. Scoop hid and watched the kids head closer to the compound. The three people stooped low to the ground and then disappeared as if swallowed by the earth.

A cave entrance? Weaver wished he'd have found it since it would've been more comfortable than the ledge he'd been on. He became a barely moving, breathing part of the ground and crawled on.

~~~~

Security from the surrounding houses on duty also witnessed three intruders on camera. Silent sensors tripped, guards made a visual, began texting. Most of the time the sensors were activated by wildlife or the rare stray hiker.

~~~~

Josh, Sara, and I entered the mouth of the cave by squatting, kneeling, and then stooping to get in. The ceiling was too low to stand up in places. My knees were dirty, and my dress was a mess. Only a few feet in, the cave opened into a bulbous vestibule for us to sit comfortably on the dirt.

Josh said, "Isn't this place totally cool? What did I tell you? Wasn't it worth it?"

Sara replied, "Awesome," as she looked around with her cell-phone flashlight. "How did you know about this place? I can't believe you kept it a secret." Josh pulled over some flat smooth rocks for Sara and me to sit on. Caveman chivalry is not dead.

I, on the other hand, was not so impressed. My dress had torn after getting snagged on the rock. Even wearing his beautiful suit, Josh thought nothing about sitting on the ground with all the creeping crawlies.

I couldn't take my eyes off the petroglyphs on the wall. I shone my light on them. Carved on the cave wall was a prehistoric picture of a great beast. It was a bear with human legs standing upright. It had a beautiful mane of human-looking hair, and on its shoulder was a huge bird of some sort that was staring out in defiance. People and other animals were holding some kind of gathering and dancing around it. One dancer wore attire similar to pictures I had seen of a medicine man. I stood up and reached out to touch it. My fingers gently outlined its shape, and I felt the texture, smooth now after eons. I closed my eyes and muttered softly, so no one could hear, "Wow, man, this is totally chill, amazing. I've been here too all this time." I felt the tribal people that first contacted spirit bear right here practically in my own backyard. My back was to my two friends. I looked like a student writing on a black board. I felt a warm electric current go through my arm, up to my head. I touched the petroglyph with both hands now and put my head against the cool wall.

I sat back down, pensive and introspective, and then pulled my knees close into my chest in the dank cave. I caught Josh stealing a glance at my thighs and wrapped my dress more snuggly around my knees. Sara noticed and giggled.

Something tugged at me, not physically. Two things. I felt the power of a drumbeat in my heart from a time long ago. I was being beckoned, called out to. The drum and the vibration of my soul hummed synchronously. I began to feel less dense, floating. But this place felt so wrong. I could feel a sadness, a wound coming up from the ground into my body. I knew it was important to know this place. Or better yet, somehow I already did. I had memories of Honon.

It was here that I felt the cold, empty blackness. I could feel it again. I went into my stare with my head down. My breathing slowed. I tried to stop it, control it, not wanting it now when I was with my best friend and Josh. They already knew about my so-called strangeness—everyone did by now—but that didn't mean I wanted to demonstrate it in front of them. It was like trying to stop a sneeze, a split-second reflex that shoots air out of your mouth at a hundred miles per hour.

Josh asked, "Katie, are you all right?"

Sara stared. "Katie? You're okay, huh? Breathe. Let's just have a good time tonight. You'll be fine. Josh, maybe we should start to head out?"

It was all I could do to get on my knees and utter the words, "We should go. This place is bad."

I heard it first. A low growling sound. I turned and peered intently over my shoulder down the long, dark, narrowing damp corridor trying to make out what was going on. I was afraid. Then I pointed my flashlight in that direction, but couldn't see much.

~~~~~~~

Axe radioed the other houses on a secure frequency. They were aware that their calls, e-mails, and other communications were being monitored. They didn't need NSA leakers and defectors to tell them that. Even when they did text, it was code. For example, the text initially sent out by house two to Axe was, "Hi, you up? Beautiful night. Want to go for a walk? We'd have to be careful though. Saw three javelina out there. I'm going out to put my garbage can away so they don't knock it over and make a mess."

That is how security reported that three people went into the cave. It looked like a male and two females. The light was low.

"Good work," he said. "Keep me posted." He spoke personally to security in his house. "No, I don't want them killed yet. We are this close." Axe made a tiny space between his thumb and forefinger and held it an inch from his eye. "We are just days from leaving this country and detonating. Our plans have been flawless. I do not want to create a scene now. We will be very peaceful neighbors until I decide not to be. They would never make it alive past point one. They're probably just hanging out at the entrance, smoking pot, drinking beer, or getting laid. Lucky boy. You say two girls went in with him? Well, just scare them off. Say boo, oh, and don't slip on a used condom. Vuuv, do you mind going down into the cave and telling those kids to leave. No rough stuff, and please be careful."

"Sure, boss. Shall I walk down there from the outside and surprise them? Should I do it cave side? If I do it cave side, the minute they hear me coming they will be so scared that they will run out without even seeing me. They will think I'm the boogeyman or something. If I come around front and confront them, they will see me, I'll probably have to have a conversation, and I will be blocking the exit."

Axe said, "Cave side, from the rear, make noise, scare them, better not to be seen."

"Yes, sir."

Vuuv was closest to the cave access through the bowling alley. He walked to the end of the alley and brushed aside the pins. He loved the sound of bowling pins being knocked over. Tapping a series of buttons summoned the elevator, up through the floor. The third access point in the house was through Axe's bedroom closet.

Vuuv rode down the elevator doing the odd things so many people do while alone in an elevator. People sing, make faces, dance, or simply pick their noses. He exited at cave level one still humming and chuckling to himself. As he walked he wondered how he would simply scare those kids off without being seen. He didn't look intimidating.

Vuuv googled animal sounds on his phone, looked up mountain lion sounds. The distant echo of this sound at the end of a dark cave corridor should scare the crap out of them.

He was correct.

Vuuv entered the cave, slinking along with his back to the wall. Not being accustomed to this sort of physical espionage, he enjoyed getting out of work for a while to play.

~~~~~~~

All three of us heard the low growl this time. Josh said, "Holy shit, we better get out of here."

I looked over my shoulder and peered down the hall with my flashlight. Josh was yelling, "C'mon, Katie. Hurry up." He waited for me then grabbed my arm.

Sara shrieked, stood up too fast, and hit her head hard on the jagged cave ceiling. She staggered, and a large rock fell on her head. Sara's hands went up to protect her skull. The lighting was poor, but she had slick wet hair and palms.

I remember from honors biology that the scalp has several layers. Beneath the skin there is connective tissue.

The scalp's blood supply is rich. Blood loss from being scalped is excessive and leads to a severely bad hair day. We had just spent so much time washing and blow-drying our hair.

Sara dropped the cell phone, which fell with the flashlight facing up, and I could see blood dripping down her face.

I pulled my arm away from Josh, put my hands out in front of me, and on an exhale, I screeched sounds of the earth and wind in some unknown tongue as an intense blast of air ten times faster than any sneeze shot down the long and narrow corridor like a bullet through the barrel of a gun. The acoustic concussion was so intense, the recoil knocked Josh back. I fell on top of him. Rocks fell on both of us, and the dust was blinding, choking, and thick. The mouth of the cave was collapsing all around us.

The three of us barely made it out of the cave alive before a large plume of debris entombed the cave's entrance. I heard a big crack like a collapsing wall from an earthquake come from the direction of the house. We were frightened, coughing, and covered in dust, sweat, and blood. So much for a romantic get-to-know-you first date.

~~~~~~

Axe's people checked their equipment and then went down into the labyrinth to find Vuuv who was now a half buried lump of clay on the ground. His head hung at an unnatural angle where a rock had fractured his fifth cervical vertebra and the base of his skull. Blood congealed around his nose, ears, and eyes.

Security and Axe were trying to understand what blew up. Later, they would need to run a complete system check. For now all visual contact was lost.

Axe became quiet; digesting the news about Vuuv wasn't easy. He moved his mouth and chewed his lips but made no sounds. His face turned red, eyes bulged. Vuuv was his technical director and one of his few remaining confidants, though he wouldn't call Vuuv his friend. No one was Axe's friend, but Vuuv would be the closest thing he ever knew to one. Vuuv was the last connection that Axe would ever have to his past. He had tried to shelter and protect Vuuv, one of the most trusted and knowledgeable people on his team. This loss would cut deep and set them back. To think that after all they had been through, all the hardships and treachery, that some teenager could get this close and do this to him was unconscionable. Some redundancy was built into the technical staffing patterns. People were crossed trained. There were only so many hours in the day, and they were working practically round the clock as it was. This would be bad for business. Uktam, a.k.a. the Axe, didn't handle setbacks or disappointment well. He had learned to suppress pain and loss, but this ripped open a primal scar that had been festering for years since the loss of his parents. Losing Vuuv brought all that to the surface.

He screamed mindlessly like an enraged, mad, frothing beast and attempted to hack one of his security agents for allowing this to happen. Violence was one of the few outlets Axe used to resolve his conflicts. Bugdon, the security agent, however, was only too familiar with Axe's bad behavior, having been present for what transpired with Rav, and knowing that with Axe someone's head might literally be about to roll.

Axe was acting out of sheer blind rage and making tactical mistakes, which was not a good strategy. Defending against a hatchet is exceedingly difficult. Usually no one wins. The best option is to be outside the reach of the weapon and get the hell out of there.

Bugdon parried and backed away from a swing that caused an audible whoosh of air. Axe missed. Overcommitting the forehand of his swing exposed him. The security agent took the opportunity to throw a heavy lamp at Axe's head, which connected with a thud, and then he lifted a small piece of furniture with one hand as a shield to the backhand swing that was coming down fast. The razor-sharp edge grazed the man's upper arm, and he scrambled to raise his weapon, a semiautomatic hand gun. Axe closed the distance and with his free arm punched his security agent in the face so that he moved backward and got off a single shot before escaping out the door into the night.

Uktam threw his axe at the guard and missed. It stuck in the wall where Bugdon's head had been a second earlier.

Axe was in pain and shocked by the bullet wound to his lower leg. He screamed, in pain and anger, "I will kill you if you don't bring me that girl." Then he thought, I will get you even if you do. Axe came to the conclusion that he wanted the girl because he was cunning, could read the tea leaves. He wanted the girl's powers working for him once he figured out the girl in his cave was the girl from the TV.

The security agent left the property in a hurry and made his way into the night.

CHAPTER 18

JOSH STRUGGLED to hold onto Sara, who was dizzy, bleeding, and barely functional. Her right eye looked like a raccoon's. She had stopped crying or saying much, which was very unlike her. He and I were trying to prop each other up. I was totally spaced out, which is what happens to me after one of these storms in my brain. Doc calls it a postictal equivalent. It's similar to what happens to seizure patients. They get into an altered state after the seizure. My events are obviously different. After the discharge from my brain lets loose with an explosive energy, I am totally spent and badly need some rest.

Nothing appeared solid to me. Everything was a wavy energetic space. There were no clear boundaries where one object started and another stopped. Things were flowing.

What looked like a boulder jumped up to grab Josh. I thought that my mind was still playing tricks on me. It took me a minute to realize it was a man. We were so badly shaken in the dark, running on fumes, that we didn't hear a word that was said. Josh let go of me with his right arm and threw a wild roundhouse punch at this stranger's face.

The stranger, who had looked like a boulder in the dark just a second ago, blocked it with his left forearm, brought his right arm under Josh's right triceps, and spun him around so that he had Josh's back. Sara slumped to the ground. The man, dressed in military uniform, put his left hand over Josh's mouth and pushed a foot in the bend of Josh's knee, forcing Josh to the ground. The soldier yelled, "Quiet, calm down."

I thought that I heard him say he was from the government and was here to help. This made me want to turn and run back up to the cave. I have a problem trusting men dressed in military uniforms who ambush me in the middle of the night, especially this night.

"I'm not going to hurt you. My name is Weaver, and I'm with US border patrol. You're safe with me for the moment. But we need to get you outta here fast. Can you all make it? If not, I'll radio for a helicopter extraction."

Josh nodded. I didn't know. I needed an inhaler. We were losing Sara fast.

Weaver picked her up in a firefighter's carry and hauled her out of the desert wearing night-vision goggles. "She's going into shock. We need to move fast. I'll radio for an ambulance when we get clear of here and into safer territory," he said. We followed closely behind.

I wondered why the heck we were being escorted out of the mountain by the freaking marines or whatever he said. I asked him what was so unsafe about this territory, as he called it, other than a small cave that I collapsed back there. I realized that I unfortunately probably killed the poor mountain lion that we startled. It was probably its den. I felt bad, but that didn't make this unsafe territory. This wasn't the Middle East; we were in the north Tucson foothills. This wasn't even the 'hood or the barrio in south Tucson. Territory? Was this guy for real? Arizona hasn't been a territory since 1912.

As we progressed down the hills in the moonlight, because Weaver said no flashlights, Josh took my hand. We held on to each other, struggled to keep up, and fell a few times. The ground was very hard and painful.

The trail we took was steeper and faster than the way we came up. The gravel and caliche were loose underfoot, and our footwear was far from hiking apparel. Glad I chose flats.

Josh whispered in my ear, "I'm very sorry I brought you and Sara up here tonight."

I looked deeply into his eyes. "I'm sorry too about the force I used. I'll never forgive myself if Sara isn't okay." I wished that I hadn't asked her to go up to the cave at the dance.

Josh looked at me and said, "Forgive yourself for what? It wasn't your blast of wind that caused Sara to hit her head. It allowed us to escape."

"Thank you for saying that, Josh. But I . . ."

"But nothing."

"I knew we shouldn't have been there. It's no one's fault, but I wish we could have left quietly without any trouble. I feel awful and guilty."

We heard the propeller sounds of the approaching helicopter. As it descended, sand and debris blew everywhere. The welcome sight of police cars and ambulance strobes cast an eerie red and blue sheen on the dust in the air. I watched particles move in a random fashion.

My biggest fear right now, apart from Sara, was the world of trouble I would be in when my parents found out. I felt sick watching paramedics strap Sara to a board with full cervical spine protection, start an IV in her arm, attach a monitor, and haul her onto the helicopter. I quickly rushed to her side, held her hand for a second, and told her, "Sara, we will not let you go. I will see you soon at the hospital. I love you. We need you."

The paramedic made a whirly motion with her hand signaling the patient was secure and ready for takeoff. She told me to move back. "We have to move her now. We have to go."

The chopper blades whirred loudly. Sara's medical status was deteriorating.

"Trauma one, this is medevac six. Do you copy?"

"Go ahead, six; what you got?"

"We are transporting a teenage female hiker with head trauma."

"What's her status?"

One of the paramedics tried talking to Sara. He shone a light in her eyes. He looked a little concerned and rubbed a knuckle on her chest as if he was trying to see if she would wake up. Nothing. She had dangerously weak vital signs.

"Trauma one, patient becoming unresponsive. Do you copy?"

"Roger that six. Initiate shock protocol. We are awaiting your arrival. Do you have an ETA?"

"Sara, stay with me. Chris, we're losing her. Open IV lactated ringers. Get the atropine, epi, and code cart ready. Tell them that her pupils are unequal. I think I can feel a depression under the scalp laceration. Can't rule out skull fracture."

"Trauma team red said they'd have STAT scan and OR ready. They have a call out to neurosurgery."

The pilot said, "ETA five minutes."

"Make it three. We might not have five."

Seconds later, in a renewed flurry of dust, they were airborne and on their way to the nearest trauma center. I felt scared and alone.

Other paramedics attended to us. It's called triage. Prioritize. Sara first, and then me. Throw Josh to the dogs.

They checked my vital signs, cuts, and scrapes. There was one that they thought might need stitches. They cleaned, steri-stripped, and fussed. I told them I was fine and that I wanted to go to the hospital to see Sara, not as a patient. They said that my parents had to be contacted since I was still a minor. I gave them the evil eye for that one.

Josh was similarly beat up. All he kept saying was how terrible he felt for going up there tonight. It wasn't totally his fault.

I explained to the police what happened. We went up hiking after the formal and sat in a cave. We heard a growling sound. I thought we were going to be attacked by a mountain lion. They all knew who I was from the news. I didn't come out and admit that I sent that shock wave that led to the collapse. There were still many skeptics who thought I was a nutcase.

~~~~~~~~

I stood next to the deputy listening to him make the dreaded parental call. I kicked the dirt, but I could still hear every word.

"Mrs. Jackson?"

"Yes, who is this?"

"My name is Deputy Bruce Carter. Pima County Sheriff's Department. I'm calling regarding your daughter, Katie Jackson. She is your daughter?" Carter was serious and to the point. Polite but matter-of-fact.

"Oh my God. What's happened? Is she all right?"

Mother must have had the phone on speaker because I heard my father yelling in the background.

"Yes, she is my daughter."

"She's okay, ma'am, but there's been an accident."

"No, please. What happened?"

"She is safe and with me now. Apparently, she and two friends were hiking up near the Finger Rock trail and an old cave system they were in collapsed. Paramedics are here now on the scene. She sustained some cuts and contusions. She is walking and talking. Quite a young woman you've got there, Mrs. Jackson; I saw her on the news."

"Oh my God, thank you. Thank heaven."

"She is requesting not to be treated in the emergency room. We need your consent to withhold medical transport."

"Can I speak with my daughter?"

"Yes, ma'am, hold on." He handed the phone to me. "It's your mom."

"Yes, officer, I kind of gathered that. If you could have delayed making this call for a few months, I would have turned eighteen." I held out my hand. With my other hand I held a bottle of water. Around my shoulder was a blanket, thick and scratchy. "Hello, Mom," I said sheepishly.

"*Mijita*, are you okay? What happened, sweetie?"

In between rasping sobs, I tried to explain what happened to Sara, the cave, me, everything.

Within a minute the sweetie stuff was over. Instead, she snapped, "What do you mean you went off hiking in the desert with a boy and Sara after the party?" The cop, who could hear her yelling, smiled to himself and looked at the ground as if he were getting yelled at by a universal communal mother.

"You stay put, young lady. Your father and I are on our way. By the time we get through with you, you'll think you would have been better off going to the emergency room or staying in that cave. You'll be grounded for the rest of your life. Do you understand?"

"Yes, Mother."

"Poor Sara. Have they called her mom? We'll pick you up and go to the hospital together to see her. How's that boyfriend of yours? Did he get hurt?"

"No, he's fine. Well, not fine exactly. He's sorta like me, all 'stove up' like dad says after he hurts himself." I was hoping to get a laugh. No way, not tonight, no points for cuteness. I whispered and covered the phone so Josh wouldn't hear. "He is not my boyfriend, Mom."

It was not good for me that the events at the cave had awakened my parents from their precious sleep. My father especially did not like having his sleep interrupted. Dad had been to one of those sleep labs where they torture you all night and expect you to sleep while being watched on an uncomfortable bed hooked up to wires.

I knew that given those conditions the results would not be optimal for me.

Mom did better on less sleep, although she became more tightly wound like air shrieking from a balloon with its mouthpiece pulled tight.

The two of them together and sleep deprived wasn't pretty.

While I stood there waiting for my parents to arrive at what looked like a crime scene, though I'm not sure we even committed a crime, I thought about them. Mom handles pressure better than Dad. She has patience and is able to wait and see how things develop in the face of adversity. Dad, on the other hand, wears his heart on his sleeve, which is partly why he's so lovable. No pretenses, but impatient and wants answers now, even when there aren't any. I was sure that Dad would be tired and cranky in the morning. He would have been anyway because he doesn't sleep well when I'm out late. He worries and waits up in case something terrible happens—like right now, for example.

I noticed Weaver and the police scratching their heads and conversing. I heard one detective say with force and optimism, "We now have probable cause to go in, investigate, and search Axe's house tonight."

Axe. Where have I heard that name, I thought? Then I remembered. Bear told me that an evil dude named Axe was up there. I recalled the cold fetid darkness.

The cops were planning to get a search warrant from a judge. Getting one in the middle of the night wasn't going to happen. For investigators, tonight was a hopeful turn of events. They might have to wait until the morning to get all their ducks in a row. Their premise was that they were just following up on a disturbance and injuries. Neighbors reported a loud noise. Kids were hurt. They thought there may have been a mountain lion sighting. They could ask to look around.

<center>~~~~~~</center>

Axe's entourage flocked to him from within the main house, the caves, and the other houses' underground passages.

His personal medic assessed his injuries. He had a new laceration to add to his collection and a gunshot wound to his calf that was fairly superficial. It didn't tear the tibial artery or nerve. The clean entry was adjacent to the tibia bone, which was not broken. The exit wound in the calf muscle was star shaped and jagged. The shot took a small morsel of muscle. It was painful, but he could move and feel his foot. Probably no nerve damage. The pressure bandage stemmed the bleeding. They found the shell casing and discarded it.

He had an arsenal of drugs and an infirmary down in the caves. He could not risk going to the hospital. Axe had sustained significant losses tonight, and his cave was again going to be the center of attention. Staffers fully expected the police to arrive any time now. He contemplated sending a search party to apprehend Bugdon, the defecting security agent. Deciding to be proactive, Axe called the police as a concerned citizen might. Axe thought that preventive measures were his best next step as he dialed 911. He did this to avoid raising suspicions about why the home owner wouldn't call authorities about this incident. He explained that there was an explosive noise on his property. It sounded like a small earthquake.

No, he didn't smell gas, and no, he didn't need an ambulance.

His staff gave him an injection of Rocephin intramuscularly, a powerful antibiotic. But he refused to take any pain pills, for fear of having his senses dulled. Axe and his team were too close to achieving their diabolical goal. All he was willing to accept were oral anti-inflammatories, an ice pack, and some lidocaine squirted on the wound periodically with a syringe. The burning sensation of the lidocaine liquid applied to the wound was worse than the wound, but once the anesthetic kicked in, he had much less pain for an hour or two. It gave him a warm and heavy numbness down to the bottom of his foot.

~~~~~~~~

After receiving the call placed by Axe to 911, Weaver's boss along with the Pima County Sheriff's department decided that Scoop and the officer on the scene would go up to the mansion. There was much discussion about whether Scoop should go. Assuming Axe was home, he might recognize Scoop from when they were in Mexico at the border. Scoop hoped that Axe would recognize him. That was the point—to start letting Axe know that he was under close scrutiny, rattle his cage, and slowly close the noose. The hope was that he would start to make mistakes. Scoop wanted to put himself out there as bait.

On the way up to Axe's compound, they listened to police chatter on the radio. The Sheriff's SUV slowed as they approached the gates followed by a fire engine paramedic unit. A brief conversation took place between police and paramedics.

The sheriff advised, "It is unclear if there are any safety issues after the collapse, but given the history of this bad dude Uktam the Axe, it is probably looking more like a criminal investigation, with us in the forward position." The engine was instructed to stay back a few hundred feet and out of harm's way.

Gravel crunched beneath the rubber tires. The powerful V8 engine idled with a burbling sound. Deputy Bruce Carter opened the driver's door to get out. Before he put a foot to the ground, the electric gate opened letting them through to the second set of gates. After those opened, the police cruiser climbed the steep drive lined with lights, exotic cacti, boulders, palm trees, cameras, and who knew what else.

As they approached the massive front doors, Carter killed the engine. They got out and the two doors closed with a thump, thump. Boots on the ground.

Axe opened the door to greet his new arrivals. He was in a handsome red silk bathrobe, wore flip flops and carried a walking stick.

"Officers, thank you so much for coming." He limped outside to greet them.

Carter pulled out a notepad. "I'm Deputy Carter. This is my partner, Agent Weaver."

"Agent? Why an agent?"

Weaver answered, "I'm with border patrol, sir. There have been reports of some illegals coming up through these hills, living in small caves around here, and disturbing the residents, so I came along."

Axe and Weaver made eye contact. It took a second before Axe recognized him. He said, "Illegals, I see."

Carter continued. "You called nine one one. What is your name?"

Uktam gave his correct name.

"Tell us what the concern is tonight. What's happening?"

Axe looked down and noticed a rivulet of blood down his leg collecting between the big and second toe of the flip flop.

"Sir, are you okay? It looks like your leg is bleeding."

"Wow, well, I'll be darned. Crap. I could tell you that I cut myself shaving, but you wouldn't believe me." Axe thought fast. "Well, that's why I called you. The bang was so loud that it startled me, and I hit my leg falling into the sharp edge of a glass table. It's nothing serious."

The deputy asked, "Would you like medical attention?"

"No, no, I'm fine. Really, I am. I was just shaken up that's all. I'll just go in and bandage it." Axe had beads of perspiration collecting on his brow.

Weaver felt that he was lying and said, "Mind if we come in, Uktam?"

"Umm, of course not."

Weaver and Carter cautiously entered one at a time. One left, the other right. The human brain filters out many details not required for its survival. To really see and experience more than a sliver of reality takes great skill and energy. It's not possible to maintain this level of perception indefinitely. It only works for short spurts of time.

In this instance, Scoop concentrated, shut his filters, and became acutely aware of his surroundings, noticing and registering everything. For example, when he asked Axe if it was okay to go in the house, the way Axe squeezed his walking stick until he had white knuckles was perhaps an important detail—a signal of worry, anger, anxiety, or simply pain. Scoop could smell the dampness of fear. Scoop Weaver and the sheriff were encouraged and given permission to enter by Axe without any wrangling, which ordinarily has important legal ramifications. In this case it could be a trap, Weaver thought.

Axe limped off to tend his wound after one of his people came out to entertain the guests. She offered them refreshments. They declined, looked around, and Carter noticed the large crack in the wall. He pointed it out to Weaver, took notes, and snapped a picture with his cell.

After a few moments, Axe returned, newly bandaged.

Weaver wasted no time and asked, "Mind if we see the broken glass table you were referring to?"

"Well, gentleman, we had it taken out of harm's way."

"What's that dented lamp over there? Did someone throw it, drop it, or did it dent that badly flying across the room when the explosion occurred?"

"We've seen this exact sort of pattern in many domestic violence calls," Carter added.

Weaver said in a mildly antagonistic tone. "Is that how you got that purple eye that looks like it's about to swell shut? It's a beauty. Might wanna put some ice on it."

Axe looked as if he were debating having them eliminated right where they stood, but Shane figured that Axe couldn't afford to start a war with the local cops tonight.

"Sir, it's interesting that there is a bloodstain here on the carpet where I'll assume that you fell onto the glass table and cut yourself. But, that was, what, only an hour ago?" Weaver looked at his watch. "I don't see any marks on the plush rug where the legs of a heavy glass table would have been. I guess you could have had those little carpet things that keep the rug from getting compressed, but somehow you don't seem the type."

"Well, officer, if I may interrupt, that is a very valuable Persian rug. The knot count is very high, and the rug costs more than you and your sidekick over here make in a year. Even though it is plush, as you say, it is tight and flat. It's very old, and you could park a truck on it without leaving a mark. Why the interrogation, may I ask? I called you to report a problem."

The pay-grade comment made Weaver's blood boil. He continued. "And it looks like over there was another stain of some sort rather hastily cleaned up—might have been blood, too. It's in the shape of a comma, not a dripping pattern. Looks like someone moved fast while they bled. Sir, was there a domestic violence incident here earlier this evening?"

Axe didn't answer. Weaver was getting a bad feeling, like they were outnumbered and outgunned. He tried to get a sense of how many people were in the house but was unsuccessful. He wished he had forensics to collect evidence.

Axe asked, "Do you officers know what the loud noise was? We didn't smell any gas."

Carter responded, "Have you noticed the big crack in your wall over there?"

"Why, yes."

"Apparently, sir, the cave beneath your house collapsed. Hikers in the area were injured, one seriously, two others mildly. We've notified utility companies, and other inspectors will be notified for your safety.

There will probably be an investigation of the structural integrity of the house."

"No way," Uktam said, with false horror. "That is terrible. I didn't know. I'm so sorry there were injuries, and now I'm worried that it happened on my property. I don't want trouble or liability."

Weaver concluded, "Just a few tips. Take a good look at my face again, and burn it into your memory. I recommend that you evacuate the house, since it's probably no longer safe. There's a motel down the road. Who knows—this whole damned McMansion may need to be condemned. But don't leave town. Maybe you ought to talk to one of your lawyers. You are most definitely a person of great interest," Scoop said with a smile. "Oh, and by the way, whatever happened to those missing cave explorers? I'm just saying. You know that murder investigations never expire. It's still an open case. Let's get out of this rat hole, Carter."

The two officers turned and started to leave.

Axe yelled menacingly, "I'll be the one pressing charges around here. What the hell were those kids doing on my property anyway?"

Weaver stopped dead in his tracks and stated in a cold hard voice before turning around, "No one said anything about kids, Uktam."

"Well, tons of kids hike up around here; it's practically a lovers' lane. What, you think some old farts from the foothills are going to be wandering around here at night? Of course it's kids. Yes?"

"What's with the yes crap, Mr. Clean? You were, what, about twenty or so when your parents were murdered, weren't you? Is that how it started for you—I mean, this path that you took?" asked Shane.

"Now, now, agent, I know a little something about you, too. Too bad your gorgeous wife left you. I hear she was a real firecracker. All she needed was a well-equipped man, not your little badge and big ego. No? See, I have my intelligence and secrets, and you have yours. Am I starting to get inside your head, Mr. Weaver?"

The two stared each other down hard, with a look of death. Scoop wanted to kill him.

"Train your sidekick well, Agent Weaver. I'm sure that he will amount to more than you ever did. I think selling candy in a little border town is more your speed."

Carter had to firmly say, "Let's go."

Weaver practically needed to be restrained. Weaver looked up at Uktam, who said, "Yes, I know you and burned your face into my memory long before you knew who I was."

"Save the hard stares for prison, Uktam. Why the hell did you call us again? Dumb move. I'm sure many more mistakes will follow. Enjoy your stay here in the Grand Canyon State."

"Look, either arrest me if I've committed a crime, or get the hell out of my house. Next time bring a search warrant because you have overstayed your welcome." Axe had a sardonic grin that was more of a black slit in his face as he whispered, "You should be afraid, very afraid."

Weaver and Carter got back into their cruiser and headed down the hill. They took it real slow discussing what the heck had just happened.

Weaver said, "That guy was right about one thing, he got under my skin. It turned into a real rank-out contest up there. Ever do that, Carter? I mean, like when you were a kid in the school yard, two kids ranking on each other. 'You are so low that you look up to an ant.' 'Yo mama.' 'Don't be bringing my mama into it.' Huh, Carter, ever do that?"

Once they got off Axe's property, the deputy took the SUV off-road close to where the hikers had been. He put on his search lights. The ride was bumpy, but the four-wheel suspension soaked it up. With the beams on, the world seemed like a dusty black-and-white photograph with a short focal length. They were close to getting back on the road that led to the parking lot. Carter glanced over his left shoulder. "Did you see that? Probably a rabbit."

"Big-ass rabbit. Stop the car. Let's have a look-see."

"Look-see? My dad used to say that when I was growing up. I haven't heard that expression in years." Hastily, Carter threw the car in park, which made it lurch forward and stop. He got out; Weaver followed. Weaver collected the Mossberg tactical shotgun that was in back, and they both approached the area where Carter had spotted movement.

A man sprang powerfully to life, sprinting for the SUV, but Carter tackled him. It was a simple, football-style, go-for-the-legs, take-out-the-center-of-gravity tackle, which remains a formidable maneuver especially when it catches someone off guard. The man ended up on top, and Weaver immediately smacked him upside the head while yelling, "Police!"

He continued, "Up on your feet now, hands on your head. Carter, get up. Dumbass, on your knees. Hands behind your back and face in the dirt. Now, move it."

"Hey, Carter, you okay?" Weaver didn't wait for an answer, just yelled "Good."

"Carter cuff this moron and read him his rights. Take him into custody." Weaver noticed that the man had a bloody gash in his arm.

"Axe got you good," Weaver said.

No answer from the man, just a spit on the ground.

"You put a good hurt on him, too. Wanna tell me about it?"

Weaver said real loud, "Great job taking down this knucklehead, Carter. You might have a future yet."

CHAPTER 19

SARA LAY on a gurney, white as the sheet. Monitors blipped; IVs dripped. She was being rushed into emergency brain surgery. The neurosurgeon, Dr. Marlz, introduced herself to Paula, Sara's mom, and tried to quickly bring her up to speed. The patient care technicians wheeled Sara toward the operating room. Paula had to stop at the swinging double doors that said, "Authorized Personnel Only," "Radiation Danger," "Must Be Wearing OR Attire Past This Point." The neurosurgeon stopped and looked Paula in the eye. "I will do everything I can, Ms. Nathan. Any last minute questions that I haven't answered?"

"I wish I could be in there with her," Paula said leaning into Dr. Marlz.

Paula could not slow her shaking hands. Trembling, she signed the surgical consent forms for her daughter with jagged handwriting. It was an illegible scribble of nervousness. The technician took the documents from her, and the nurse squeezed her arm reassuringly.

"Please save my baby. You look so young. You've done these before? Any success?"

The doctor squeezed Paula's hand and said, "I have, and I intend to do everything in my power to help save Sara."

And with that, the medical team and Sara disappeared behind the double doors of sterility and clinical science. Mrs. Nathan stood alone and then went to the waiting area, her tears laden with fury and hope.

~~~~~~

Walking over to the X-ray box, the doctor studied the brain scan again and then walked over to Sara and asked for help slightly repositioning her patient to optimize the approach for surgery.

Next, she shaved Sara's head in the left parietal region close to where the fracture was, which she examined in further detail. The break was in the parietal bone. It pushed down on the brain. Everyone's bones are of a different strength. Some are porous, some are as strong as ivory.

Yet in this case, given the amount of trauma she had been informed about, and what she could feel, Sara's skull seemed a bit on the thin side. As she continued her examination, she noticed a sharp edge or spicule of broken bone that nicked her glove. She stopped what she was doing, changed her gloves to maintain sterility, and asked the anesthesiologist to double-check the antibiotic orders to prevent infection.

Beneath the skull are the meninges, the membranes that line the brain, along with many blood vessels, which were bleeding and continuing to place life-threatening pressure on Sara's brain tissue.

The neurosurgeon walked back out to the big stainless steel sink, tapped a fixture with her knee to turn on the water, and scrubbed again at the sink with a brush and chlorhexidine for a few minutes, thinking about what lay before her and how she was going to handle it. The CT scan revealed an epidural hematoma and a skull fracture. Sara was deteriorating neurologically, and the blood needed to be evacuated, but there was no guarantee of success because there was also evidence of blunt traumatic brain injury. This was an emergent surgery, not the best of circumstances. She looked through the window at the anesthesiologist and the breathing tube down Sara's trachea. The doctor took a moment to close her eyes, breathe, and pray as she did before every surgery. She prayed that her mind and hands would be guided to do well for her patient and her patient's mother. But she had a nagging suspicion that something still didn't fit.

Sara had several medications on board dripping through her veins that included anesthetics, antibiotics, and medications to tightly control blood pressure. Bags of clear fluid dangled from a pole. A massive dose of steroids was given to help reduce brain swelling. The plan was for her body temperature to be lowered to also help with brain swelling and inflammation.

Anesthesia has three medication components. Pain control with opioids, amnestic drugs so that are no memories of the surgery, and paralysis with agents such as succinylcholine to minimize extraneous movements, especially during delicate procedures. This way the patient won't buck the respirator, or fight the surgeon.

X-ray and electronic brain wave equipment was wheeled into the room.

The surgeon backed into the room with wet hands. The lights were bright and the institutional blue-tiled walls were shiny in the bustling theater.

The team gathered to save Sara. All eyes were on Dr. Marlz, who was five feet tall and would need to use a stepping stool for parts of the operation. Also present were the anesthesiologist, his resident in training, and the neurosurgeon's intern. The surgical techs were checking and rechecking instruments. The circulating nurse held up a sterile gown and helped the doctor get in it, tying it off in the back as the doctor twisted around in a well-rehearsed dance.

The doctor noted the time on the wall and asked for the drill. "Everyone ready? Let's do this. Hang on, Sara."

All went swimmingly initially.

Dr. Marlz asked her intern for more saline irrigation. The exhausted intern allowed a gentle stream of saline to wash the wound. Marlz used gentle suction. "There. Do you see it?" Off in the depths of Sara's brain was a pulsatile mass not much larger than half an inch that was leaking blood.

The emergency scans and history led everyone to believe that this was a trauma case. There was no time or reason for an angiogram. No one suspected an aneurysm.

The surgeon barked orders for the intraoperative microscope to be brought in and for endovascular surgery to be paged stat to the

OR. She announced that this would become a multihour micro-scopic procedure.

She thought quickly on her feet, weighing options and making judgments. She considered clipping the saccular aneurysm on the circle of Willis or going for an emergency angiographic endovascular coiling. The luxury of time for planning all this out in great detail was gone. Dr. Marlz felt that she was working against the clock. The best theory she could hypothesize was that this was genetic. The trauma weakened the wall of the blood vessel like a weakened tire tube. She asked the medical student to open the chart and started firing questions. Any history of Ehlers-Danlos, polycystic kidneys? The medical student rifled through the notes. "Negative."

"You sure?"

"Yes. I asked her mother. On the dad's side there was a history of aortic aneurysm. Nothing else."

"Good work." Under pressure, Dr. Marlz comported herself in a compressed, quiet, cool, if not icy, manner.

Anesthesiology can be boring 95 percent of the time and scary the other 5 percent. Just as the hardest part of flying a plane is often the takeoff and the landing, so, too, the hardest part of anesthesiology is putting patients under and waking them up.

Another big concern is that the patients are sedated and cannot tell the anesthesiologist how they feel. The doctor depends on monitoring equipment, and it becomes difficult for an anesthesiologist to remain vigilant every second, much like keeping alert during guard duty at night.

The EKG monitor revealed that Sara's heart rate was dropping again along with her blood pressure and the amount of oxygen getting to the brain. It was noticed immediately. The surgeon stopped what she was doing with the aneurysm to let the anesthesiologist manage the acute change in medical status.

Within another thirty-second period Sara coded. Her EKG flatlined twice, and her blood pressure was immeasurably low. Immediately, the team went to work performing advanced life support. A full code blue was called.

~~~~~~~

Sara felt a tug. It was as if her entire body was a suit of clothes that she was stuck in. It wasn't painful or unpleasant; it was more like someone or something grabbed her sweatshirt over her belly and pulled through her chest and arms.

There was a loud pounding sound that confused her. Her senses became altered such that she could see the sound and not just hear it. It appeared to be dark and wet, sucking and muddy. Something slimy that made her nervous. Then, with a sudden jerk through her skull, she was free. She never felt better.

Sara looked down at the panicked team who appeared to be speeding about, tearing open packages, starting new intravenous drips. She didn't know what all the fuss was about.

Doctors and nurses were sweating, swearing, and calling out. One doctor stood at the head of the table shouting commands. Someone dropped her pen. It was oversized, black, and shiny. Sara admired the way it looked—so smooth and elegant. An instrument of precision. Sara went over to the busy nurse and tapped her on the shoulder. "Excuse me, ma'am; sorry to bother you, but you dropped your pen." The nurse ignored her. Sara never liked being ignored. She preferred attention. She would much rather have had the nurse tell her to go away because she was busy.

Sara tapped her shoulder again, harder. The only thing that happened was that a tiny breeze moved the nurse's hair causing her to turn her head and scratch her chin on her shoulder. Sara bent over to pick up the pen, but it wouldn't budge; the most she could do was barely get it to roll just slightly in the direction of the nurse who did finally notice that her pen had fallen.

Eventually, Sara left the room to go and get her mom. She wanted to go home.

Experiencing a peculiar lightness of being, Sara floated down the hallway and went to the waiting room where her mother sat wringing her hands, pulling back her hair, massaging her own temples, closing her eyes, and praying. Sara realized that she had just died because the area in which she now found herself was full of others like her. Multitudes were passing on and through with lists, stories, and explanations of how they too passed on.

Sara gently landed next to her mom and tried to get her mother's attention, but her mom wouldn't listen. "What else is new? Mom, hello, yoo-hoo. Let's go home now."

Sara's mom stood and started pacing the room. Sara kept trying to tell her mom that everything was fine. She felt great, and she loved her mom and felt loved in an intense way that she couldn't even describe and had never known before. If only she could stand on a mountaintop and tell the whole world to chill and love each other, but she guessed that eventually they would have to figure it out on their own.

Suddenly, Sara was on the move, inexorably drawn toward a brilliant energy field shimmering through a huge, cone-shaped portal. She felt pure and utter joy and could see the sweetest sounds. Each note was a colored sparkle, and every chord produced gem stones and rainbows of purples and reds. She was not alone. She had never felt less alone, but she couldn't see anyone. It boggled her mind that she could see sound and hear light; they were one. She was melting into it and becoming one with it.

Her senses became heightened but not in a way she was familiar with. The peace and serenity were overwhelming. She felt as though she was in a crystal pool of warm water. She could breathe it in. Next, she was in the clouds, nothing more than eyes that could see and awareness that knows. She was informed that her earthly body had stopped functioning. Her body was an empty husk. Awareness was all that she was and would ever need to be. This was a pureness of consciousness that she had never known could exist during her young life.

Points of light like orbs that were energy forms began to coalesce into fibers of rope light and then into larger strands of every color. The strands braided into bigger knots of light and melody, and then other ropes joined and gathered into a lattice or network that created a cocoon of safety for Sara. This net mathematically encompassed and connected everything to everything else, like some artistic fractal.

Sara was one of those points of light becoming bound into an ocean of light and love, like sea life caught up in a warm oceanic current. She shifted into an area that while dark was drenched in something divine and brimming with a silvery purple sheen that allowed infinite vision, like a full moon over the mountains. There was a shiny, silver, screen-like appearance.

Next to and around her she was greeted by beings she could only describe as nameless spiritual guides. They communicated without words since human language, as she had already realized, was a poor vehicle for transmission of ideas in this realm. Sara saw one who shone from within, gold and purple, and who communicated that Sara should concentrate and decide. It was her free will to do so.

It was explained to Sara that she chose this life as a very young soul. She was being given the choice to come back home, perhaps try again at some other point, or go back. In a flash, the guide presented Sara with a depiction of a past life. She could see everything, including who she was between lives, her current life's experiences, and lessons as a spiritual being. She was reminded that she was always loved and never alone. She understood and received messages from the other side about love, compassion, humility, and forgiveness far beyond her years.

She came to know that the love she felt for the oneness of this field was the same love that was felt for her. Since she was part of the one, therefore it stood to reason that she was to love herself. This included those she perceived as enemies and all living, sentient beings. Cause and effect were fully operational. Sara was separate from nothing as everything emanated from and was part of the one field.

She looked beyond and saw animals, too. A bear and others sent her messages that she was still needed. She next had a vision of herself as a mother holding a baby, then as a baby being held by her mother.

She didn't want to leave this place. It's where she ultimately belonged. It was home. Sara felt the prayers of her mother calling and pulling at her as if across a canyon. Sara made her choice, and for a second time, she was tugged but now the other way, back from where she started. Space opened, and time reversed. All the other souls around her sent her love and observed. It was as if the universe applauded, cheered as Sara headed back through her cone-shaped tunnel returning from her out-of-body, near-death experience.

～～～～～

Paula sat with Sara in the ICU and held her hand, a vigil that had gone on for almost twenty-four hours; she took little naps in the chair with occasional bathroom breaks. She fasted, although the nurses urged her to go home, get some rest, and eat something. They promised to call her right away if anything changed. As much as Katie wanted to stay overnight, too, her parents insisted that Paula needed time alone with Sara.

There was one small important change in Sara's condition. Tears collected and ran down the side of her pale young cheek. Only Paula saw this, but didn't understand that each drop of joy contained her daughter's distilled experience. Each tear was a universe unto itself.

Sara opened her eyes. Her mom noticed and shut her own eyes tight, whispering, "Thank you."

Sara felt something very painful. She couldn't talk, and her head felt like it was being crushed. She thrashed and grasped for her throat.

Paula ran out to get the nurse and yelled, "She's awake."

The nurses came in and saw that Sara was fighting the ventilator. She no longer needed it. Within minutes they got the doctor on the phone who gave the order to have respiratory therapy ex-tubate her patient.

After the tube was pulled and the coughing fit subsided, Sara made an attempt to speak but couldn't.

Paula broke down and sobbed and squeezed her baby, practically knocking down the IV equipment.

CHAPTER 20

IMMEDIATELY AFTER the cave collapse, phone calls, e-mails, and tweets poured in. My parents and Doc S. decided that it would be acceptable for me to appear on *Focus*, the morning news talk show, since there were more news reports about mysterious happenings surrounding me, the new teen superhero. I was hoping to make the cover of a magazine, but morning TV would have to do. I must admit, making a local buzz and having my moment of celebrity was appealing. Things were looking better. Josh was cool. My parents believed in me. I was still maintaining a solid B plus grade point average. No major acne outbreaks.

Unfortunately, Sara's progress seemed agonizingly glacial. Having survived a near-death experience, Sara was still in dangerously bad shape. I was by her side when the nurses allowed it. Sara went through bouts of fever. Her blood pressure would bottom out and then skyrocket. She had to be placed back on the ventilator again and then taken off. Her legs swelled. When she puked, horrific shocks of pain went through her broken skull. She had to be heavily sedated to prevent her brain from bleeding or swelling again. Her legs wouldn't support her, and she could hold virtually nothing down. Intermittently, she would get panicked and agitated, tearing at all her tubes. At least she could move. When she could communicate a few garbled words, she tried her best to explain her near death. I could not understand. It made her cry and become frustrated that she couldn't communicate. She shook her head, which obviously was painful. Sara grimaced, winced, and with extraordinary effort said, "Can't. Too hard. No live."

I tried to be strong for her and told her to hold on. "Each day will get better, Sara. You'll see. We will be together and live to have more fun. Do stuff. Hang out after school, meet boys. Please, Sara, hang on; do this for me."

After a week of this torture, she remained weak as a kitten, her thinking foggy. She had mildly blurred vision, and her speech was still garbled. Sara still could not swallow thin liquids; they made her choke. She drank shakes and ate puddings. She swore that she would never eat a living being again and became a vegetarian.

The doctors said that she was improving steadily and had the potential for a great recovery, but it would take time, hard work, and rehabilitation. It was unclear whether she would be able to graduate with us, which I felt terrible about, and which Paula took hard. Still, we were all thankful that we didn't lose her. Her personality seemed a little different. Sara seemed more insightful, joyous, and apprecia-tive of each moment. She was very loving and simpler. The people in her life meant everything to her now. With a sense of equanimity she proceeded to simply be.

Doc S. as I now often called him wanted to see me before the news show. My parents agreed. I reviewed everything that happened at the cave that night with him. He had become my life coach and lifeline.

I recounted a recent dream that I had in which I was on a vast sea. Various animals appeared from the south or the west. They were trying to communicate with me, but I couldn't understand them. Next, I was on a boat. A fisherman caught a large fish, which was flopping and couldn't breathe. The fisherman mocked the struggling animal who did finally communicate to me. "Please help me fellow earthling. I need to be free. The ocean currents are awaiting me, and I am full of eggs. I have a community. What humans are doing is wrong. The plastic garbage islands are killing us. Soon we will all be gone. Extinct. You are taking way more than you need. We can no longer keep up. Please.

"I don't want to die just to be your food. I have a mother, too. I am alive. Your kind rarely even gives thanks anymore."

In that moment I completely felt her pain, her struggle to live. A pang of anxiety gripped me as I became the fish. The fisherman, a horrible man with scars and gold teeth, laughed and plunged a knife in my belly, filleting a piece of my flesh and then eating it raw while I was still alive and writhing. I heard the scream. It was me. I woke up screaming and sweating. I have not been able to touch fish since.

We were in the professor's office at the university. It was an extension of his house, his persona, his mess. There were artifacts from all over the world. Doc S. listened and said nothing for a long time, thinking about what I had just told him. I waited impatiently, anxiously.

He walked over to the window and looked out over the old stone wall. The trees played with light and shadow. Beyond, students scurried to and fro, some on bikes. The light rail car came to a stop as a bus lumbered by. He scratched his stubble with the back of his hand, which sounded like sandpaper, kind of loud in the silence of the room.

Mindlessly, he began to tap with his left hand and picked up a small sculpture with his right which resembled the markings on the necklace he gave me. I asked him about it. Staring at it he said, "Spirits are communicating to you. What are they? They are forces moving in or through us. Katie, you are changing and developing. Evolving. These forces usually cannot be contacted during the mundane waking state but require an altered state such as dreams.

"As an anthropologist, I can tell you that spirits have always been and continue to be a fundamental, ubiquitous part of humanity. They may guide or deceive you, help heal or destroy. Some are the servants of death. You must learn discernment. If you dare to open your soul to these forces, you will be transformed. There is great danger in doing so. Your dream speaks of dark times to come.

"Life forms are depending on you for their existence as they are mocked by some evil danger. When you open yourself to these forces of nature, you will be altered. One of the keys to training novices worldwide has been developing advanced skills of mental imagery and stabilizing the mind. In other cultures this has been accomplished by methods that our society would consider extreme—fasting, long periods of dancing, abstinence, sleep deprivation, acoustic stimulation such as loud drums, hyperventilation, and the consumption of certain natural substances."

"Doc, that sounds like the life of most college kids I know—except for the abstinence."

The professor laughed so hard that he turned red, his belly shaking up and down. He shook his head and grabbed his gut as if to gesture his sides hurt. On his hand I saw that he was wearing a very large gold signet ring that I hadn't noticed last time. I couldn't exactly make it out. It was old and worn. The design inscribed on it had the same markings as my necklace and the small sculpture.

Doc S. kept lecturing. "Traditional religions to this day find that fasting can deepen one's prayer and meditation. Psychological studies have shown that any one of these techniques can be mind altering enough to create visions. After the visions become clear, controlling them is the next step. In this way some masters are able to receive wisdom beyond the usual constraints of known space and time. Likewise, the medium may contact spirit masters, the deceased, angels, guides, or whatever label we wish to give. A dialogue can then begin, but sometimes it is they who open the dialogue with us."

Doc was weirding me out. I asked him, "Do you do any of these practices or take these so-called natural substances? What is that ring you are wearing?" Rings, necklaces, spiritual practices, so called natural substances, it was beginning to feel like a cult. I was getting paranoid.

He just stared, contemplating his response, and smiled.

Doc explained that my dream was a symbolic call for a needed change to the physical environment and that the precise information about animals in the east or west has specific meaning about life and death corroborated by the blood and the alteration in weather with the rain that I experienced.

He told me that I would be receiving more so-called instructions from spiritual teachers as I tapped into the collective repository of consciousness. He emphasized that these beings are real, not fiction or fantasy. However, they exist in another realm that we can tune into and envision. Just because most of us currently cannot see these entities doesn't mean that they don't exist. At one time we couldn't see bacteria, but they were there. There was a time when we didn't know about atomic energy, but it was waiting—same thing for electricity and the telephone. We used to think that the world was flat, too. These entities do coexist in their own reality and probably have since the beginning.

"Katie, we have great limitations to our ability to know, which is very humbling. Do not underestimate the wisdom, knowledge, and power that patiently sits latent within you." He suggested that I go back for another acupuncture session, which I blew off because it's my choice, and I have no time for Merna Lee with Sara being so sick. I am so done being tested every which way. No more. Now that he had all the baseline data, including when I ate dinner, he wanted me to receive an acupuncture treatment that would strengthen the effects of some of the essential elements. His theory was that it would give me more power where needed. This seemed sketchy since I felt out of balance enough of the time as it was. I could just do more caffeine and sugar, right? He was convinced of my abilities. He and my parents agreed it was time to refine and cultivate them.

The next night in another dream vision, Honon expressed displeasure over my appearance on the news show. It was a terrible night of wrestling in the sheets with her. She said that it was too egoistic and prideful and wasn't in keeping with why we are here. It was a digression that was taking me away from our real purpose. It even had the potential for danger. She was angry that I was being sucked into the whole celebrity hero thing. I, on the other hand, was superexcited.

I expressed to her that she chose the wrong person for the job. So there. I resign effective immediately. Better yet, she's fired. Don't let the door hit you on the way out. Pack your stuff in a box and get out.

Honon the Bear answered that it was I who chose this challenge before I was born. It was Bear's job to make sure, to the best of her ability, that I stayed on task and fulfilled this destiny bestowed upon us since many lives were at stake. I got angry at her archaic spiritual chatter.

"Wah, wah, wah, whatever, already, okay! I am so done with all this spirit crap. I'm a teenager, and I want to live my life and have fun. Just leave me alone. It's my life, and I'll do whatever the hell I want. Why don't you go back to being a petroglyph for another million years?"

She tried to explain that my existence here wasn't entirely mine and that apart from my free will, my soul belonged to the one source. My life, as she called it, was part of all life. My little spark of it was on loan.

"No, damn it. I was the one who saved that little boy. I am the one dealing with all this pressure. Just go away. I'll call you if I need you. Why don't you go back into hibernation?"

I woke up crying, gasping. I think that I lost the fight. Honon communicated to me that she was always here and would never leave me. She has always been here to guide me, but that she could not tamper with my will even if my choices were adolescent.

"Give me a break. Two parents are bad enough; now I have three. It's like two parents and an overbearing aunt."

〜〜〜

I spent time thinking, trying to relax, and getting ready for the TV show by polishing my nails, all twenty of them, in cool colors. Polish was on sale at the drugstore for two dollars a bottle.

On the day of my appearance, I was escorted to a room at the TV station. There were trays of snacks and drinks and someone to apply makeup. Wardrobe decided what I was to wear. I was so busy getting ready that I barely had enough time to attack the cheese and fruit platter. I did manage to cop a scone. They even referred to me as the talent. People ran all over the place as if their hair was on fire.

Someone knocked on the door and poked his bald head in. "Five minutes, kid," he said. Then his head disappeared just as quickly. The interview was going to be prerecorded, not live, so I was told not to worry, but I was nervous anyway.

"Hey, you're the hero girl. Good luck; break a leg. You'll do great," some random stranger offered.

"Just be yourself," another advised.

I wasn't sure what that really meant anymore. Who else would I be, a bear? What is the self anyway?

I was escorted to the set. It wasn't like what I had seen on TV. Instead, it was small with lots of wires, duct tape, poles, and equipment.

I met Dan Harrison, the news anchor. I'd seen him on the tube before. He was shorter than I thought he'd be, but then I've only seen him sitting behind that desk on TV. He did ooze charisma. His hair was perfect, the suit expensive. Harrison took my hand.

"Katie, I'm Dan Harrison," he said and then paused to allow the resonance of his baritone voice to sink in. His startling eyes said he was used to people being impressed. The smile revealed perfectly white, expensive dental work. He must have practiced the look and the greeting a million times. So far I wasn't impressed. I was thinking about what Bear said.

"In a few moments, I'll introduce you. You will be seated right over here. The interview will last about an hour, but we won't use all of it. Are you ready?"

I looked around at all the equipment and people with headphones monitoring the audio and visual.

"You are going to do great, and our community is proud of you."

I was floating in the moment and took my seat. The music started. It was one of those dramatic news sounds—a click, a gong, and a drum. Then the power went out.

"Seriously?" I said.

Darkness and panic ensued, followed by light and buzzing. I covered my eyes to adjust to the lights coming on. I hadn't moved, but the staff hadn't stopped.

Backup generators were up and running. The staff reported that they just got word from weather that the area had been hit by a very rare and unusual electric storm and that the station had sustained some serious damage. Many of the circuits were fried. The interview would have to be postponed.

I was extremely bummed. Unconsciously, I yelled, "Honon!"

Harrison asked what I had just said.

"Oh, nothing. Just an old family saying when gremlins take over, like 'cripe's sake,' or 'son of a buck.'"

"Honon? Gremlins? Right, of course," said Harrison, clearing his throat and seeming irritated over his wasted time. "Well, my secretary will see you out. We will be in touch when it's time to reschedule. Thank you very much for coming in today, Miss Jackson." He winked at me, flashed his big teeth again, then moved on to the next thing.

CHAPTER 21

BUGDON, AXE'S newly arrested security guy, was read his Miranda rights, cuffed, and placed in the rear of the SUV. He wasn't even given the courtesy of having his head pushed down. Instead, he was chucked into the back like a side of beef, his head banging the side of the door frame.

"Watch it!" Bugdon yelled.

Weaver yelled, too, still angry about Axe and ready to take it out on this loser as a consolation prize. "Hey punk, you gotta name? I'm not the judge and jury, but you just resisted arrest and assaulted a cop. Not for nothing, but, um, looks like Carter over here, Officer Carter to you, has contusions, abrasions, and a sprain. He hit the ground harder than a wrestler. Make that aggravated assault. In Arizona that means you will be taking a long vacation where the sun don't shine. You'll get to make friends at the DOC—department of corrections—or to some, department of confusion. I think that you would look good in orange. It goes well with everything." Carter and Weaver laughed.

Bugdon muttered, "Carter and Weaver. I will remember that."

"What kind of accent is that, Boris? May I call you Boris Badass? You look a little more like a Doris. Well, maybe with a good derma-tologist. Maybe put a little lipstick on the pig. What are you some kind of Russian spy?" Weaver asked.

After he stopped laughing, Carter added, "Man, I'm sore. Hurts to laugh. I landed on a rock. Feels like I cracked a rib. We can take him over to Shannon and book him over there. Then we'll get him medical attention if he wants it."

Boris answered, "I do not want a doctor. You are very weak men. You people run to doctors for every little thing."

Weaver added sarcastically, "Guess he's refusing medical care. Please document that in your report."

"Roger that," said Carter.

"It's going to be a long night, Doris. You hungry, need to pee?"

Bugdon was taken in but not booked, photographed, or finger-printed—just detained by US Homeland Security. He was placed in a generic room, modern and square, with commercial linoleum tile on the floor, fluorescent lights above, ceiling tiles stained from the last leak, a plastic table, and folding chairs. A soda machine buzzed and hummed gently in a corner.

The cops knew they had approximately twenty-four hours to either book or release him before some court-appointed lawyer showed up and made a stink, assuming anyone even gave a damn. Maybe Axe, the Russian Embassy, or a family member might claim him.

Sometime around the fourteen-hour mark, things started to thaw. Bugdon was smelly, tired, and rumpled. Sitting in the plastic folding chair got old. He stretched out on the floor and dozed for a while, but the cops took turns waking him up and asking him more questions.

The coffee was old, burnt, and bitter. So was he. His arm throbbed and swelled. He remained in handcuffs. The hours dragged by agoniz-ingly, second by second, breath by breath, tracked by the big battery-operated clock on the wall. It was a small luxury to at least know the time. The only decorations on the wall were a picture of an American flag, a picture of the police chief shaking hands with the governor, and a poster listing "Your Rights as an Employee." The only other color in the room was a well-lit exit sign. Exit. How Bugdon wished he could do so, but the door to freedom was locked and guarded.

The security agent finally gave up his name. Bugdon Verdovnikov realized that if he went to jail, Axe would have him killed there. He would be a hunted man. He despised Axe, and while he was on a need-to-know basis about Axe's scheme, he knew enough, maybe too much. It was unfortunate that he didn't kill Axe yesterday. Axe was a formidable foe. Bugdon did not agree with Axe's insane plans of world domination through destruction.

Not that he wasn't willing to accept an exorbitant salary to protect the man and keep his mouth shut. Bugdon was after all a bottom-feeding opportunist who realized that the game had changed and that he had been dealt some new cards.

Bugdon was guarded by an armed, uniformed grunt. It would have been relatively easy, especially in his younger days when he was training heavily, to take out multiple officers, even while cuffed. This was different. He was safer here.

His prospects were limited, and he was in the custody of the Americans who, to this day by international standards, still treated their prisoners much more humanely than most countries. If he could negotiate his freedom, then perhaps he could access his accounts in Switzerland and live out his days in comfort. Instead of breaking the young man's neck, he asked the officer if he had cigarettes, to which the officer replied, "I don't smoke; it's bad for your health, and this is a nonsmoking facility."

Weaver and the team discussed the slowly evolving situation. This guy Bugdon was here illegally. He was potentially a high-value detainee. If Axe's people found him, they would terminate him. He was closely involved with Axe, who they had been tracking for a long time. If he was an enemy combatant, they could sweat him and threaten Guantanamo. It meant the ability to stall on formal charges. It gave them a little wiggle room to operate the old-fashioned way. Either way, the decision was made to contact the FBI, which didn't make the Pima County Sheriff's Department happy. Weaver rested awhile but couldn't sleep, so he got up and had a big breakfast before he went back in to see the detainee.

"Hey, Doris. Sleep well? I understand that your real name is Bug man. I like it. I brought you a pack of cigarettes Bug dude. I heard you were asking. Don't tell my boss, as a two hundred dollar cleaning fee may apply. Maybe a little Febreze will do since this room doesn't have windows, which I'm sure that you noticed. You know, if you didn't smoke and were in better shape, you might have made it to the SUV or beat Carter last night, and then we wouldn't be wasting our tax dollars on your ugly-ass carcass."

Bugdon looked like he could eat the whole pack of cigarettes.

"We talked it over among ourselves. In summary, you're screwed. There aren't very many options for you. If you never saw the light of day again, no one would give a rat's ass. You are here in the States illegally. Then you tried to steal a cop's car and assaulted him while resisting arrest. We also have reason to believe that Axe, your prior employer, has been linked to global terrorism, dealing in weapons of mass destruction. Since you are probably part of his gang, that makes you an enemy combatant to the homeland, even though we don't technically use that term anymore. Get my drift, Bug juice?

"Option one, we let you go where we found you. Either you get Axe or he gets you, but you probably wouldn't last a day up there. Axe's team would hunt you down, finish slicing you up, and send your parts home in a Ziploc. Plus, we have no intention of letting you go. Option two, you spend the rest of your days in Camp Gitmo or worse. I'll let the FBI or CIA decide that one. Option three is interesting. Pay attention, Bugsley. At this time you are a belligerent detainee. You may be subject to a tribunal.

"We can give you witness protection while under detention. The operative word is witness, like informant. Quid pro quo. You get placed in one of our safe houses. You will be treated well. One false move, or if I detect that you are misleading us at all, I will personally drive you back and dump you on Axe's front yard wrapped in duct tape with a red bow on your ass.

"If the information you provide is accurate and useful, leading us where we need to be, and if the outcome is successful, only then can we make you any promises."

Weaver postured, pointing forcefully with his finger. "We are aware that you crossed our border illegally from Nogales, Mexico. We will deposit you back in Nogales free to find your way home to Russia, Switzerland, the moon, or the bottom of the ocean for all I care." Weaver unconsciously tightened his body, telegraphing male dominance, expanding into a V shape. "At that point you are on your own, never to return, persona non grata. That will be your ticket out. Understood?"

CHAPTER 22

I SAT alone with Sara in her hospital room, and even though she was weak, Sara glowed as though illuminated from within. Her eyes were more alive than I had ever seen them. In a strange way, her out-of-body journey had agreed with her. All her tubes including her IV were gone. She could sit up and eat solid food. The doctors said she would need physical rehab to help her regain her balance and strength on the weaker side of her body. She'd also need a speech therapist because her speech was a little off due to conditions called dysarthria and aphasia. Sara had mild difficulty formulating and pronouncing words. She laughed at her own garbled speech. The staff came in and gave her ice cream.

Sara said, "Wanem?"

I said, "Huh?"

"Wanem?" She pointed to her lemon ice cream.

"Oh? Do I want some?"

She nodded her head.

"House Tos?" Sara asked.

"Slowly, Sara. Go real slow." I enunciated slowly and loudly but then reminded myself that she wasn't deaf.

Sara replied, looking intent, her concentration complete, her mouth and jaw making many extraneous movements like someone with palsy.

"How eth Tosh?"

I puzzled over her words. "How is Josh?"

She nodded yes, without even wincing said, "eth."

I whispered in her ear, "Tosh has a cute tush."

We giggled so hard that I had to get a napkin and help Sara wipe the ice cream from her mouth.

"No, really, Sara, Josh asked if it would be okay if he came to visit. He still feels to blame."

She agreed to the visit, not the blame.

We were communicating well and had no trouble finding stuff to laugh about while poking fun at the staff that marched in and out of her room. Tomorrow she was scheduled to be discharged from this part of the hospital and sent upstairs to the rehab unit. The TV had lame *Gunsmoke* reruns from my grandparents' day, but the game shows were kind of fun. I felt sleepy and wanted to curl up next to Sara and nap.

Out the window the sky was infinitely blue and cloudless. It whispered its breezes and tickled the gently swaying palm trees. The weather was what I call sweet and sour, with its warm sunshine and cool air. We could see another part of the hospital across a courtyard—another window, another sick patient. I saw movement, illness, and in my heart sent a healing wish. I was genuinely happy to be there with my dearest friend.

A whirl of activity outside the doors made me nervous, reminding me of infections, disease, and suffering. I tried to suppress my fear and anxiety about being around a hospital's nasty germs and the potential threat of an Ebola outbreak. I will decontaminate when I get home.

Sara's room was fragrant with flowers. This was a relief that distinctly contrasted with the odors out in the hallway where the combination of food, bodily fluids, and medicinal smells was nauseating. Cards and colorful balloons softened the room's true clinical purpose. One balloon kept finding its way back into the draft of a nearby vent and rhythmically circled. A small teddy bear with a *Get Well* T-shirt sat in the corner.

We discussed whose parents were the angriest about what happened and compared notes. As far as our parents were concerned, we kids mutually decided to leave the premises and go off cave exploring. We were not pointing fingers or casting blame. No one was forced to go. We all went voluntarily. Well, sort of.

Sara's mother arrived at the hospital after she got off work, looking haggard. I was that freak who had become a bad influence, the one whom she held responsible for what happened to her daughter, the one who is lately always followed by calamity, police, or reporters. She looked at me like something in the air smelled bad.

I stood up and moved away as she entered the room. The way she sighed and threw down her purse was her way of asking me to leave.

"Well, I'd better get. I have homework and a project due in the morning." I went over to hug Sara, said good-bye to her mom quickly, and slipped past awkwardly.

～～～～～～

The desert night sky was cool. Across the thin, limitless canopy, the freeway and railroad tracks made a distant din. Trucks passed, and crickets chirped. There was no human pedestrian activity at this time between night and dawn when Bugdon was moved to a safe house. He was cuffed, wore a black hood over his head, and was escorted to a windowless, nondescript, white, government-issue Ford van with a license plate that started with the letter G. He muttered something about defecting.

The ride was nearly an hour with three vehicles in procession. There was a lead police car and one behind the van Bugdon was in, so he was well guarded.

Upon arriving on a patch of scrub that was back of beyond near the Pinal County line, Weaver was waiting in the double-wide trailer that was to become Bugdon's new cage. Weaver drank his coffee. Cream, no sugar. The bagel he munched was toasted with eggs, tomato, and cream cheese.

After Bugdon's clandestine entry, the hood was removed. With a mouthful of sandwich, Weaver cheerfully greeted Bugdon, "Good morning, Bug. Want a bagel?"

The day quickly got hot. Not much progress was made. The swamp cooler kicked on, and fans droned. The only thing Bugdon said was "How come you people don't have more solar power?"

At around nine o'clock, Scoop became fed up with his detainee. He wasn't cut out for interrogation. He'd rather just shoot the bastard and be done with it. He thought about using his Taser as a way to get information. He remembered back to his early military days when some young bucks chose data-gathering interrogator training; it might as well have been called inquisition school at Gitmo University where one can specialize in water boarding. Early in their training, they would spend all day screaming at each other and practicing to become pricks in a world with a disturbing addiction to hatred. Can you imagine the breakfast line? Screaming. How would you like your eggs? What the hell is that supposed to mean? Who's asking? Good morning and screw you.

Some of those kids started out looking like kittens that couldn't coax a fox into a chicken coop. Yet there have been psychological studies on how easy it is to encourage indifference and brutish actions by humans.

Bugdon told Weaver, "I do not wish to be dumped south of the border in exchange for information. I want access to my Swiss account and political asylum with full immunity in exchange for everything I know."

"I'll look into your requests," Weaver said; he then turned and left.

He stepped outside and called his superiors to apprise them of what the detainee had said and was requesting. They kicked it around. He listened intently and then snapped the phone shut and shoved it in his pocket.

Scoop Weaver took off in his car, adjusting the visor to block a low-hanging sun. Several letters fell from his visor onto his lap and shoulders offering a crude yet effective reminder to pay his mounting bills. Recalling that he had noticed a small, rural US post office a short way back, he decided to stop in, thinking about Bugdon as he drove.

The government was stretching the limits of the law by detaining him this long. If the media or the ACLU got wind of this, there would be hell to pay, but the stakes were too high. Weaver was following orders.

Scoop walked into the post office and up to the desk. A woman with tight red curls said in a nasal voice. "Take a number, please."

"I'm the only one here," said Scoop.

"Sir, this is the US Postal Service. Everyone takes a number."

He obediently did as he was told. "Look, I have number one."

"Everyone gets number one around here, sir. Next."

Scoop's cell phone chimed. He was informed that Bugdon wanted to talk and had something important to say. "I'll be right back."

Weaver hopped back in the car. The American V8 roared. With plenty of power to spare, the machine fired straight and true. Scoop opened the window, threw the flashing light on the roof of his unmarked car, and floored it. He walked back in the safe house.

"This better be good, Bugdon. I was at an important federal meeting with a very pleasant young woman." Weaver scraped a chair across the floor and straddled it. "Well, what do you have to say for yourself?"

In a thick Russian accent, Bugdon announced, "I vill hef de Begel."

Weaver squinted and placed a cupped hand around his ear, not sure if he had heard correctly. "You want half a bagel?"

"Officer, coffee, and a bagel first, please. Ask yourself the following question," said Bugdon acting like for now he was calling the shots. He continued whispering in a heavy Russian accent leaning in on the table. "Why would I allow myself to be caught? Not so long ago, even a warrior like you would be no match for me, probably still. Maybe my boss Axe put me out as bait, gave me a little nick on the arm so that you could taste blood. Ever think of that?" he asked with a sly grin, wrinkling his nose. "Perhaps, it is a setup, and my body is chipped with GPS." He touched his side.

"Very soon you could be surrounded by overwhelming force. Americans, such amateurs. You worry about charging me and your stupid lawyers. In my country, if you were the detainee, believe me, we would know what we wanted, and you would be dead already—if you were lucky. I hold you in captivity, Officer Weaver. You need me desperately right now."

"Well, dry my tears. If I smoked, I'd be lighting up with my hands shaking. Is this what you called me back for, to waste my time on our taxpayers' dime?" Scoop got up and walked to the door.

"Wait."

Weaver didn't turn. He just stopped at the door.

"Axe is planning something very bad here in the States. It involves catastrophic casualties. Weapons of mass destruction. If I help you, do we have a deal?"

"If you are here as the canary in the mine shaft, or bait, how do I know we can trust you?"

"Because it is so bad that all the millions of dollars that I have waiting for me won't matter. Unless we get very far away, we will all be killed. You see, Mr. Scooper man, I too have a desire to live and eat. If I wish to defect here, then maybe I have a vested interest. Or, maybe I have a conscience, remorse. So far all you have offered me is a shitty bagel."

Weaver closed the door, sat down, and unfastened the top button of his shirt.

CHAPTER 23

THE BIG brass at the air force was leaning on corporate to finish a prototype that wasn't quite ready. That meant long nights and deadlines for engineers like John Jackson.

Success meant landing a huge government contract or losing it to the competition in the military–industrial complex designed to keep the homeland secure, and the rocket's red glare, the bombs bursting in air.

John's marriage was on the rocks, so he was hitting the gym more to burn the fumes.

His locker read J. Jackson. It was a top locker made of stained pinewood, skinny, deep, and rectangular. He left a few personal items there. Some of the other men kept an entire wardrobe neatly tucked in there along with every kind of toiletry. Other guys had science projects growing in there.

He changed into work-out shorts and a T-shirt. All John had time for was a thirty- or forty-minute cardio workout, so he decided to torture himself on the stair stepper where he could also watch TV. He walked into the gym, which was kept at a cool sixty-eight degrees. There she was—Darlene, the waitress with a penchant for low-cut spandex clothing.

Whenever John saw her at the gym, he puffed up, walked taller, flexing a bicep here, flashing a smile there.

She said, "Hi, John." His heart sped up. Darlene was maybe ten years younger than him. Five foot three with a bouncy blond ponytail, she wore a tight tank top that was little more than a bra; her chest was perky and protruding. Her belly was exposed to below the navel, which revealed her cut abs. Darlene's black tights were very revealing. When she got on all fours to do yoga poses and leg lifts to strengthen her cute little butt, which already looked like a teenage boy's, she looked at herself in the mirror and caught John staring longingly. She smiled.

Darlene got herself a towel and an alcohol wipe. She cleaned off the cardio elliptical machine next to John's and began to effortlessly rock her hips in time to the music that was playing.

Distracted, John began his work out, not needing much help to get his heart rate up any faster or harder. More blood to all his parts. John jokingly said, "We have to stop meeting like this."

She giggled and asked, "Where else would you like to meet, John? You look like you've been getting into even better shape lately."

He immediately felt ten years younger, anxious, excited, and guilty all at once. He was burning a lot more calories than usual on that damned stair stepper, and he wiped his forehead with a towel. There was awkward silence for a moment.

A bit winded, John breathily asked, "Want to get some frozen yogurt across the street when we're done?"

They were both now looking straight ahead into full-length mirrors. She nodded her head. "Yes, that would be very nice. I love frozen yogurt."

John was as mixed as a vanilla and chocolate swirl. He had just stepped in it big time. He had sort of hoped that she would say no and give an excuse, like allergies. John imagined that she might have said, my large boyfriend will beat you up if he finds out, or your jealous wife will tear my eyes out before she kills you when she finds out. But no. She said yes. On the other hand, his ego soared. He thought it was a palpitation but didn't know the difference.

"I'll be done here in five minutes; then I'll freshen up," said Miss Darlene all twinkly eyed.

"Okay, I'll hit the locker room. Meet you in the lobby?"

"Perfect." She giggled.

John rinsed off and sat in the hot tub for a few moments to collect himself. Feeling a bit shriveled, he was already having a twinge of buyer's remorse. He couldn't hide out and not show up. How bad could it be to sit under the fluorescent lights in a public place and watch that gorgeous doll lick an ice cream cone? John positioned himself so that the jet stream from the hot tub pointed at his sore knee, an old college injury.

Another man stood there, buck naked, holding a bottle of water. He got in the tub, raising the water level. His gut was huge, veiny, and taut. A hernia protruded through the umbilicus, like his belly had a belly. Loud and obnoxious, he limited his conversation to how much money he made or some expensive trip he had taken. He brought a newspaper into the hot tub, trying not to get it wet. After unusual bubbles percolated to the surface, John got up and left. "Well, looks like I'm overdone here, feel like a lobster."

John shaved at the sink and then applied deodorant, antifungal foot spray, and cologne. After combing his hair, he used some mouthwash.

He fidgeted nervously in the lobby hoping not to run into anyone he knew. While waiting, he realized that he was not cut out to have an affair. He knew people who did. The stress of having a double secret life was unfathomable. These guys had to work incredibly hard to cover their tracks—running home to intercept mail, getting the credit card or phone bill. It was nuts.

Darlene emerged. She was breathtakingly stunning tonight, and John Jackson's heart melted a little.

They took two cars; their destination was only a mile away.

The yogurt shop was dead. They smiled like kids tasting different flavors and toppings.

~~~~~~~

It looked like life was grand for dear old Dad until I walked in with Josh. That's how I found out about perky little Darlene, the home wrecker.

"Hi, Dad, what are you doing here?"

At first I was just a little uncomfortable running into my father while on a date with Josh. I looked around the store.

"Where's Mom?"

He was obviously caught off guard and shocked, but he tried to stay cool, eyes wide, and then looked down into his hands. "Hi, Katie. Hello, Josh. You remember Darlene. We just finished working out and decided to get a snack before each of us went home separately in our own cars."

Darlene stuck her hand out. "Hi, Katie. I've heard so many wonderful things about you. Your dad is so proud of you. And our whole community is thankful for the amazing things you have been able to do. It's such a pleasure to talk to you." Josh leaned in also and shook her hand.

The only thing I could think was *puta*. Instead, I said, "I recognize you from the restaurant where you work. I think we've met."

I squinted at her. It started thundering outside. Father just shook his head, not knowing what to expect before the wind blew the front window out. With a loud bang, glass shattered to the floor. Darlene may have rocked my father's world, but I rocked the ground she stood on. She screamed. The kid behind the counter slipped. My father hunched his shoulders, hunkering down. Josh dove under a table. After it was all clear, he poked his head out and stood next to me dazed. Before grabbing Josh's arm to leave, I caught a glimpse of my father and the home wrecker's reflection in a hundred pieces of fractured mirror. The yogurt machine exploded. Cookie dough–flavored yogurt splattered on the walls. A customer yelled, "Help! Run! Earthquake!"

Josh and I spilled out onto the street. Before long we heard sirens. I saw my dad talking to Darlene in the parking lot. It looked like they were saying their good nights. Brief hug and small talk. Their cell phones were out. I pictured them exchanging numbers or e-mail addresses. Darlene slinked into her coupe and quietly rolled away.

"What the hell was that, Katie?" Josh said in a hoarse whisper nudging me into a corner beneath an overhang as if to take cover and have some privacy.

"This is ridiculous. Being with you is scary. You can't do stuff like this every time things upset you. You need to get control. Take an anger management class or something."

"Wow, Josh. Don't tell me what I can and can't do. You can't take that tone with me."

"Damned straight I can. I feel like yelling, turning, leaving, and never talking to you again."

"I'm sorry, Josh, but seeing my dad with that woman . . . Did you see them? That was a date, like us. Totally gross. My stupid father is on a date with the waitress. Well, how original."

My arms were flailing.

"The bitch."

The two of us moved forward toward our cars. People were staring, at the shop, at us. I was feeling sick of it all. Doc was right; I need more time, more training.

Josh kept at me. Chest forward, veins in his neck protruding, bent forward.

I could smell his angry breath in my face, as he said, "What I saw, Kate, was two happy people having a good time and enjoying themselves eating yogurt like we were about to." He slapped himself in the chest.

"End of story. Period. Why did you read into it? It's not illegal to eat yogurt in public with a friend. The other thing that I saw was a jealous daughter with uncontrolled anger and powers that are attached to her emotions at any given time."

Now we were yelling at each other in the parking lot. I pointed my finger at Josh and was about to punch him.

"Jealous? Is that what you think this is? I'd like to see you do any better with those perfect parents of yours. My parents have been fighting. They don't sleep in the same room; you can cut the tension with a knife in my house. Now this? I'm scared that my parents are going to split up. Maybe they should. Maybe we should. Damn you and them. I can't wait to get the hell out of my house, and this town, far away. I'm so going to college out of state. And Sara, my best friend, look what's happened to her." I cocked my head accusingly.

"It wouldn't kill you to go and see her. If it wasn't for your stupid idea to go up to the cave, she wouldn't be fighting for her life."

I held my head with both my hands and shook it.

"You'll go on with your charmed life. What about Sara?"

Josh looked at me and pointed to himself. "Me? My idea? So like it's all my fault now? I didn't twist her arm. She was all for going up to the cave. And it was you who caused the collapse. I've been in that cave a hundred times and never had trouble until you came along. I used to call you freaky. Now you're just plain trouble."

That was it. I got in my car and rolled the window down.

"Yeah, right, Josh. What were you doing up there a hundred times? Getting drunk? I'll have one less problem without you."

"I can't do this either, Katie. Even though every time I think of you I want you in my arms, we are just too different." Josh was calm and quiet now, resigned.

I said, "Is it us that are too different, or me?"

Josh glanced at me, ignored the comment, and added, "Maybe it's just better, safer, if we don't see each other. I don't want you, or me for that matter, to be scared or hurt. We all deserve a shot at happiness, including your father. I don't think we can make each other happy."

I replied, "Your happiness is not my responsibility. Go and make yourself happy."

Josh got into his car, too, slammed the door, and screeched away. I stayed behind because I couldn't drive, couldn't move; I could barely catch my breath. I banged on my steering wheel, tore the necklace that Doc gave me off my neck, and threw it out the window. I looked up and saw my father waiting patiently for me. Heading toward me, he picked up the necklace.

He knocked on the window. I rolled it down.

"I think you dropped this, Katie."

He handed me back my necklace and said calmly, "Please move over. Let me drive you home. I'll come back and get my car later."

CHAPTER 24

THE UNIVERSITY'S humanities Building was still. All that remained of the day's human efforts was scuff marks on the tile floor. A new posting swayed lazily from the bulletin board screwed to the sterile block walls. It read, "Discover the Benefits of Studying Abroad." At night the empty corridors of higher learning took on an eerie green tinge. Limited fluorescent lighting for nighttime use hummed. There was a faint echo in the building. Someone knocked gently on the professor's office door.

"Yes? Come in, come in," Doc S. said softly, feeling interrupted. Concentrating intently on his books, he fingered an old tobacco pipe. Classical music played on his simple radio. Lately, he needed stronger reading glasses, the kind with the built-in miniheadlight for studying documents. The door opened slowly with a squeak. Four slow, shuffling, yet purposeful steps were made to enter, and then the door closed again with a click.

Without looking up, Doc S. said, "Office hours are over. How can I . . ." He looked up and peered into the shadows. It took a moment. Recognition gave way to a look of shock and disbelief. Fear suppressed any sound he might have emitted.

A very imposing man, obviously not a student or someone from housekeeping, looked at the professor almost humorously. With a strange accent the man, who was wearing latex surgical gloves, said softly, "Good evening, Herr Doctor. Surprise." Axe spoke with his palms facing the ceiling as if to say oops.

"I am so sorry to startle you at this late hour. I understand that you are a very busy man and a mentor. I must get down to business and ask you a few questions about someone that we both have in common. I would love to stay and socialize, but time is of the essence."

The professor looked angry, put on his best threatening voice, and demanded, "How did you get in here? What do you want?" He lifted the receiver. "I'm calling campus police. Get out."

Axe pulled out a revolver that had a silencer screwed on the end of the barrel. "I wouldn't do that if I were you, Doctor. I'm here because I know that you are working with Katie Jackson. Don't you remember me?"

Axe pulled up his sleeve and revealed the tattoo that matched the insignia on the professor's ring. Doc's eyes refocused. He exclaimed, standing suddenly, "Of course, I recognize you, Uktam."

Axe took a step closer, out of the shadows. "No sudden moves. Sit down now, please. You probably never thought you would see me again. Did you miss me?"

"What do you want this time, Uktam?" asked the professor, who remained standing.

"Same thing I wanted then."

"Axe, you fool. You barely escaped with your life then, threatening nature and the spirits."

"You hurt my fragile ego. Unless you do as I say, you will not escape alive today." Axe began to walk around the office casually lifting and examining the professor's trinkets as if he were a welcome guest. "Doctor, I remember your research."

Axe scratched his head trying to recall. "Indigenous medicine men of the Amazon. Comparing the ayahuasca vine that they used to peyote used by the Native Americans of the southwestern United States. Is that what drew you to Arizona? I was sure that your studies would win you a Nobel Prize or something. You had botanists, chemists, and anthropologists from all over the world assisting you, as I recall. You created a broth. It contained herbal vine juice from the Amazonian rain forest. It was part of your plan for everyone to drink this stuff, hallucinate with the natives, and get all the answers to the universe. But it was more, much more. The powers it gave the user were and still are my desire.

"Apparently, we were both so taken with the experience that you had a signet ring made, and I forced the local chief to mix the medicine with ink and tattoo it on my arm."

"Yes, Uktam, as I recall you tried to steal our secrets and use them for evil. The natives knew your intentions and finally drove you out. I'm only sorry that they didn't finish you off."

"I'm sure you are sorry, since I'm the one standing here with a gun. Save your tired old story, Professor. You were seeking glory and fortune no less than other men such as yours truly. You turned those people against me when I saw your power grab. Now you are up to your old tricks taking control of young Katie Jackson's mind. But how and why?" Axe scowled and moved closer, circling around the room slowly. "That is what I'm here to find out." Axe waved the gun, and the professor sat down, the air exiting his body.

"Schlisselvasser, I do not believe that you are noble. How much are those parents paying you to manipulate their daughter's mind? What spells have you cast on her? Such a benevolent and kind doctor. Are you her agent, too? Will you get a piece of the tell-all book and the appearances?"

The professor tore off his reading glasses and threw them hard on a table in defiance. "Bastard. Damn you. Jealous, Uktam? That young girl is the real deal, unlike you. You never had the power and never will. That's the difference. You're a fake, a charlatan. You can read up on it and practice channeling all that you want, but you will never get it. Never. Do you hear me?" Doc S. yelled.

"This is because your true essence, the light of the vessel that shines within you, is so crusted and filthy that the light is either out or so dim that you will not be able to access this field."

"Well, if I can't, then Katie will either do it for me or I will snuff her light out as well as yours, something I'm good at. No?" Axe smiled.

"The more that you behave this way, Uktam, the further away you get from ever accomplishing your goals."

"That's where you are wrong, Professor. I want any files that you might have on her. Her address and any other related information about her powers. While you are at it, tell me more about her. What are her likes and dislikes? Who is that boy she keeps company with? And of course, I'm offering you one last chance to teach me how to acquire her powers before I terminate you. What spirit did you infuse into her being? I know your tricks. Was it a bird or a lion this time?" Axe cocked his head questioning.

"Are you mad, man?" The professor pointed at Axe. Perspiration ran down his temples. "She has these powers intrinsically. She is a gifted spiritual high priestess. You don't seem to understand. Yes, I've guided, channeled, and enhanced her ability to see more clearly what is already within her. We've only just begun. I've never encountered anyone anywhere, not even among the indigenous peoples, who has what she's got. With me or without me, she will blossom." The professor looked down for a moment. He may have said too much. Then he turned his chin up and looked defiantly into Axe's evil eyes, which looked like the holes of hell.

Axe walked around the office and saw the books lying on the table that Doc used to educate the Jackson family on what was happening to Katie. As Axe lifted the books, CDs, a flash drive, and some papers fell out onto the floor.

The professor grew ashen, mortified that Axe had found the file he requested.

"Ah, now we are getting somewhere. Her parents' names and numbers, too. How convenient." Axe rifled through the professor's office for thirty more minutes while unpleasantly interrogating him.

As Axe left the office with the confiscated materials, he shut off the light, closed the door behind him, and slipped down the stairwell wearing a hoodie and dark glasses.

Later that night, housekeeping made the rounds. Armed with a pushcart and other supplies, the custodian began to vacuum the rug while listening to music. Per her custom, she moved the chair from behind the grand old mahogany desk so she could get the vacuum under it. The professor got annoyed when dust bunnies accumulated.

The vacuum banged into something. Sometimes the professor left his garbage pail under the desk, but that made a loud clang; this was silent and soft, like a sack of meat. The housekeeper looked under the desk and screamed when she saw Doc's lifeless body stuffed under his desk. She dropped the vacuum cleaner, which dispassionately sucked up blood and dust.

Police and forensics converged on the scene, collecting evidence that might yield DNA, developing a plan, and checking all the professor's contacts, students, and associates. The investigation was on. The university went into lockdown. How could this happen? Some parents requested that their students come home. The media circus was frenetic.

The president of the college and local law officials kept the public informed. Classes were cancelled; students were urged to remain calm and stay in their locked dorm rooms. Police were beginning to clear the campus. Politicians stated their deepest regrets and condolences for the enormous loss while assuring the community that all possible leads were being investigated. The police would not rest until the person or persons who committed this heinous crime were brought to justice.

Axe watched the news and poured himself a cold one.

The next morning, Dog licked my face; I couldn't get back to sleep, so we went for a walk.

To keep Dog from barking, I gave her my sneaker. She gladly took it and ran circles around me while making guttural playful sounds to show me she was wildly excited about going out.

Meanwhile, I was hobbling next to her wearing only one shoe. I wrestled the sneaker away from her, and before she could start barking, I gave her the leash, which she whipped back and forth in her mouth with glee. Now there was the definition of happiness. I stuffed a few plastic grocery bags in my pocket so that I could pick up after her.

A big, green garbage truck lumbered through our development. Dog sniffed at everything. She had a crazy amount of energy. Like most young dogs, instead of walking straight down the hill, she quickly paced from one side of the road to the other traversing it like a novice downhill skier. A scent got her attention. Dog squatted to defecate.

Dutifully, I pulled a grocery bag out of my pocket and made sure there were no holes in it, as that can cause big problems when scooping. I placed the bag over my hand. Dog was pulling. She likes to leave the scene of the crime immediately. I lifted the wad and kept walking. After a few moments I noticed an empty garbage pail on the street where the garbage truck had just done a pickup. The lid was open. Mindlessly, I tied off the bag and lobbed the dump in the garbage pail. Two points.

Meandering down the street listening to my music, I heard someone yelling. "Hey, you." I kept walking minding my own business. Again I heard, "Hey, you."

I turned around and looked over my shoulder. "Yeah, you. Come back here right now and get that bag of dog shit out of my pail."

I think I walked a little faster. The man, who was even older than my parents, turned the pail over, dumped out the bag of poop, and started coming after Dog and me. I was quite pleased that I did such a good job of packaging the plastic bag that it was still in a neat bundle.

He finally caught up to us. He was standing there waving the bag of feces around, demanding that I take back to my property, and yelling about how I dared to throw the bag in the garbage pail. I hoped that the bag would break. I refused to take it from him, so he put it on the ground and gave it a little kick toward me. This jerk was starting to get under my skin. My emotions were twisting in the wind. I looked down, squinted, and stared, but nothing happened—no thunder, lightning, or wind—nothing, not even a cough or a sneeze.

Finally, this friendly neighbor did an about-face, abandoned the bag on the ground in front of me, and left muttering.

I lifted the bag and walked away, head down. Hey, shit happens.

I came back around to the neighbor's house, and when no one was looking—please forgive me—I emptied the contents onto the neighbor's driveway and ran home with Dog.

Mom stared at me when I walked in. I knew something was wrong. At first I thought the fecal neighbor had called my house.

"Katie, oh my God. Have you heard the news?"

Mom looked exhausted.

"What, Mom? Are we at war again or something?"

"Oh, sweetie, I'm so sorry. I'm devastated. It's the professor. He's dead." Mom touched by arm, then hugged me.

It didn't quite register at first. Like a fresh injury, it started with a sting. Moments later the agony began to set in.

I wanted my dad at that moment. He had been spending less and less time at home. He was beginning to isolate himself more, checking out of the family unit. He did sit me down and tell me how much he loved me and that, regardless of what happened between my mother and him, he would always be there for me. It was very painful, and I had weird dreams that I was looking for him but couldn't find him, and in the dream he just wouldn't come home some nights.

I stayed in my room and cried for hours. Eventually, I had no more tears. Completely washed out, I needed to talk. For an instant I thought I'd call the professor and tell him what just happened. Then the realization hit me again.

I went over to the physical rehab hospital to talk to Sara, who was making a strong recovery from her injuries. The moment she saw my face, Sara knew something was wrong. Before she could get the question out of her mouth, which was a bit slow on her lips since she was still in speech therapy, I hugged her and started bawling, explaining what happened to Doc.

Sara was becoming much more independent with her activities of daily living and slowly walked with me to the cafeteria using her walker. We both had Cokes. Sara was able to swallow the drink now. It required concentration, and she had to clear her throat and cough a few times. She still did a little better with thicker consistencies such as pudding. So we both had some. It went down smoothly for Sara, but I choked on my tears, and my nose dripped.

She told me, "It's fine to miss him. But I know with all my heart and soul that he is home again and in a place that is indescribable. We should feel worse for those of us left behind. Let the police do their jobs now." She was beginning to tire from the effort of walking and talking. She added, "Katie, I will ask the doctor if I can get a pass to leave the hospital for a few hours and go with you to the funeral. My rehab is going so well that I am scheduled to be discharged home in a week." I love Sara. This was great news. I looked at her and smiled. What a roller coaster. Sara on the mend; Doc dead.

Dusk settled again as it always does, like nothing happened or ever changes—utter universal indifference to tragedy. Everything took on an orange hue; the mountains in the distance looked like purple puffs. There was something about the alluring mystery of dusk. Everything seemed more alive and peaceful when the sun set but before night fell. The slipping light and changing shadows gave Josh a visceral glow. The whole world seemed to become pastel. Tonight, the sky remained on fire with swirls of color. He put on his clear racing glasses.

The evening criterium bike race was about to start. More than thirty riders congregated, ready to compete. Josh Ryan was among them. After our fight outside the yogurt shop, he texted me and told me he had thought about not riding tonight, but I said that he needed to burn off some energy and knew the ride would do him good. Josh decided to ride his featherweight, fourteen-pound carbon road bike with electronic gear shifters.

Josh had invested about ten grand into the colorful blue and white Italian rig that he was sporting. Sorry, helmets are ugly. He looked like a Martian with half a watermelon on his head. Safety first. The tight racing jersey and shorts I could live with, especially in his case. Some older guys have no business in tights. It's up there with a Speedo—plain wrong.

I was still in a state of shock. Aimless and powerless, I felt like a lost kitten and decided to go down to the race anyway and see Josh ride. I brought Dog to keep me company. He was so cute and cheered me up. I don't even know why I went. My eyes were puffy and red.

If people looked at me the wrong way, my lips quivered, and my eyes moistened, which can be helpful in the desert where many people suffer from dry eyes.

I wanted to see Josh and apologize for how I behaved at the yogurt shop; plus, I didn't want to be home. My actions last night were no different from a temper tantrum, like someone smashing dishes or punching a wall and then feeling remorse later. Before the race maybe I could wish him luck. I knew how important these events were to him. He beamed when he saw me. I felt a sad smile coming through.

Josh introduced me to his buddies as his girlfriend before the race was about to start. Suddenly, he grabbed me and hugged me tight, whispering, "I missed you so much." Then he kissed me. I felt woozy. I don't drink, but this must be what drunk feels like. The kiss was gentle at first but got more urgent. My insides felt hot and weak. His kiss was an announcement to his racing buddies that I was his. Feeling self-conscious about his friends, we stopped.

Lately when my emotions rolled like this, the environment shifted. I was pleasantly surprised that nothing happened externally, no sun or wind. Maybe I was gaining control? I enjoyed the moment of teenage normalcy if one can even use those two words in the same sentence. I thought, I must tell the professor. Then I remembered again, and the pain hit me; I cried softly. "Poor Doc."

Josh sweetly held my face, looked into my eyes, and kissed me repeatedly.

The race was a one and a half mile loop around an urban neighborhood closed off to traffic. A cop was directing traffic away from the race, which made me feel safer for these riders. The one who completed the most laps in a certain amount of time won.

After the first few laps the leading group out front began to form. It was very tactical and involved not just brute strength but a game of nerves. Watching some of these riders try to pass each other, wheels inches apart at twenty-eight miles per hour, was nail biting. Daylight faded. Riders switched on their lights, which added a new dimension of risk to the atmosphere.

I learned a lot from listening to Josh talk about racing, and I could begin to see the strategies in action. Waiting too long to hold a front starting position can make the rider's legs heavy. It's impossible to hold that position throughout. Riders can get overanxious about moving up in the flow. They look for an easy wheel, or for the pack to slow so their momentum can carry them. Every time I saw Josh round the corner, I'd yell, "Go, Josh." The experienced riders tapped the breaks as late as possible before leaning sharply into a turn. If a rider in front of him slowed down, Josh would not slow down or hit the brakes; instead, he moved over and cut through. These riders were working hard, in pain with lungs burning. Last month a crash resulted in someone fracturing a pelvis.

Position is important midrace. The middle is the best place to deal with attacks. I could smell the adrenaline and testosterone during the last lap. Maybe it was just body odor?

The riders stood in their saddles, bikes rocking hard back and forth under them. These guys were on an anaerobic sprint, their faces determined. Although this was not the final sprint down the Champs-Elysees toward the Arc de Triomphe, it sure felt like the Tour de France to me. Josh came in second, which was amazing.

After the race I was going to meet Josh and his friends. The riders needed some time to pack up their gear and cool down. I walked around the dark quiet block to my car with Dog. Businesses were closed. I held my keys and the leash a bit tighter.

A black Cadillac Escalade slowed down on my left. Two men were hanging out in a doorway a few feet ahead, joking, laughing casually, and not paying me any attention. The passenger window of the Escalade opened; Dog growled low. I thought someone would ask for directions or make a catcall. Instead, I felt a sudden sting and a burn in my left upper arm. I reached with my right arm to see what happened, which jerked Dog's leash a bit. I had been shot with a dart. I staggered.

I watched as Dog attacked one of their legs, biting hard. She barked a menacing sound before clamping down and shaking her head, tearing into clothes, skin, tendons, and bone. The other man kicked Dog hard, like a soccer ball, in the ribs. Dog yelped, flew backward two feet, and then shook it off. She had been through much worse with the last loser she lived with, so a kick wouldn't stop her. All it did was make her turn, baring her teeth, hunkering down with lowered ears, slitted eyes, and a foaming mouth. She leaped for the villain's throat but caught his chest instead as the man instinctively moved back and put his hands up in a protective posture. Dog ripped. First at his chest and then she tore his thumb like a chicken drumette, partially disconnecting it from the kidnapper's hand. Becoming dizzy, confused, and sedated, I was forced into the back of the Cadillac.

The last thing I saw was that Dog turned and started after the Escalade but door was already closing, pulling away. She jumped at the vehicle, but it was no use. Dog took off after us before everything went black.

CHAPTER 25

KATIE LAY unconscious deep beneath the earth, held hostage in Axe's labyrinthine cave system. On the ground above her, he lounged at the swimming pool. Quite content with himself, he contemplated the valley floor beneath his mansion as he looked at an olive before biting it. Lately, he favored the green olives with the pits. He liked nibbling around them but hated when the pitted kinds were mixed in with the unpitted ones. Annoying. One time he bit down too hard on an olive with a pit, and it broke one of his remaining teeth, which is not saying much about his foul and gold-ridden dentition. Heaven forbid he should see a decent American dentist while he was here.

As he sipped a mimosa, Axe wished that all these last-minute complications could have been avoided. He didn't like having to tie up loose ends—like Katie tied up in the dungeon, for example.

The girl could prove useful, he mused. He imagined that it didn't hurt that she was a tasty little morsel, which appealed to his animal desires.

He took a phone call and simply said, "Yes, of course, you fool."

~~~~~~~

Moments later in an instant explosion, a concussion and ball of fire consumed the side of the federal safe house. The guards were transformed into a fine mist. A short time earlier, at the far end of the trailer in the back bedroom, Weaver and Bugdon had finally begun to negotiate a deal in earnest. The blast knocked them both over. Bugdon went down hard. He couldn't hear or see well, and confusion overcame him. Weaver managed to roll under a desk holding his own head and reaching for his shotgun. The high-pitched ringing in his ears was painful. He opened, closed, and clenched his jaw a few times.

Two trained mercenaries entered their room in defensive tactical formation. Weaver pumped the twelve-gauge shotgun twice from the floor in their general direction, and then they were gone. He pumped again. A third man entered with an automatic and fired at the desk on the floor. Wood chips and wallboard flew everywhere. Weaver rolled left and fired. An eerie quiet ensued. Dust and gunpowder clogged up his nose.

Bugdon stayed down, mortally wounded. Weaver crawled to him, demanding to finally know what Axe was up to. He shook Bugdon, yet held the slumping man, compressing his gushing wounds. Before the life finally drained from his gray dull eyes, with a raspy voice Bugdon whispered, "Underground nukes here in Tucson."

～～～～

Josh called Katie's cell. He called her home. Message after message. Eventually he went home. The glow of the race was gone.

～～～～

Weaver declined medical attention after the blast that killed Bugdon. Other than a splitting headache, mildly blurred vision, and hypersensitivity to sound, he seemed to be doing reasonably well. He was very irritable, and his jaw was tender. Chewing hurt, so he decided to drink instead. Needing to think, which was difficult at the moment, he decided to hit the bar and self-medicate with beer. He had a favorite Mexican haunt close to where he lived. It was packed with a solid clientele, not upscale, and no troublemakers, usually.

Some guy was hovering over three bar stools playing musical

chairs, trying to save them all. He didn't even have any extra articles of clothing to throw over them to make them look occupied.

Weaver limped over. The guy said, "These are taken."

Scoop was in no mood to bicker or deal with anyone and replied, "No one is sitting here. It's first come, first serve at the bar, like it always is." The guy quickly waved over the two women he was apparently saving the seats for.

Scoop said, "Look, pal, I'm just going to order a beer." Right then, a shriveled looking blonde with a page-boy haircut and blue eye makeup sat on the stool, cutting Weaver off. Her head was literally an inch in front of his nose. "Really?" Weaver asked.

He could see every strand of dyed hair perfectly styled into place as if glued. By now he wanted to strangle someone, throw this lady off the bar stool, and kick the guy. Instead, he coughed hard into her hair. Then he faked a sneeze on her neck. Hacking down the back of her shirt, he feigned an apology, saying, "She's too close, and I'm violently allergic to many scents. Must be the perfume." He faked a few wheezes.

When the bartender finally brought his beer, Weaver accidentally on purpose knocked the bottle over, spilling it onto the guy's lap. He paid his bill and said, "Next time, mind your manners." He walked out.

~~~~~~

Josh tried calling Katie's house again, and her mother finally answered, hoping that it was Katie calling. Katie's mother was obviously disappointed to hear from Josh. On the other hand, she didn't want her daughter driving in a car with a testosterone-laden, inexperienced boy who raced bikes.

Josh was polite but concerned, and Rena said that Katie wasn't home yet, which at least led her to believe that Katie and Josh weren't in a car together.

Rena wrung her hands, pacing back and forth. Looking out the kitchen window past the shades hoping to see Katie coming up the driveway, John and Rena shot worried glances at each other. Katie's dad checked his cell phone every few minutes. When nothing happened, he finally became impatient and dialed 911. The operator at first was of no help. She tried to calm the Jacksons down, but they tried to explain that their daughter didn't and had never behaved in this manner. The police explained that maybe Katie was at a friend's house. They asked if she had gone out alone or with others. Rena responded that Katie took her dog with her when she left earlier. This barely classified as a missing person yet.

Fury, agony, optimism, and despair gripped John. He tried to beat down thoughts that he might never see his daughter again. Deputy Carter was on duty when Katie's parents called 911, the same cop involved when the cave collapsed. Unfortunately, the police were getting to know them, as if they were a family with too many domestic disturbances. Detectives were exploring leads after what happened to the professor, which also led back to the Jackson's house. It didn't take very long for the cops to connect Katie's disappearance and the professor's death.

〰〰〰

The drugs that had been shot into me slowly wore off. In a twilight between phases of consciousness, I dreamed of my dad. I was a little girl, and we were running errands together early one Sunday morning. He took me to an old-fashioned diner with a soda fountain, where I sat high on a stool that spun round. Old men were sitting to our left and right discussing the problems of the world. Dad was introducing me around and bragging about his great kid, Katie. It was the first time I tasted tea, though it was more milk and sugar than tea. I also had toast with melted butter and jelly. It was the best thing ever. I was happy. I looked to my right at one of the other patrons; it was Honon Bear who said, "Girl, it is time. You are prepared, and we will never leave you alone. It will be difficult, but we know you can do this." Strangely, Bear had a heavy Caribbean accent, which I found rather becoming. I'm surprised that she didn't say, "Welcome to Bermuda; pass the rum." The only item missing was a steel-drum band.

Then I looked in front of me, and the server behind the counter was the professor. He smiled at me and told me he was doing great and that it would be quite a few decades before I could join him behind the counter, but that he'd be waiting with a delicious cup of tea. He told me not to fear. "Fear what professor? Death?" He didn't answer.

During the solitude of captivity, I felt darkness descend upon me as well as violent shaking, loud wind, words of fire, and finally lights so intense I thought that I might explode. The lights were beams that were like branches of a tree leading back to its trunk and roots, to which I was attached.

My head hurt. I felt dizzy. My mouth was parched. I began to cough and opened my eyes. It was frightening waking up in a strange place that could become a sepulcher. Oh my God, the last thing I remembered was Josh's bike race. How long had I been here?

The lights were dim, and the smell was moist. Not an entirely unpleasant odor, but musty, organic, and earthy. I was lying on a cot. The floor, walls, and ceiling were all stone.

A woman entered. She was wearing a white lab coat. With a thick accent that sounded Russian, she said in a stone-cold voice, "Drink these; vill make you feel better." She handed me a big mug of steaming broth and a tall, sweating, cold glass of orange juice.

At first I refused. "Get lost, Natasha."

The woman was insistent. "You are dehydrated. Need fluid, yes? Drink. My name not Natasha."

I was too weak and thirsty to say no. So I drank. The soup felt great going down, though the broth was a little bitter, with an almost smoky flavor. It also could have used a little salt, maybe paprika. "Where am I?" I asked.

The woman started to walk away.

"Hey, wait, I need the bathroom."

She turned and pointed to it and then left me alone.

CHAPTER 26

THE FBI and Homeland Security didn't take the threat of weapons of mass destruction lightly. They jumped on the possibility of WMDs on US soil. White House situation room personnel located in the basement of the West Wing were all briefed. In attendance today were President Timothy J. Scott, the vice president, a National Security Administration advisor, an officer from Homeland Security, the FBI director, and two Pentagon generals, with live air-force feed.

At fifty-five hundred square feet, the situation room is capable of giving the president of the United States encrypted command and control of threats both foreign and domestic. Run by the National Security Council, the room was established by the late John F. Kennedy and operates 24-7. This month's bout was shaping up to be Axe's basement versus the White House's basement.

Davis Monthan Air Force base was put in a state of high alert. The NSA combed through phone numbers and data, trying to bracket any trends that they could isolate.

Josh was questioned several times as the last known individual that Katie was with. The poor guy was distraught at having been labeled as a person of interest. The police had great cause to be concerned for Katie's safety now. They finally believed her parents after they found blood less than a block from where the race was. Forensics asked her parents for her toothbrush, hairbrush, nail clippers, or any other object that might have her DNA on it. There was no match between the blood found at the crime scene and Katie's DNA. Oddly, the preliminary results revealed that human blood was mixed with nonhuman blood that appeared to be canine, but Dog was nowhere to be found. Final DNA results would take days—time they did not have.

That Bugdon said the words *nuke* and *Tucson* before he died legitimatized and initiated probable cause for search and seizure. Of course, now no one could prove he said it.

〜〜〜〜〜

Axe realized that he was a marked man. But first a shower and a shave were in order. He lathered to the blasting music of Rachmaninoff and then thought about how he hadn't expected the professor, Weaver, or Katie to complicate matters. It was time to retreat underground. Axe considered his next step while dressing.

He advised the surrounding houses to be at code level red. At the first sign of any intrusion, they were to let him know and execute emergency protocol.

His facilities had significant defense capabilities, not the least of which were shoulder-held rocket-propelled grenades and other anti-helicopter, laser-guided, ground-to-air projectiles that he had bought from odious figures. Many of Axe's personnel did not know the extent of the diabolical plan and were expendable. Mere collateral damage.

He advised his technical team in the main house to proceed below to level three, where he would join them shortly. Axe originally planned to be long gone at the time of detonation. It was time for Plan B as the opportunity for an early departure had eluded him.

〜〜〜〜〜

The task force Shane Weaver was attached to had the county plans of Axe's house spread out on a table. As far as SWAT could tell, there was a wine cellar and either some sort of racquetball court or bowling alley down below in the basement level. Nothing below that was recorded. Utility records, however, showed that Axe's place pulled enough amperage to run a hospital and light up a football stadium. It was one heck of an electric bill.

This local threat of WMDs drew the ire of the White House. The decision to deploy a predator drone to and above Tucson from its own local Davis Monthan Air Force base was discussed in the situation room and the Pentagon.

From thirty-thousand feet, all the drone would see was a house with nothing in particular to shoot at. Drone reconnaissance was still no replacement for human intelligence gathering. Fighter jets were camouflaged like bees in a hive ready to be scrambled, but to do what exactly?

Colonel Frank R. Bury, the commanding officer of the 355th Fighter Wing, Davis Monthan Air Force Base, Arizona, was fully briefed and in command of more than seven thousand airmen, twenty-five hundred civilians, and more than one hundred aircraft.

If it were true that someone was threatening the homeland with a rogue nuclear device, then the federal government needed to consider destroying that target even if it meant casualties, otherwise known as a surgical pinpoint strike. The lives saved would far outweigh the minimal sacrifice of innocents and friendlies. This hadn't yet been presented to lawmakers in Congress. The media and public outcry would be staggering. Not to mention that it is a big no-no for the US military to shoot upon its civilian citizenry. The Pentagon had no credible evidence that there were WMDs in Tucson, other than the dying words of a thug.

Another option was to evacuate.

This presented an interesting challenge. The only freeway that ran through town was Interstate 10, which was one of the best things to come out of Texas. A million people on that road would turn it into a parking lot. There would be panic, a stampede. It was also possible to get out of Tucson using highway 77. In addition, anyone with an all-wheel-drive vehicle might take rugged country roads up into the mountains.

Greater Tucson had a less than optimal evacuation plan. The White House contacted the governor of Arizona.

Houses three and four on Axe's estate detected a rapidly approaching Black Hawk helicopter from the Marana National Guard. Houses one and two noted a caravan of quickly approaching vehicles raising dust.

Axe gave the order, "Hold your fire." He wrapped up a few details and walked into his bedroom closet, opened his exotic-wood watch-winder box, and tilted one of the winders, which activated the elevator doors. Axe stepped in and was sucked deep below ground.

CHAPTER 27

TEAMS IN place; perimeter established. Weaver approached the front entry to Axe's estate for a second time, but this was no practice drill, and he had serious backup. Just then a limping, panting dog matted with a bloody coat cautiously drew near. Obviously exhausted and injured, the mutt came up to him tentatively without overt signs of aggression and therefore gave no reason to shoot it. Weaver bent and put his hand down in a friendly gesture, and the dog sniffed and wagged. Scoop checked. The dog had a collar and tag that bore the Jacksons' name and number. Scoop opened a bottle of water, for which the dog was grateful. He slowly poured it so the dog could turn her head sideways and lap some directly from the plastic bottle since no one had a bowl and no one offered a helmet. He poured the rest on the dog's head and ears to cool the panting beast. While fishing for a power bar in his pocket to feed her, it hit Weaver.

"Oh, wow, Katie Jackson, the missing hero chick, the girl I rescued from the cave right over there. She was in cahoots with that dead professor, and now her dog is here?" The dog grabbed Weaver's arm, pulling him in the direction of the collapsed cave where she must have picked up a scent. Weaver said, "Good dog" and realized that the Jackson kid could be in there somewhere on premises and radioed in the new wrinkle of a possible hostage situation based on a dog and a hunch. He wondered what the heck kept bringing the Jackson girl back here to this spot.

Battering rams crashed through Axe's front door. No one was

there to greet them this time. The team exploded into the house in formation, with Weaver up front and the dog following. She was the newly deputized volunteer SWAT dog. It was problematic that this dog was a wild card and could give away their position by running through the house and barking. But so far the new canine behaved well. She was quiet, cunning moved instinctively. The dog's sense of smell could come in handy; plus, getting rid of her would be a big ordeal right now. Could he still just shoot her? His judgment was to go with it and let the dog stay. The house seemed silent but not to the dog. She could hear things no one else could and was on the move again.

A mug of still-warm coffee sat on the kitchen counter. Weaver radioed. "Someone saw us coming and left in a hurry. We will move and clear room by room. Lock down perimeter. Oh, and lock down the whole damn town, buses, freeway, and airport."

The team methodically searched the entire mansion in full gear. At the end of a corridor of bedrooms they heard low voices, maybe a radio? They used hand signals and nonverbal communication. Weaver believed in the element of surprise. If they had to strike, it would be best to do so without the enemy taking precautions. He believed that one method of survival was the ability to remain fluid during quickly escalating tensions.

They had abandoned the classic diamond or column formation. Their training was not to form a mass of flesh clogging a corridor since that would make them an easy target. Instead, they made themselves small and low, hugging floors and walls. One disadvantage to this was greater opportunity for shooters to get away, but it improved the safety of the police. They were taught that under extreme duress of battle, perceptual distortions were inevitable such as tunnel vision, limited focus of attention and comprehension. During an exchange, IQ drops to zero. Training, strategy, and tactics must compensate for this. The use of cover, concealment, and movement were paramount. Movement of a pod can be too slow and cumbersome.

Weaver preferred well-trained, thinking, resilient fighters; they approached the door from behind which the voices came. The point man gestured closed door right. The left flanker shifted behind the point man and stacked behind the right flanker. The left flanker squeezed the shoulder of the right flanker to let him know he was ready. The right flanker squeezed the shoulder of the point man, who was Weaver, indicating that he could now move past the door. Both Weaver and the right flanker moved past it, pushing the dog out of the way. The two flankers, who were now in cross fire position should someone suddenly make a break for it, decided who would open the door. The right flanker closest to the door's hinges reached across to grab the knob with his gloved hand. The door was opened, and the flanker entered, followed by the breaching flanker going in the opposite direction of flanker one. A rear guard remained in the hall giving cover. The dog remained with Weaver. No one breathed. Then there was a deep sigh that smelled of fear.

"All clear, false alarm. It's a damned TV talk show."

Weaver whispered loudly, "Good job, but we need to keep moving. There are a lot of rooms to cover. We also have to check the basement level."

~~~~~~

Police revisited the Jackson home. Deputy Carter had new information to share. Standing stiffly in the doorway, he informed John and Rena, "We found your dog loose on the property of a home several miles from here." Carter's look of concern deepened.

Katie's mom asked, "Is she all right?"

"Mr. and Mrs. Jackson, may I come in? We need to talk."

Rena tried to be polite and offer him a drink, but she was nervous and her hands were shaking.

"No, thank you, Mrs. Jackson. I'm fine, really. As you recall, we rescued Katie and her friends from a cave collapse recently."

John commented, "How could we forget?"

His wife shot him a dagger and gestured to Carter. "Please sit."

Carter sat down politely and continued. "After the rescue we took someone into custody who we believe was living on those premises.

Additionally, the owner of the property is a person of extreme interest to authorities in the US and many other countries. It would be safe to say that he is not a good guy. Our people on the scene described the behavior of Katie's dog as similar to the behavior of some of our search and rescue canines. The dog is stressed, suffering from exposure, and may have been in a fight."

Carter sighed heavily, swallowed, felt parched. "Ma'am, maybe I will have that water. We suspect that Katie is in that house. If so, possibly against her will."

John fell into the chair and rubbed his face. "Well, can't you go in and get her?"

"I'm afraid it's not going to be that easy. You see, we have reason to believe that the compound is highly armed and dangerous."

Rena began to shake uncontrollably, dropped the water pitcher, ran into the bathroom, and threw up. John went in after her.

Carter shook his head and waited while his radio beeped and dispatchers called.

John and Rena returned, and John asked, "What do these lunatics want with our Katie? Is it ransom money?"

"We don't think so, sir. Can you tell me more about what relationship, if any, Katie had with the late professor?"

"Look, Officer Carter, how many times will we be asked the same question? We've been through this a hundred times. Asked and answered."

"John, please," said Rena.

"I know that this is extremely difficult, Mr. and Mrs. Jackson, but please bear with me and help us to help Katie."

The Jacksons looked at each other, nodded, and began to explain how Doc was mentoring their daughter. Carter was well aware of Katie's actions as seen on the news.

"Mr. Jackson, I know that you hold very high clearance as a lead investigator with Pantheon Elway munitions. I have been given orders to disclose something to you."

Carter had learned that John worked as an engineer at Pantheon Elway, called PEM, in Tucson. It was a huge company with a long heritage in Arizona. It employed thousands and was a small city unto itself, with its own zip code, fire department, and clinic. John designed sophisticated weaponry systems and collaborated regularly with air-force brass and the fighter pilots regarding human-equipment interface and applicability of these designs in the field. John had a few retired fighter pilots who now flew commercially and worked for his team as consultants. This was similar to a drug company that did clinical trials on people. John met, had coffee with, and even occasionally played golf with Col. Bury, the commanding officer of the air-force base, who had even been to the Jackson house a few times.

"Mr. Jackson, at this point we don't know if the owner of the compound is trying to ransom your military weaponry expertise in exchange for your daughter. We don't know if he wanted her in connection with the professor; perhaps she found out things she shouldn't have while exploring the cave. It may be that the owner wants to exploit Katie's talents."

Rena said, "I knew I should have never let her go out with that boy."

"Mr. and Mrs. Jackson, before you hear it on the news, we want you to know that the owner of that property may be planning an act of terrorism against our city and country. At my pay grade, all I'm told is that all options are on the table regarding how to neutralize the threat."

John screamed, "My daughter will not be collateral damage."

CHAPTER 28

EVEN BEFORE exiting the elevator, Axe immediately commanded attention, barking orders at his engineers to initiate the final sequence. Their eyes opened wide, shocked by the order and the surprise visit from their boss. They snapped erect in response to the authority.

Axe asked where the girl was. The woman who brought Katie soup showed him.

~~~~~~~~~

I imagined what my captor would do to me if I didn't fully cooperate. One option was to cover me in wet blankets and slowly simmer me in a pot of boiling water until I was juicy and tender. The other was to slit the bottoms of my feet, cover them in honey, and tie my legs in a cage filled with starving rats. These were some of the favorite punishments of cruel Roman emperors. Perhaps this was a medieval dungeon equipped with a rack.

The nausea induced from drinking the broth had subsided. I felt like my mind was opening. Visually, I began hallucinating. I would look at a wall then stare into it. The wall went from a block of rock to patterns of repeating color and shapes that made up the rock, and then ever smaller subunits until the wall was nothing more than open, breathing, living space. From this space, I perceived that the universe was aware, pulsating, and watching. Then I felt a knowledge that there were other universes, multiverses. I tried to breathe and focus on each exhale, which helped. I wished that I had learned to properly meditate. I imagined what it might be like to disappear physically but still be awake and present. If I get through this ordeal, I'd like to work on that.

Even though I felt as though I was underground in a basement of some type, from the dampness and smell, I experienced a vast open sky above me that was entering my being. I had prayed that whatever powers I temporarily had and wished would go way so that I could be a normal kid would now return. I tried to connect with the image of Professor S. in my recent dream about the coffee shop. Despite all of his advice, fear took root deep within me. It was true fear—the kind that becomes like a friend when it's time to survive. I closed my eyes and asked Honon what to do. My breathing became labored and rapid.

"Shush, little darling. I am here, never left. We are okay. Yes, the fear is your friend now. It will empower you." I felt like singing a few bars of one of my parents' favorite songs: "Caribbean Queen, now we're sharing the same dream, and our hearts, they beat as one."

When Axe entered the room, he brought a smell of fecal decay, sulfur, and sewage. "Ah, so you are the annoying little girl with all the so-called powers. Welcome to the beginning of your demise. Don't fret; we all must go sometime. We start to die the day we are born." Axe explained this as if he taunted people in a dungeon routinely.

"First, I'd like to tell you what you tampered with and why I am so unhappy with you that you must be destroyed. There isn't enough room for both of us here."

"I'm happy to go somewhere else," I said.

"The man that you killed in the cave with that thing that you do was my closest confidant."

"What man? I didn't . . ."

"Silence," he shrieked. "Don't lie to me. I know what you did."

"No, you don't understand. We were hanging out, that's all. There was a roar, like a mountain lion. It was dark. I didn't mean to hurt anyone, and I'm not looking for any trouble. We were just resting after a hike."

"Well, my dearest, it is you with the lack of understanding. You see, sometimes even when we are not looking for trouble, it has a way of finding us. There are also times when you just want to walk away from trouble, but the other person won't let you—like now, for instance. I will mean to hurt you even though you say you didn't mean to hurt my friend, and when I'm through with you, I'll do to your boyfriend and that other girl what I did to the professor."

"What did you do to Doc, you bastard?" The ground shook and the walls cracked from my sheer anger, informing me that my abilities were returning.

He put his face inches from mine. Gross me out. Germ alert.

Axe stroked my head, played with a lock of my hair, smelled it and me, like the morning coffee, and said, "Ah, lovely." His breath stank like the rotten smell I experienced when Bear first took me flying on her back. I vividly recalled her giving me the tour and the black foulness I encountered. It was him. This was why I was here. "Your beloved professor and I go back a ways. He is not the wonderful benevolent man you thought he was. We met in the South American Amazon jungle. He was after fame and glory, and I wanted the secret power that you now possess. The professor spent a great deal of time living among the natives and studying their ways. Medicine men and women are extremely secretive and only use oral tradition to keep records.

"He ingratiated himself into their good graces the same way he fooled you, buying time so that he could perfect the infamous elixir of the vine. He almost succeeded until I spoiled the party. He believed that the correct sequence of chants, meditations, and the juice could lead a person so deeply inward that great powers could be unleashed that would repair the world. Like any self-respecting pagan idolater or sorcerer, I wanted those formulas so that I might bend the world to my will. That is why I spiked your broth earlier with the fruit of the vine. I drank from it, too. Think of it as sharing a toast. Soon our conscious minds will join, and I will know your powers.

"I have the late professor's full dossier on you. He mistakenly placed a great deal of faith in you and thought you were the authentic heir who should know the full plan, when it was me all along. Were you aware that he manipulated you? He would drink and use his training to channel that bear nonsense into your mind. He used you. He puffed you up like a stuffed teddy bear or marionette. You are nothing without him, and you aren't much more with him. He was planning to use you for his own plans over time." Axe peered into my eyes hypnotically, pupils dilating. "Don't look so surprised. I came to realize that the professor was also a powerful mystic." Anger toward the professor rose in my heart. I felt used, violated.

Axe rolled up his sleeve and showed me his tattoo, the same design as on the professor's ring, statue, and my necklace. "We were both part of the same secret society that went underground nearly a thousand years ago."

As Axe stared into my eyes, the tattoo on his arm began to move and writhe. It crawled down his arm and into the palm of his hand. He cupped his hand, which was smoking. Then he inhaled it. What was left of the tattoo slithered to his ring finger and began to twirl around it slowly, hardening and forming into the same signet ring that the professor had worn. I could not believe my eyes. Then, when I looked back up at Axe's terrible face, it was no longer him. He was the professor.

I heard horrible unrelenting screams. I didn't realize it was me.

"Remember me, Katie? Miss me? You see, I never really left. I am still here for you. I'm here to help you, dear. I changed places and forms with that monster up in my office. It was I, your doc, who survived and Axe who perished in my office that night. So don't worry. Now we can pick up our work where we left off. I know all about you, Katie Jackson. Your parents are worried sick. I can get us out of here. Come with me; join me. We have so much to do, and you have so much yet to learn from me."

I looked at him incredulously.

"You see, *mijita*, it's really me, the professor. I know everything about you. We first must get out of here and then finish blending our minds and powers." He gave me his hand. I started to believe him. He touched my head with his ring, and it burned.

Somewhere deep inside me, a tiny voice whispered no. I shook my head violently. "Liar. You will never get away with this."

"What is a little punk like you going to do about it?" His disgusting face changed back into the monster he really was. "You know," he said as he marveled at himself, "I might spare your life if you'll allow me to harness those powers. It might also be acceptable to become part of my organization and use those powers to strengthen us both. With me you will be very rich and powerful. Your parents could live like royalty. We would make a beautiful team, far better than what that quack had planned for you."

"I might consider working for you if you stop whatever evil plan you have going on down here."

Axe stroked my face gently with the back of his hand, and I reflexively recoiled. "You will submit to my wishes."

"Never."

He backhanded me. I tumbled to the ground. The tears began to flow, which made me angrier.

"Tears will do you no good, you little witch."

In a low growl, I said, "What did you just call me?"

"A witch. Why do you ask? That's what you are, yes? You no like, my little witch?"

"Yes, my tears will be very helpful. No one calls me a witch. My name is Katie Jackson. Just watch me."

I struggled to put my hands together forming a diamond with my thumbs and forefingers. I thrust my arms forward and blew an intense steamy blast through my fingers. It seared Axe's face, smashing him backward.

Bear danced in my heart, and I felt my thousand-yard stare and trance begin. I could no longer differentiate between what was happening in my mind and what was happening on the physical plane. More tears streamed. The water table beneath the cave system converged. Underground lakes and rivers from the Pacific to the Mississippi sent their cherished waters to the grounds beneath the parched desert. At first it was one water drop for every tear, some salty, some fresh. Then water rose in a torrent. The underground aquifer water system for miles around began to drain in my direction like sinuses clearing out after an infection.

Salmon were tempted to turn and swim back downstream. Axe's technicians detected dangerous rapid elevations in the water table on underground sonar that had been installed. Outside, it was as if tens of millions of butterflies began to flap a sinusoidal, other-worldly resonant frequency, and the winds responded by delivering a gale force. The more Axe pressured me, the more fiercely the weather picked up. Sheets of rain blew sideways at seventy miles an hour, then eighty. The news stations blamed the extreme conditions on global warming. Unfortunate junior reporters were seen on television wearing designer storm gear telling people to stay indoors. Their fancy storm equipment left them unprepared and speechless.

~~~~~~~~~

John Jackson worked tirelessly, having no mercy on himself, which is what he did best under stress. Exhausted, he slumped forward with dark puffy rings under his eyes and then put in a call to Colonel Bury. John was very close to putting the final touches on a weapons system that was ready for field trials. Even though it was still experimental, it was the only way he could think of to help his daughter. His weapons system came from the medical field where he had been collaborating for several years.

John had a bad bout of kidney stones that required two treatments. One was extracorporeal shock-wave lithotripsy, and then he needed a follow-up regimen of laser lithotripsy to break up that nasty stag horn sitting in his kidney. The idea behind these treatments was to minimize collateral damage to the healthy kidney tissue, while allowing minimally invasive procedures to get the stone out. In this case, Katie was the healthy kidney tissue to be saved.

John spent his career believing that, sadly, war was a reality—an unfortunate cost of being an earthling in a fallen world, the price of freedom. Rather than just praying for peace and a better world to come, he used his brilliance to devise weaponry that destroyed property and weapons, sparing life when and where possible. He also supported the drone program because it was intended to decrease deaths. John Jackson believed in using surgical strikes, which seemed to be less deadly. Reading about an innocent civilian being killed in a drone attack broke his heart, made him work harder to increase the pinpoint accuracy of the drone strike program. It infuriated him that hardened fighters by day blended in among civilian populations, and wondered what he would do, where he would go, if the United States were under attack. Now, his own daughter could become the victim of the same collateral damage he helped to create.

Humans can be excellent, efficient killers. John Jackson's newest weapon was a high-powered shock wave that sent an acoustic pulse of enormous magnitude. If the composition of the targeted structure was known, a frequency could be calculated that would weaken it internally. For a given architectural design, weight-bearing pillars and joints could be specifically targeted, causing cavitation and excessive shearing forces that would collapse a structure. This was followed by a series of laser shocks that isolated and destroyed. He designed it so that it could be outfitted to just about any attack helicopter in the US arsenal. While a building collapse would clearly maim or kill people at ground zero, casualties and collateral damage were mitigated.

Police had reason to believe that Katie was in some sort of basement level. A bomb that left a deep crater in the ground would kill her for sure. John had to convince the Air Force that bombing was a bad option. Trying his weapon could reduce the structure to rubble at ground level, and then troops could search and rescue. Either way Katie's chances weren't good. Not to mention having the US military blow up American civilian targets was not cool.

From everything he learned, the weaponry was a personal gift and best effort to help save his daughter if John could convince the colonel. John knew of at least four helicopters equipped with his weapons system sitting in Colonel Bury's war chest. His weapons system program was called Operation Staghorn until they could come up with a more formal name. Maybe they would name it after his daughter? Katie's Fury had a certain ring.

"Good morning, JJ. How are you holding up?"

"Best that I can, Colonel."

"I can't imagine what you and Rena must be going through. We are doing everything we can here under the circumstances."

"I know you are, Frank, and it gives Rena and me great comfort to know that you are on our team and a dear friend."

"You know I love you guys, and this is far from over. When all this is resolved, we will have a beer and play a round of golf."

"Thank you. From your mouth to God's ear. The reason I called you, Colonel, is to discuss Operation Staghorn. It's ready to go. I have dotted every *I* and crossed every *T*. I've reviewed it with the pilots again. Sir, I am one hundred percent confident that it's time to be deployed in field exercises."

"That's excellent news, John. Why don't you take some time away from work? Stay close to home. You and Rena are under a lot of stress. You didn't need to bring this in ahead of deadline."

"Well, Frank, you should know me by now. This is how I deal with stress, burying my head in the books and putting my shoulder to the grindstone. Here's the kicker, Frank. I'm requesting that the field trial begin now. Here in Tucson at the place my daughter is thought to be."

"Oh, I see."

"Look, Frank, if we do nothing, my girl . . . you understand . . . this is very difficult for me. Katie is probably history." It killed John to be talking about his daughter as an objective in a prospective military exercise. He coughed, choked, held back his tears, and sipped water.

"John, if what we have been briefed on is true, it's worse than we thought." The colonel and John Jackson were on a secure encrypted line given their clearance. "The nutcase in charge over there has apparently threatened to detonate a bomb, possibly a dirty nuke. We are still trying to confirm that."

"Then there's even more of a reason to act sooner than later. The equipment, pilots, helicopters are all ready. This will level the place with minimum cost to life . . . my daughter . . . Frank, please . . . help me."

"John, stay by the line. As you know the White House is monitoring this situation very closely. I'm going to get someone at the Pentagon on the phone who will be in communication with the Situation Room. I will get back to you. Keep the faith, brother."

John called Rena on his cell phone. She was staying in Catalina with her parents since John was working around the clock, and they were taking time away from each other.

"Rena, hi. It's me. Can you do me a favor and ask your dad a question? It's for Katie."

"Of course. You hear anything?"

John knowingly violated his security agreement, which could cost him his job, by disclosing to his wife that there was a suspicion of nuclear activity under the house where Katie was being held captive. At this point, he didn't give a damn about the breach. "Ask your father if he knows of any old inactive mines from back in the day up in the area where Katie is being held."

"Okay, John. I'll call you back."

Rena explained the crisis to her father, often having to speak loudly and slowly, repeating herself.

There he stood, one leg forward wearing cowboy boots and a western shirt with snaps, just like always. Cowboy hat on. One hand in his pocket jiggling change, toothpick in his mouth, oversized bifocals from the eighties low on his nose.

"*Si, mijita.* Way up yonder under Finger Rock trail is that old mining shaft—you know the one, with those heavy old timbers. Lotsa little connected caves there, good well water, too. Cold and deep. Let's saddle up some horses, and I can show you."

"No, Papa, we don't need to go up by horse."

"Maybe you're right; pack mule might do better, huh?"

"Well, my car sure won't make it." Rena laughed and cried at the same time.

"Rena, the reason we couldn't mine that area was because there wasn't much ore, it would be too expensive to get at, and folks were awfully mad that we might foul the water table. Don't you remember when you were little, and I used to pack you kids up? Took you there myself on our horse Blue Boy to play camp and explore before all those fancy houses went in."

Rena stiffened suddenly. "That's it? That's the place? Of course, I remember. Oh, thank you, Daddy! I love you." Rena gave her dad a big hug and a smooch. He looked down and smiled, his cheeks flushed. He scraped at the floor with his boot.

Rena called John back. "John, I spoke to my father, and I know exactly where the mine shaft is. I used to go there when I was a kid. I can show whoever needs to see it."

"Please go home, Rena. I'm going to call the police and tell them. I'm waiting by the phone for a call back from Frank Bury. I love you." He hung up abruptly.

Rena stared at the phone a minute as if it were one of those eight-ball games and would give her advice.

John called Detective Carter and explained that they knew of an access route into the mountain.

Carter told John that he would meet Rena at the house. First, he had some logistics to deal with and wanted to get word to Weaver of the new information. The shaft's safety was one major problem. That thing had been out of commission for years. They would need to find people from Pima search and rescue who had the equipment to descend.

~~~~~

Rena waited at the door for Carter with hiking shoes on and was ready to go.

Carter drove up the trailhead with Rena in an all-wheel-drive vehicle to the place where the search and rescue team was assembling. They were advised to wear some lead for protection and drop into the hole with radiation detection badges and equipment to assess levels. They weren't happy about the extra weight, but tough luck. It was easier than hauling out a 250-pound hiker who was injured.

Informal introductions were made all around. The group made Rena feel special, and under better circumstances she would have swooned being surrounded by these mountain men. She didn't even notice. John would have been jealous.

Rena remembered exactly where the mine was and led the party right to it. One of them commented to her how this would have been easier to get to on horseback or mules. Rena smiled to herself and thought about her dad. To her left was Finger Rock, and to her right she could see in the distance the house where her daughter was being held. She screamed, "Katie!" The cops tried to calm her down. Rena had the urge to go up to the front door and knock. Little did she know that the dog and Weaver were three steps ahead of her.

It appeared to be a small cave not unlike the hundred others around. The mouth of the cave wasn't more than six or seven feet high by four feet wide. The old timber was rotted. Rocks crunched loosely, the footing steep and uncertain.

Two team members were lowered and climbed down 250 feet. Their lights helped but couldn't penetrate the cool, thick darkness. Farther on, the temperature dropped and rushing water was heard. A tunnel system branched toward the mansion. Radiation levels rose the deeper they went. The fact-finding mission was aborted, and the climbers ascended.

Returning Rena to the front door of her house home was no easy task. It was like having a pacing mountain lion in the backseat. She was angry and agitated. Why couldn't anyone get to her daughter by following the caves? What was being done to get Katie out of there? Carter tried to explain the radiation danger and that they wouldn't rule out a deeper climb with more equipment. She wanted to know when. It could not be soon enough. Carter wondered aloud with Rena about lowering inflatable flotation devices into the water, or sending people to follow the cave down to where the house was, if not for the damn heavy isotopes.

John dozed off at his desk and was startled by the phone. After he woke, he took a second to get oriented.

"John. Bury here. We have a green light on your stone buster."

"Thank you for going to bat for us, Frank. How can I ever repay you?" John smiled, rubbed his hands together with the phone tucked beneath his chin, and looked at the ceiling like it was heaven.

"Wasn't me, JJ. Your work is well respected in high places. I just ran it up the chain of command. One of the reasons the Pentagon has great interest in your project is because your stone buster is also a potential tunnel buster. There is increasing demand for that technology by us and certain allies. Also, we don't want it falling into the wrong hands. Underground threats from tunnels beneath borders are happening more frequently both domestically and internationally. The idea is ancient. As far back as the American Civil War, we have had an interest in this. General Ulysses S. Grant's army dug a long tunnel for explosives that he wanted to use against Robert E. Lee's forces. It backfired then. It won't now will it, JJ?"

"No, sir."

"Good. We have four AH sixty-four E Apache Guardians equipped with your devices. As we speak, they are being readied for deployment. We have all the drawings on the target compound and will dial in resonance frequencies per your protocols. We will hit it from all corners. It's not all good news, though. We need a victory, and we need it fast. We now have credible intelligence that there is a nuclear threat under that compound that runs very deep. Your wife led searchers to a cave that uncovered this finding. John, I'm not ever going to ask how Rena got into the fray. Leave it to Mama Bear.

"If your tunnel buster can open the way for us and create a large diversion from above, we are planning to send special ops down that hole and try to infiltrate from below. They will come in from Coronado or Pendleton ASAP pending availability. We're a bit stretched thin at the moment."

John responded, "Yes of course. Understood."

"The problem is radiation down the shaft. Levels could be dangerously high, and outfitting our troops with protective gear will make it slower going, but I'm sure they can handle it. My orders are that if this doesn't work, then unfortunately we will have to dig deep and hard and turn that place into a crater that will look like a meteor hit it. Do you understand?"

"Frank, it'll work—it has to. Look, how long can you keep this radiation meltdown deal a secret anyway?"

"The president spoke with Governor Jennifer Brooks. She has met with her team. Arizona scores poorly on large-scale disaster planning. It might even make New Orleans look good. It's based on private automobiles and few roads in or out. An all-out evacuation would be like Thanksgiving traffic times a thousand. Some state officials believe that our great state should abandon the idea of evacuation altogether and work on shelter safety instead, which translates into stay home and kiss your ass good-bye."

〜〜〜〜〜

When Katie was a small child, there had been a wildfire in the hills near the Jackson home. Fire trucks came to their neighborhood and told everyone including the Jacksons that they had exactly two hours to evacuate. No one knew what to take, so they loaded up their cars with pets, photos, documents, computers, things of sentimental value, memorabilia, and small valuables.

The Jackson's neighbors down the street threw an evacuation party. They broke out the grill, iced down the beer, and weren't budging. The website on evacuation is weak, reminding people to shut off the lights, lock the door, and turn off the stove. Don't forget to bring the kids, or not.

Arizona's leaders and their advisors had to do something, but not much could be done. The risk of doing too much was as great as doing nothing at all. Creating mass panic could be deadly. Politicians might offer pat advice before hopping onto a chopper. Sorry, folks, gotta run.

The governor checked to make sure she had no lipstick on her teeth before going on the air. She was stiff and stressed as she placed her arms on the podium. "My dear fellow Arizonans. Today I come to you with a heavy heart, great sadness, and resolve. We potentially have tribulations ahead that we will see through together. Please do not fear, and most of all do not panic."

The governor swept the hair out of her face. "We have just learned that the northern foothill region of Tucson is having an underground radiation leak. As we speak, first responders are on the scene, having already risked their lives to assess the situation. Local citizens together with law enforcement have come forward to help. The National Guard has been called. Be confident in the knowledge that your government at every level is now involved."

Governor Brooks swayed and rocked slightly from side to side, looking at the teleprompter. "The situation currently unfolding is that absent any nuclear facility near that location, we are unable to rule out terrorist activity. Arizona is a young state but geographically an ancient land. This is one of our magnificent treasures and a weakness. We do not enjoy a rapid mass transit system that can help us today in our time of need."

Brooks pointed to herself and briefly turned to acknowledge her team. "We have weighed our options and are ordering an evacuation of the area. After I conclude this evening, there will be further instructions regarding which areas we plan to preventively evacuate peacefully. Looting will not be tolerated. We must work together. At this time all infrastructure is operational. We will provide details by radio, TV, and Internet. The full weight of the governor's office will engage the assistance of private and public airlift, railroads, buses, and all other means of transport. Pickup stations will be announced. I know that some people will not be able or willing to leave their homes, and my staff will be advising shortly on shelter safety protocol."

Pointing to the cameras, she continued. "If you live in the area of Tucson, Arizona, north of River Road, west of Sabino Canyon, and east of Highway 77, begin to gather a supply of bottled water, canned goods, medications, and any other essentials. Lock your residence, meet your families, and await further instruction. Begin using bottled drinking water effective immediately. We are currently examining the extent of radiation leaks to the underground aquifer."

The governor had a determined yet kind expression. "Whatever this threat is and whoever is responsible for it, know that we are stronger, and will rise above it. Those responsible will be brought to justice. We will not be terrorized. The resolve of Arizona and the United States must not be underestimated or trifled with. Arizonans will not retreat from who we are and what we stand for. I am planning to board a helicopter and head for ground zero in the Tucson foothills. My staff and I are not planning to leave until this ordeal is brought to its natural conclusion. I will be conducting the duties of governor from Tucson. God bless you all, and God bless America."

CHAPTER 29

AXE SCREAMED at me as an inch of water gushed into his precious lab. "Make it stop or I will destroy you immediately." He threw me to the wet floor. "I will crush your bones until your mother's milk oozes from your marrow."

"Okay. Ow. I'm not doing it, whatever it is. I can't make anything stop, only you can."

Defiantly, I added that I wouldn't stop it even if I could. Maybe not a great comment given the circumstances.

Outside lightning tore into the top floor of Axe's house. All the circuits were fried and power lost. Within moments generators were humming. When the lights came on, I stood towering above him in the form of a giant, salivating grizzly bear with the face of my great grandmother. With claws and fangs, I roared, and the wind outside howled, tearing a huge chunk of his roof off. I was enjoying doing all this in conjunction with Bear, who guided me. That juice I drank was good stuff but was starting to wear off. For the first time, I thought I saw a glimmer of fear in the eyes of that bastard who said, "How are you doing this? You have shape shifted into that bear."

I said, "Back at you for showing off, taking on the face and voice of the professor earlier. Two can play that game." I think that I wowed him.

~~~~~~

Inside, Weaver looked out the window quickly at formidable skies. White and blue veins of lightning scorched the sky. Thunder pounded. It rained sideways through the vents, closed windows, and doors. He and his team finally cleared the master bedroom.

Quietly, Scoop Weaver walked through Axe's lair trying to get into his head. After searching in drawers and behind paintings, Weaver walked into the enormous closet. The large open case of watch winders caught his eye. In Scoop's younger, misguided inner-city days, this kind of watch collection worth several hundred thousand dollars might have made for easy loot. If it weren't for the military, he would probably be in jail now like so many of the other guys he hung out with on street corners. His street smarts paid off in his current job.

In his haste, Axe made a tiny error, or was it a trap? He forgot to reset the winder mechanism sealing the elevator from intrusion. It had a time-out mechanism that would have automatically done so, but that was still a few moments away.

Weaver loved a good watch, but these were way over his pay grade. He feasted his eyes upon museum-quality pieces that he had only heard of. A few times on payday, when Weaver felt wild, he got an Invicta, or a G-Shock—but this? One by one he lifted the watches to have a closer look. There was a Rolex, a Cartier, and an Audemers Piguet he'd seen in a magazine. When he got to the solid gold Patek Phillipe Nautilus that retails for $90,000, it caught. He jiggled and turned it when a sound began. Then he heard suction like a central vacuum cleaner. He yelled, "Down."

The team dropped into position. A wall of mirrors slid away, and an elevator door opened, with a hiss. Chimes and a voice like that of an expensive European car's navigation system played through the speakers. An international computerized female-sounding voice said, "Welcome. Please watch your step and the closing door. Hold onto the guard rails. Next stop level C."

Weaver, a guy who instinctively ran toward trouble instead of away, rolled into the elevator; the dog followed. Three more team members followed suit. The doors automatically swallowed them.

Weaver's team was shocked. This elevator was not on the floor plan, and being in it now was not in the plan at all. This was not a good time to be improvising. Without prior intelligence, backup, or contingencies, they were trapped. When those doors opened, they had no idea what or whom to expect. Standing in an elevator, they would be fully exposed. Weaver looked up to see if he could get into the shaft of the capsule.

〜〜〜〜〜

Until now the largest known earthquake around Tucson happened in the 1880s. Chimneys toppled, and buildings cracked. Railroad cars were spontaneously set in motion. People said for miles around that it sounded like prolonged artillery fire. In 1959 there was a 5.6 magnitude quake in Arizona. Another in New Mexico was felt in Tucson in 2014. I felt that I could beat them all because this hatchet-faced guy called Axe was really beginning to get on my nerves and made me rage. No, like I'm not even joking about this moronic bully. I looked at the floor below me and exhaled powerfully, slowly. I made a hissing sound, which willed the ground to shake. The walls cracked, people fell.

Axe was urgently called away from battering me because of the elevator breach.

〜〜〜〜〜

After dark, four Guardian helicopters flew at an altitude of six thousand feet and made their final descent into position, encircling the compound despite deteriorating conditions.

Pilots spoke to each other about their orders to use the new weapons. Their mission was to destroy the compound and cavitate the ground, exposing tunnels and structures with minimal loss of life. Pilots were ordered not to fire their machine guns or other conventional explosives unless fired upon. They were briefed that the weapon designer's daughter had been taken hostage underground and of the nuclear potential, another reason to exercise caution before ordinance. At this point it was unlikely that using diplomacy such as yelling for the bad guys to come out with their hands up was going to be productive.

After the aerial mission was complete and the ground softened, a team of special ops would drop down the mine and onto the exposed areas left by the helicopters.

Without emotion, warriors engaged.

"Staghorn one, this is staghorn two, out."

"Yes, two, go ahead. What's your status? Out."

"We have a visual."

"Copy, staghorn one, on final approach."

"Staghorn three and four, final formation."

"Roger that. Final formation a go. No signs of trouble."

"Let's do it, and maybe we can catch the end of the game."

Gunners smiled at the confident bravado and hung out the sides of the aircraft.

The Apache Guardian is a monster. Technically, it's an army chopper, but don't tell that to the air force or National Guard. With quiet rotors it maintains an eye in the sky. It can control predator drones and carry enlarged payloads at combat speeds of up to 189 miles per hour, day or night. Its sensor and computer capabilities allow it to take in and evaluate large amounts of data while under heavy fire, helping the pilot create the best combat strategy. This bird can take punishment but prefers to dish it out.

The Guardian can warn ground soldiers of potential threats. Troop morale improves knowing that Apaches overhead have their backs.

Four helicopters were in position and began to deploy John's weapons. Each one targeted a specific structure of the compound to inflict maximum property damage. The noise was skull splitting. Pilots wore special ear protection, kind of like noise-deadening headphones. Even from way below ground Katie could hear a strange thumping sound.

The surrounding houses radioed Axe that there were incoming

attack helicopters to the main compound. Axe gave the order to fire at will.

From rooftops in a tempest, Axe's guards opened fire with shoulder-held, large-caliber antihelicopter bullets that explode after impact for maximum damage. A half dozen wild shots in the wind were leveled at the closest Guardian. A rotor was partially torn off, and the chopper went into a wild spin.

"Mayday, Mayday, going down hard and hot."

The Guardian crashed in the desert.

The two helicopters farthest from the gunfire flipped 180 degrees. Tracer rounds lit those buildings up, unleashing hell's fury upon the rooftops. In less than a minute, all shooters were ripped apart, and the buildings were riddled and on fire. The remaining helicopter continued the shock-wave destruction until the other two rejoined, following orders of engagement to use all needed devices if fired upon. And they did, regardless of who the hell's kid was down there.

One corner of the main compound collapsed like a panting fighter going down on a knee.

Pilots emptied everything they had into corners of the compound. The building collapsed. A powdery gray ash rose instead to take its place. The odor was burnt wood, metal, and plastic.

The Guardians next turned their surgical attention to any tunnel structures and began drilling at them like a dentist. They were carefully picking away at structures presumably because of the kid's safety.

Four special ops hung out of the helicopter in the rain and fast-roped in a couple of miles south of the mine to avoid detection and enemy fire. Rugged desert hills bore an eerie resemblance to terrain they had recently been deployed to Afghanistan.

The quietest way uphill the last two miles in this weather was on foot. Clay, mud, and loose rock were proving hazardous. Boots were sinking, pushing, and grinding it out. Rain soaked through clothes and went down collars; there was blinding, driving rain everywhere.

The small but highly lethal team of four descended the mine

shaft into what was now a raging underground river. The dank narrow shaft was a respite from conditions outside. Without their powerful lights, they couldn't have known that the underground river was more than sixty feet wide. Troops were equipped with an inflatable CRRC zodiac forced insertion extraction rescue raft. Bats darted endlessly.

Police tried to inform Weaver that they had reinforcements coming in from the caves below the compound. No answer.

～～～～～

Axe's entire laboratory was now shin deep in water, and the level was climbing fast.

I blew out a door that closed behind Axe with wind that erupted from my gut. A console nearby with electronic equipment, computers, and two people working there received similar treatment.

Axe turned and approached me with murderous rage in his eyes and a hatchet in his hands. Now a desperate man, his face was bloodied and burned from where I got to him earlier.

～～～～～

As the elevator descended, Weaver whispered. "Who farted? It's hanging around in here way too long."

No answer. Awkward silence. Finally, "Sorry, Scoop. I get gassy when I'm nervous. I think it was that damned burrito."

The doors opened, and nothing escaped except the odor. Weaver, along with three men and the dog, hit the floor, which was nearly submerged in gushing freezing water. Cold and gasping, they were immediately shot at by Axe's awaiting security. Dog jumped ahead against the tide of water in search of the Jackson girl.

Weaver made it under the cover of a metal cabinet lobbing flash-bang grenades in the direction of the incoming fire. Then Scoop came out blazing with both barrels. Peripherally he thought he saw someone resembling the Jackson girl running from Axe. She or it looked half human, half beast, half mad. He fired, Axe ran, and Scoop pursued, stopping long enough to ask, "You Jackson?"

"Yes, Katie. You're the guy from when the cave collapsed."

That confirmed, Weaver had to decide whether or not he should go after Axe. He wanted the girl to stay here, wait for help. But maybe Katie would be safer with him, rather than down here alone with that lunatic on the loose.

"I'll be okay, I think. Please stop that maniac," Katie said.

"Katie, are those powers that we hear about real and intact? We sure could use all the help we can get. Maybe there's not enough oxygen down here, but a moment ago you looked half human, half animal."

Katie touched her body and face, made a muscle with her arm, and feigned a smile. "Yes, I'm powered up."

"Good, because Axe is planning to detonate a device underground. I'm sure that it's here somewhere. With the water and crumbling walls, it won't be easy to find. There's probably not much that we can do about the bombs. Can you find the electronics and use whatever it is to destroy them while I look for Axe?" He squeezed Katie's shoulder, looked her in the eye, and said that he had the utmost confidence in her.

Katie felt panic race through her heart, pounding in her chest and throat. "Don't leave." She really missed her mom right then and thought about how worried sick her parents must be. The water was up to her hips. She didn't know how or if she'd make it out alive.

Weaver turned to go, and Katie followed, having changed her mind. There was no way she was staying there alone with Axe's goon squad. Dog swam hard toward Katie Jackson barking. Security looked in their direction. Katie reached, grabbed and hugged Dog who's entire body wagged. Warm licks on the girls face were a welcome contrast to the cold water. Whenever she came upon an electronic console, Katie blasted it with her palms, which were now shooting intense heat. This alerted the remaining armed and dangerous security detail of their location. Fortunately, most had fled.

Weaver and Katie saw Axe at an underground lake on which a

sizable raft was moored. With the changes to the water table, the lake more closely resembled a choppy sea. As the outboard motor came to life, Axe turned and yelled. He might have waved, but it looked more like an obscene gesture.

Whipping around a tight corner at a steep angle, four soldiers in their motorized raft fired on Axe's position. The lighting was poor, the water white capped. Bullets ricocheted off cave walls and ripped into the water. Weaver pushed Katie down, yelling, "Get down, and stay low." He took up a better position.

The special ops team came upon Axe's boat yelling orders that they were planning to board.

Axe had a flare on board and waited until the special ops got closer. He shot the center of the raft with a flare gun and hit a soldier. The boat temporarily floundered. Axe pulled ahead full throttle. A storm of fire power poured down in Axe's general direction. Although it wasn't clear if he had been hit, the evil man went overboard and disappeared out of sight into the murky drink.

CHAPTER 30

"LET'S GO. Axe is down," Weaver ordered. "We have to go back into his laboratory and destroy what we can."

The three remaining troops who were standing saw us. Weaver waved. Grateful for the help, we waited. They knew exactly who we were, and Scoop, as he said was his nickname, brought them up to speed on what was happening back at Axe's place. They threw both of us leaded vests. Scoop joked and wanted a longer one so that he could protect the family jewels from radiation. We didn't know it at the time, but with the extensive flooding and dilution rates of fast-moving water, radiation levels were at acceptable levels. No worse than being in the hospital for a week or two getting daily CAT scans or X-rays, which I'm told is not an uncommon event.

Special ops communicated to the surface that the girl was alive and relatively unharmed. Axe had been taken by the wash. They had one wounded.

The six of us headed back. The wounded soldier was burned but making it. The orders back to the special ops were to neutralize the threat and get the hostage out, or the White House was giving the order to scramble jets and destroy the complex. Even if it meant casualties, the greater populace would be protected.

~~~~~~~

Axe clung desperately to a rock, gasping for breath. He was bleeding but not dead, a state of affairs he had known many times in his life. Being wounded only made him more dangerous. Flood water surged around him. He came up for air periodically. Although he didn't deserve the slightest moment of respite, the cold water felt good on his charred face.

When he planned this underground escape hatch, he had not considered the possibility that it would be flooded. He had planned to comfortably negotiate his way in the raft until he could walk out in a cave and into a remote culvert system farther downstream to be picked up by the late Vuuv. Now he was seriously hurt, and the place was deluged, so there was no telling where he'd end up, and he certainly couldn't head back to his lab. The only option was to let go of the rock and let nature take its course. He knew that by foot it took approximately five minutes to jog out of here. The water was rushing three or four times faster than a person on foot, so he figured that he would be submerged for a minute or two. With any luck he would find another place to catch his breath along the way. He was claustrophobic and deathly afraid of drowning, but he had no other choice except to face his fears. There was also a chance that he would snag on a rock or branch and get stuck.

The water was cold, but he took off his outer shirt and undershirt, tied off the sleeves to his T-shirt, blew as much air into it as possible, and used it as an emergency life jacket. It minimally improved his buoyancy. He didn't want to shed his boots; he'd need those. He let his precious axe drop in the water and also dropped his belt. Then he took everything out of his pockets to lighten the load but kept his ID, cash, and knife. The cell phone was probably dead, so there was no need for it. He stuffed the gun in his pocket and kept his watch; it was a good one, waterproof, though he was afraid it would get badly scratched. He chuckled at himself and his stupidity about watches. The water slapped him in the face again and made him cough. He took a deep breath and let go.

~~~~~

Weaver, the four troops, and I got back to the lab. Waters were rising quickly, and time was running out. I closed my eyes and yelled, "Honon, help." Without knowing why, I looked at the palms of my hands and held them about a foot apart until I felt them get hot. It felt like I was holding a basketball, but there was nothing in my hands. Between the palm of my hands, it seemed as though time itself was concentrating. I could knead it, pull it, and compress it like dough made of time itself and all the energy stored within. And then this basketball of time burst away from me as both my hands opened. It was like a basketball player passing the ball quickly to another player. I threw it into the heart of the workstation that was still above water.

A blue-green shock of light buzzed, hissed, and then the entire thing imploded upon itself, sending contents flying in every direction. The soldiers who were quickly and strategically setting plastic explosives took cover, looked at each other, looked at me in confusion, and then went back to work. One guy gave me a thumbs up. Floating by was a plastic tube of the type that contains posters or architectural drawings.

Scoop Weaver grabbed the tube of drawings. "We have got to get back to the boat now and get the hell out of here before the whole thing blows."

<hr />

Axe's heart beat at its maximum capacity; he was frantic and near drowning. His lungs were bursting from holding his breath, but he wouldn't give in to lack of air, wouldn't exhale. He heard somewhere that if you puff in and out against pursed lips you can go a little longer with less pain. There was still some oxygen left in exhaled air. He couldn't make it much longer. Anxiety and adrenaline made it worse.

He recalled that when people get thrown overboard while whitewater rafting, they survive best if they let their bodies relax. Go with the flow. Don't fight it, he kept telling himself. Roll, float, and let the water do the work. Up ahead he thought that he noticed a pocket.

A gap of a few inches between the waterline and the top of the cave. Air. He willed his body to float face up, flat on his back. There just ahead, he pushed his chin and face above water. He inhaled explosively, rasping and gasping at the sheer pleasure of breath, life. He was going to survive. A sharp rock jutting down from the ceiling caught Axe's chin and ripped at his face as he kept moving down stream. Remaining teeth tore away along with part of his nasal cartilage and lip. Shock and lack of oxygen made the bloody water around him seem like nothing more than an interesting color. He was in and out of consciousness, expelling bubbles and blood. His eyes were opened underwater, terrified, and he found himself looking at a bear with Katie's face smiling at him.

CHAPTER 31

THE MQ-1 is a Predator drone, an unmanned aerial vehicle used predominantly for military offensive or border patrol purposes but allegedly not over the homeland—unless, of course, it is gathering innocent data about the weather. With the Patriot Act, however, all things are possible.

This is a medium-altitude, long-endurance aircraft that can be operated from a ground control station at a great distance by satellite link. Powered by a Rotex engine and a propeller, it can fly four hundred nautical miles or loiter in the heavens above for a dozen or so hours.

The one currently deployed high above Tucson, Arizona, was armed with cameras, laser designators, and AGM-114N hellfire missiles locked and loaded, designed with a blast flow that would reach around corners and strike an enemy that might be hiding in caves. The drone was additionally loaded with MQ-9 reapers with a three thousand pound payload and was headed for Axe's compound.

~~~~~~~

Axe burst violently from a culvert and washed up on the Pontatoc underneath Skyline Drive, still breathing but stuporous. After a moment, he opened his eyes and propped himself on one elbow. He winced, and the world spun. He saw two knuckleheads who were having an extreme weather party and who thought the raging wash was a hoot. They looked like they just got back from a Colorado pot fest on the last Greyhound into town.

One of the yahoos was drinking a beer. His face was pink. When he and the other one saw Axe, they looked at each other in disbelief.

~~~~~~~

"We have movement on the ground, sir. We have a visual. Zooming in," said a remote drone pilot hundreds of miles away.

"Visual confirmed. That is Uktam, a.k.a. the Axe, our combatant. He appears injured, mobility impaired. Wait, there are two people—friendlies, civilians."

"Hold your fire. Contact law enforcement to take him into custody."

~~~~~~~

The first yahoo said, "Like, hey, dude. You okay?"

"No. Help."

"Wow, man, maybe I should call 911. What happened? You wipe out trying to tube the river? Man, it's the roughest I've ever seen it. We brought our tubes. Global warming has its pluses, dude."

"No, no, yes. I mean, no ambulance, and yes, wiped out. Do yourselves a favor—don't tube the river. Just help me up, and I'll have a swig of that beer. I'll make it home, really."

"Your face, man, it's really bad. Like, you really need a health-care provider."

The other guy, who was wearing a big woolen hat that hung low, partially covering his dreadlocks, said, "More like a plastic surgeon if you ask me, huh?"

SWAT arrived.

Axe was eighteen inches from the face of the second guy, who was now helping him to his feet. Axe staggered, almost fell. The two yahoos, being good-hearted, helped steady him. They were a bit unsteady themselves by now.

SWAT took up tactical offensive posture and yelled through a loudspeaker, ordering Axe to lie facedown, hands behind his head, now.

Instead of complying with the wishes of law enforcement, Axe hopelessly grabbed one of the yahoos. In one swift movement, the yahoo's neck was in the crook of Axe's bloody elbow. The other guy dropped his beer. SWAT had no clear shot and stood down.

Not too far from Las Vegas sat a young, twenty-first-century digital fighter pilot out of Nellis Air Force Base, eighteen minutes from the strip by car. A contemporary to the late Vuuv, he too swigged energy drinks but was a little more robust. This pilot would have been impressed by the technologically advanced yet naive and highly impressionable Vuuv.

The Pentagon ordered this pilot to fly the predator drone overhead in Tucson. He could have just as easily been halfway around the world in Saudi Arabia.

"Locking coordinates. Laser designator deployed. Please confirm, sir."

~~~~~~

Weaver helped me into the raft sporting a Patek on his wrist. Whatever. To the victor go the spoils. I was seasick in the choppy soup and really did not want to hurl in front of these serious studs.

There was no way I was able to climb out of the mine shaft by rope, so I had to be hoisted out with Dog in my arms.

Once I was pulled up and out of the caves to safety outside onto the desert, the order was given. Explosives under Axe's compound were detonated, which set off car alarms, broke glass, and made every dog within a mile flip out, including mine. Bright light could be seen for miles. There would be no mushroom cloud today.

Weaver and I were invited, more like herded into a bland, unmarked, windowless white E. Series Ford commercial van. Inside, it was a mobile office. Both of us were frantic and didn't want to get in.

Weaver yelled, "We're not done. Where is Axe? We gotta go."

We wanted to know what happened to him. I screamed, "Did he get away?"

We were given hot drinks and dry towels. I did not accept either. No time to relax with a friggin' hot chocolate.

Another agent in the back of the van studied live video feed, which we were encouraged to view to help calm us down after what we had just been through. Weaver and I wished we could have been on the scene as it unfolded.

On the screen we watched Axe on the move. He pushed a young man to the ground and attempted to run. His movement looked more like a limp, skip, and hobble, but he was making forward progress on foot. From inside the van, we heard instructions for SWAT to call off their hounds and stand down.

～～～～～～

The drone operations commander ordered, "Hold your fire, son. Track target combatant out one click south."

"Copy. Tracking target one click south."

"We are at zero point seven two clicks. Enemy combatant turning east into a more populated area, sir. Please advise."

"Deploy hellfire missile. Now. Copy."

"Roger that, sir. Deploying. Three seconds to impact."

The missile hit the ground less than twenty-four inches from where Axe stood. Before the two helpful party guys could hear anything, a mist of red and dirt plus a spray of water shot into the air. Axe experienced his death as complete, utter separation, a blackness of chilling proportions.

～～～～～～

"No. Stop. C'mon. No way. Is that thing for real?" I pointed at the screen. "Yes," I screamed. "Thank you. Thank you. I can't believe it's over." I hugged Weaver and the video guy, who tapped fists.

Now I accepted a drink and a towel.

~~~~~~~~

The first yahoo said, "Whoa, dude. Did you see that?" They looked up. Something soft and amorphous fell out of the sky and splattered the second guy. No doubt the birds would find a meal. FBI would later pick up the pieces with goo bags to confirm identity.

Governments are better at asking for forgiveness than for permission. Suddenly, the weather started to calm, the waters receded.

~~~~~~~~

The rain stopped, and Bear smiled. In my heart she thanked me and said, "I'm sleepy now; I need my beauty rest. Think I'll go hibernate under my mountain." Before Bear went back to her spiritual resting ground, I wondered if I'd ever see her again. She whispered, "Yes, you will. Remember that you are never alone, darling."

EPILOGUE

I THINK that I was in love with Josh. I don't think that it will work out. He will never allow a woman to come between him, his mother, and sports. Sounds intriguing now, but I'd like to see how that flies in twenty years when the kids are crying, there's a sink full of dishes, the bills need to get paid, and he's sitting on the couch with a paunch watching a game. "Stop nagging me. Not now. You are coming between me and sports."

I think cycling is his elusive mistress even though his mother would like to be. No one will ever be good enough for him in her eyes. And let's face it, I'm not exactly the girl next door. In my heart I believe that he still thinks of me as freaky Katie even if he's too scared to come right out and say it. He's been offered several cycling college scholarships.

After having met with the president at 1600 Pennesylvania Avenue NW, I'm going to college in the Washington, DC, area mainly because I have been deemed a weapon of mass destruction and a national security asset or threat, depending on one's point of view. Either way, men in dark suits wearing earpieces keep a close eye and tell me I might have to cut classes when I'm needed from time to time. I hope that my new professors will understand and fare better than my last one.

The long-distance relationship thing doesn't work for Josh either. I guess he doesn't like his girlfriends too close or too far away.

My parents are glad that we are splitting up, although they don't say so. I can just tell. They think I'm too young for a serious relationship and should go out and see the world.

Speaking of Mr. and Mrs. Jackson, a.k.a. the parents—they're still married and still nuts, but I love them. Dad isn't allowed to go to that gym or yogurt shop anymore. Looks like he fears for his life and has given up flirting with Darlene. I don't know if they need marriage counseling, or what. I'm never getting married or having kids. I'm going to live far away in a tree house made of books and read.

Scoop Weaver got promoted and transferred to the DC area, too. He will be mysteriously moving there at around the same time that I matriculate in college. He's a big muckety-muck in antiterrorism and Homeland Security now. My dad heard that Weaver and I are considered a team. That's news to me. I'm not going anywhere without Dog. It's all three of us or none. Dog needs to be deputized as a full federal agent of the law. Maybe I'll get him a handy service-dog vest so they have to let him into college with me.

In case you were wondering, Weaver turned in the expensive watch. It's part of evidence. He has first dibs on it when the investigation is over.

〰〰〰

After the Tucson crisis, the matter still wasn't settled.

Schematic diagrams delineating Axe's second Rocky Mountain plans were found in the plastic tubes floating in the cave.

Those plots were thwarted with ferocious dispatch and barely got off the ground.

The gravity of deploying a predator drone on US soil by presidential executive order would be debated for years to come. Naturally, some thought it was a singularly brilliant act. There was no shortage of detractors who felt like it was dangerous, stupid, and unconstitutional. Besides, someone could have had an eye put out.

Dad's weapons system was considered a success. It will be used for specialized defensive tunnel clearing and other so-called search-and-rescue missions in hostile territory. It's no longer a prototype pilot program. They have given my father the honor of naming it. We have been kicking a few names around. I like Katie's Wrath. They may stick with Staghorn. Josh thought we should name it the Axe. Luckily, Josh doesn't get a vote since it's a dumb name.

Scientists concluded that Axe's deadly intentions would have amounted to the equivalent of an underground nuke test. While highly toxic and unsafe, it probably wouldn't have been the apocalyptic blow he so desired. Some theorize that the radiation burn beneath the breached Japanese reactor will have a similar effect on humanity, which is serious and still unknown.

In the end, Axe was pathetic and deranged. Documents showed that he lived his life in fear and hate—hate of himself and the world, like most bullies and terrorists who wish to force change upon others. He lost all connection to his own tattered soul. Ruled by the ego, he came to believe that he was a separate entity. I wonder what great things he might have accomplished if he had grown up in better circumstances.

Some say that to defeat an enemy, we must first become like them. Maybe we have to think like them, get into their heads, become like them. I say, never.

Honon Bear is at rest now, and so am I. She taught me that while we are all very unique, none of us are separate.

If someone dares to terrorize us or destroy sacred lands, I will be back. Just watch me!

CPSIA information can be obtained at www.ICGtesting.com
Printed in the USA
LVOW07s1102301214

420910LV00004B/40/P

9 781627 871624